Praise for *Virgin* Mysteries

"These 17 tales of death bring Virginia to life with some rich characters, clever plots, and a great use of setting. From the mountains to the bay, with stops at historic lighthouses, homes, and even the state capitol, this anthology shines a new light on the Old Dominion."

—Barb Goffman, *Macavity* award-winning author

"Creepy, diabolical, and completely delightful! Who knew these otherwise charming authors could be so cleverly sinister? One after the other, these terrific and twisty tales tantalize you, tease you and surprise you!"

—Hank Phillippi Ryan - Agatha, Anthony, Macavity and Mary Higgins Clark award-winning author

"First came Poe's mysterious and murderous tales, and then those of Cornwell and Baldacci. Now there's Virginia Is For Mysteries, a brand new collection of wonderfully-told and cleverly-crafted whodunnits."

—Lee Lofland, author of the Macavity-nominated book *Police Procedure and Investigation*, and founder of the Writers' Police Academy

Visit the website at
virginiaisformysteries.com

Virginia Is For Mysteries

by Meredith Cole, Maria Hudgins, Teresa Inge, Maggie King
May Layne, Vivian Lawry, Michael McGowan, Smita Harish Jain
Jayne Ormerod, Yvonne Saxon, Rosemary Shomaker, Fiona Quinn
Linda Thornburg, Heather Baker Weidner

ISBN 978-1-9384676-4-6

Published by

◤ köehlerbooks™

210 60th Street
Virginia Beach, VA 23451
212-574-7939

Virginia is for Mysteries

An Anthology of Mysteries Set in and Around Virginia

From 14 Sisters in Crime Writers

Meredith Cole — Maria Hudgins — Teresa Inge

Maggie King — May Layne — Vivian Lawry

Michael McGowan — Smita Harish Jain

Jayne Ormerod — Yvonne Saxon

Rosemary Shomaker — Fiona Quinn

Linda Thornburg — Heather Baker Weidner

VIRGINIA BEACH
CAPE CHARLES

Foreword

Welcome to Virginia, the eclectic land bookended by blue herons and blue mountains. This birthplace of presidents demarks the line between the urban North and rural South. Its shores, foothills and peaks, once the epicenter of American independence, now host a cultural and geographic stew of dialects and lifestyles. It's a place prideful of its history, parochialism and gentility. Some here prefer salted pork, corn liquor and country porches overlooking hills. Others covet soy milk, Cabernet and luxury apartments in reclaimed historic buildings on riverbanks. Most prefer some combination of the above, grateful that Virginia has so much to offer.

It is in that spirit of diversity that Koehler Books, itself Virginia spawn, proudly ladles out morsels of homespun creativity. This anthology, *Virginia is for Mysteries,* offers a buffet of storytelling by a talented and imaginative group of fourteen scribes from throughout the state. Most belong to the writers' group *Sisters in Crime.* Their genre is mysteries, taunting readers with whodunnits, whimsy and irony.

Through the seventeen stories in this collection, you will see Virginia through evil eyes. This menagerie of stabbings, shootings, poisonings, misplaced blame and premeditated revenge provides a sense of place, a sense of the people who occupy that space and a sense of humor. Peruse these pages and graze on the dastardly delights served up by some of Virginia's finest imagineers. Virginia *is* for Lovers as the state proudly proclaims. How better to stoke that affection than with the whimsy of homegrown mystery?

Joe Coccaro, Executive Editor, Koehler Books

Contents

Virginia is for Mysteries
Story Locations

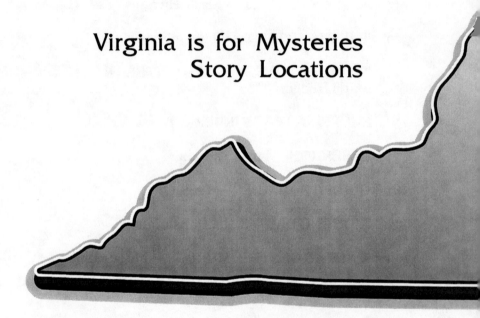

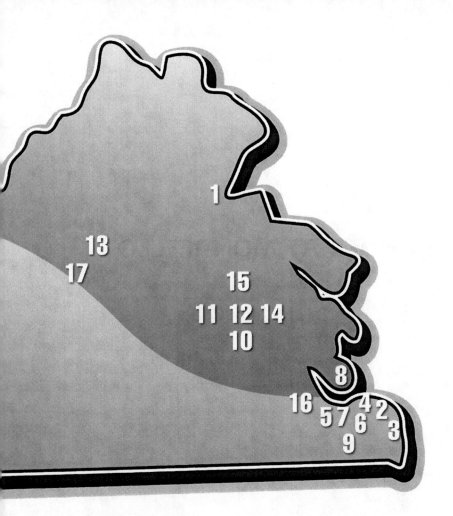

MURDER AT MONTICELLO

By Meredith Cole

AFTER SPENDING TWO HOURS trapped with twenty esteemed members of the American Historic Horticultural Society on a bus to Monticello, tour guide Rory Adams was ready to kill someone, preferably a grumpy horticulturist. But she restrained herself. First of all, murdering clients was bad for business. And second, they were finally about to arrive in Charlottesville for their tour and tomato tasting.

When Rory first conceived the idea of specialty tours for her family's DC tour company, Your Capitol City Tours, she thought it would be incredibly refreshing to get off of the National Mall and see new sights in the area. But specialty tours inevitably meant specialty interests. And these plant experts were proving to be more rancorous then her usual customers.

Rory had attempted to make peppy conversation and stay off any loaded topics, but it soon became apparent that almost everything to do with plants and history was explosive. Rory had no idea how controversial tomatoes were until she made an innocent remark about Thomas Jefferson. "The former president was an avid and enthusiastic gardener and is credited with helping tomatoes become more commonplace on American dinner tables."

The bus erupted into an argument.

"The first tomato was brought over from Europe—and not by Jefferson. He was a talented horticulturist, but this is too much," said Dr. John Powers, a feisty retiree in his eighties. "I must disagree," Dr. Randall Shuster interjected. "Jefferson was perhaps not the first to introduce the species, but his influence on the tomato is well known. His garden was both inspirational and educational." Dr. Shuster was a die-hard Jefferson fan who passionately believed the third president's efforts to import a multitude of plants to North America did more good than harm. Rory had perused his book on the subject in order to prepare for the tour.

"That's right," said Toby Handler. "Well said, Dr. Shuster." Toby was a tall, skinny graduate student whose main job appeared to be following Dr. Shuster around and agreeing with everything he said.

"Tomatoes are not native plants," said Dr. Mary Walton with a sniff, "so it doesn't matter who snuck them into the country." Mary was definitely the grumpiest member of the group. Only a little over five feet tall, she made up for her small stature with a booming voice. A specialist in native flora and fauna, she apparently saw it as her mission to rid the world of all non-native species. No one disagreed with her, but Mary appeared to take any less strident views as an affront.

Herbalist Karen Long, wearing a flowing cotton dress and comfortable non-leather shoes, had sat quietly in her seat up until now. Even she could not resist joining in. "Thomas Jefferson did valuable plant studies, but I find his use of slaves to work in his gardens disturbing. I don't know how anyone can possibly say that a slave owner was an enlightened Renaissance man."

Rory sank back in her chair and let the group argue, wondering if she should have made everyone go through a metal detector before they came on board.

Finally the Blue Ridge Mountains marched closer, and the bus wound its way up the road to Thomas Jefferson's house. The heat hung heavy over the land like a yellow haze. Rory wrenched her eyes from the view and picked up the microphone again. "Imagine approaching the house as so many of Jefferson's visitors did, on horseback or by carriage over rough terrain.

Despite the distance and exhausting trip, visitors flocked to Monticello to meet Jefferson and to see his home."

When the bus pulled up to the visitors center, Rory offered the group a chance to use the restroom and stretch their legs as she went to check on their tickets and other arrangements. "Meet me at the shuttle bus in fifteen minutes, and we'll continue up to the house on the buses provided by the house. Remember, you'll have time to shop at the end of the day before we return to Washington."

Rory got in line to pick up their tickets, hoping they wouldn't dawdle. Rory had arranged for a special tour with the head of the grounds, and she didn't want to be late.

At the shuttle bus, Rory counted heads. Only nineteen were present and accounted for. There were supposed to be twenty, and it took Rory just thirty seconds to see who was missing. *Of course, grumpy Dr. Walton,* she thought. Rory ground her teeth with frustration. They had just five minutes to climb the winding road up to Monticello, and they didn't have time to wait around for stragglers.

"Has anyone seen Dr. Walton?" Rory asked. No one had, and Rory wasn't exactly shocked. Since Mary had been arguing with most of them today, it was doubtful any of them had wanted to hang out with her when they arrived at the visitors center.

Just when Rory was considering putting an announcement on the PA system to page Dr. Walton, Mary strolled up carrying a large shopping bag. Rory wanted to yell at her for being so inconsiderate, but she managed to force a smile on her face. "Now that we're all here, let's head up for our tour, shall we?"

They all mounted the bus, and Rory took a deep breath. She only had to be with the tour group for the rest of the day, and then she never had to see any of them again. She could take it. Rory tried to relax and enjoy the view as they drove through the woods to Monticello.

At last Jefferson's home emerged, and Rory smiled when she

heard several of the horticulturists gasp. She was glad the sight of something other than a plant could astound them.

Dr. Finn Dawson, the head of Monticello's grounds, stood in front of the house checking his watch. Finn had reshaped the gardens and landscape of Monticello since he had started working there ten years earlier. The literature stated that Dawson had recreated the gardens and grounds as close to Thomas Jefferson's original vision as was possible, even though members of the staff were not opposed to using twenty-first century methods for upkeep.

Rory went first down the steps of the bus toward Finn and shook his hand enthusiastically. They had exchanged several e-mails, and she'd been so thankful that he had offered to give the tour himself. Anyone with less knowledge and experience wouldn't stand a chance with this gaggle of egotistical academics.

As the group got off the bus, Rory saw Finn frown as he spotted someone. *Who is it that Finn is so displeased to see?* Rory wondered while studying Finn's reaction.

"Welcome to Thomas Jefferson's home and gardens on behalf of the Monticello Historical Society," Finn said loudly and clearly. "We're going to begin our tour in Thomas Jefferson's flower gardens, and we'll walk around the house to get there."

"Rory, can you take my picture in front of the house?" one of the tour group members asked.

Rory had used almost every camera invented at least once, since taking photos was a common request for most tour guides. "Say *tomato*!" she said. Then Rory moved quickly to the back of the group as they followed Finn Dawson to the gardens. She had to make sure everyone stayed together.

Rory felt inspired as she strolled down the brick pathways where Jefferson had walked and planned out every detail of the house and grounds as well as his university, and she was awed by all the other amazing things he had done. She could just picture the house buzzing with activity during Jefferson's time. The place was quite busy today. Tourists were strolling around taking photos and following other guides. At the back of the house, a large white tent was set up with a sign in front announcing the upcoming tomato tasting.

During the next forty minutes, Finn gave them an extensive tour of the colorful and varied flower gardens that Thomas Jefferson had originally planted. The group was mostly respectful and polite, although one argument broke out about the origins of a flower in the garden that Rory could not follow. A born diplomat, Finn smiled politely and simply herded the group over to the vegetable garden and away from the flower in question.

Finn gave more attention to Jefferson's tomatoes, since they would be doing the tasting later. "Thomas Jefferson was really our first foodie, and he experimented with growing all sorts of new plants. Until about 1810, most people in North America believed that tomatoes were poisonous. So, Mr. Jefferson was on the cutting edge when it came to cultivating varieties.

"In this garden," he continued, "we replicated faithfully the tomato varieties Jefferson would have been growing."

Mary leaned forward and stuck her head in amongst the plants. Rory wondered if Finn was going to ask her to step back so she wouldn't crush anything, but he only frowned when she reemerged.

"How interesting," Mary said with unabashed sarcasm. "Brandywines. And Soldackis."

Randall Shuster looked shocked. "You must be mistaken, madam."

"Sir, when it comes to tomatoes, I am never wrong," Mary said indignantly.

Finn wisely ignored them both and checked his watch. "In the spirit of Jefferson and his love for cultivating new varieties of plants, we invite you to go over now to the tasting in the tent. In an hour, other groups will be joining us, but it will remain an intimate event until then."

Finn bounded away, promising to join them soon. Rory counted heads, and was relieved to find that she could still account for all twenty. Mary and herbalist Karen Long had fallen behind, and appeared to be in a heated argument. They looked furious. Rory knew she would have to diffuse the situation quickly if they were going to stay on track.

"Karen! Let me take your picture in front of the gardens," Rory said, hurrying over to the two women. Long shook her head, looking like she was about to cry. In contrast, Mary looked strangely triumphant as she walked away, head tilted upward, nose in the air. Rory escorted Karen as they made their way to the tent.

Inside, the tables were covered with white cloths, and heirloom tomatoes were artfully arranged in baskets. The tomato colors were fabulous—deep reds, burgundies, yellows, oranges, purples and greens. It was hard to believe that so very few varieties of tomatoes were actually available in supermarkets, and the rest were mostly ignored. Rory didn't know much about plants, but she knew that she liked food and she was prepared to taste everything. There were sliced tomatoes on plates in front of each basket of fruit, ready for them to try. Rory's group got in line.

Mary stood in front of Rory and sniffed disdainfully as she surveyed the scene. "Looks like a pedestrian selection," she huffed. Rory wondered how many and what kind of exotic tomatoes would satisfy her. She seemed to be disappointed by most things she encountered.

Rory's mouth watered at the sight of the tomatoes. She picked up a plate in front of the first tomato labeled "Yellow Brandywine."

Rory took a small bite and sighed when the flavorful juice hit her tastebuds. She turned and found herself grinning at Karen Long.

"There's nothing like heirloom species grown organically. The flavor is amazing," Karen said. Rory had to agree, and she rather envied Karen's waistless flowing dress. Rory would have to stop snacking when her belt got too tight.

Rory decided that no one in the group was going to interfere with her experience tasting all the varieties. She set to work sampling each one and then marked off her preferences on a card. Some were sweeter than others, but each tomato had a unique, interesting flavor. It was difficult to choose. At last she wrote "Granny Cantrell" as her number one pick and dropped her card in the voting box.

Other groups had joined them now, and the tent was quite full. At last, guide Finn Dawson stepped up to a microphone. "We've now tallied up your scorecards and the Granny Cantrell has won first place." Rory cheered along with the rest of the crowd. Belatedly, she remembered that she had a group to wrangle and began to count heads. Only nineteen. *Mary's gone again! There's always one.*

"Has anyone seen Dr. Walton?" Rory asked Toby and then each of the others in the group. No one had seen her. Perhaps Mary had gone to the restroom. But Rory hated to lose track of anyone in her charge. Rory couldn't believe Mary would have wandered off during something like the tomato tasting and missed an opportunity to declare her own winner. Rory stepped out of the tent to look around and see if she could spot Mary and nearly tripped over Mary's body, facedown in a plate of tomatoes.

— 🐞 —

The police took awhile to arrive, but the staff at Monticello was quick to take charge. Rory's group was herded off to the visitors center to an air-conditioned conference room. They all looked shell-shocked. No one had been fond of Mary Walton, but they all appeared upset that she was dead.

"Was it a heart attack? Poor old girl," John Powers said, his voice cracking with emotion.

"I hope it wasn't food poisoning," Randall Shuster quipped. "We could all be in danger."

"What were you arguing with Mary about in the garden?" Powers asked Karen.

Karen shook her head as if to shake away the bad memory. "Mary always liked to be right."

Rory wondered what Mary had said that upset Karen so much. She didn't seem to be the murdering type, but you never knew. Rory was disturbed at how quickly the seemingly mild-mannered herbal guru had jumped to the conclusion that Mary had been murdered. Karen suspected that it wasn't natural causes as soon as she had found Mary's body. Food poisoning took longer than five minutes to kill someone.

Rory's hands were still shaking, and her skin felt clammy in the cold air conditioning. "Excuse me for a moment," Rory said to the group. "I'm going to see if I can find us some refreshments."

Rory walked to the cafeteria to order the group tea, coffee and cookies. She was sure that they could all use something comforting and fortifying after their ordeal.

Karen came into the cafeteria just when Rory was packing up her order. "Tea! How lovely. Can I help you carry something?"

Rory passed her a tray, grateful for her help.

"I wanted to tell you something," Karen said. Rory froze. She hoped Karen wasn't going to confess that she'd murdered Mary. "I've known Mary for years, and she somehow uncovered a secret from my past. I worked for several years for a big agri-business company before I saw that what they were doing was wrong. I've tried to keep it quiet ever since I knew that if the information became public it could ruin my herbal business." Karen's voice sounded bitter.

Rory tried to wrap her mind around the fact that Karen had

not only worked for the *enemy* of organic food, but that Mary had had something on Karen. "I didn't kill her, but I thought about it," Karen said. "She'd been blackmailing me for years. But I'm sure I wasn't the only one."

When Rory and Karen arrived with the refreshments, the group thanked them profusely and got to work making everything disappear. Rory sat back down, cradling a cup of coffee in her cold hands. Mary Walton had been a blackmailer. Rory wondered who else in the group had secrets that Mary had discovered.

Buck Morris, an Albemarle County police officer, interrupted her reverie a few minutes later. He was a big man whose stomach stretched the buttons of his uniform. "You're the tour group from DC?" he asked in a slow country drawl. "I need to ask you a few questions about Mary Walton."

"How did she die?" Randall Shuster interrupted.

"And you are . . .?" Morris asked.

"I am Dr. Randall Shuster from Yale University." Randall puffed up like an indignant rooster.

"Are you the leader of this group?" Shuster asked the pompous PhD.

Rory stood. "That would be me," she said, hoping she had managed to keep the sigh out of her voice as she introduced herself as the representative for Your Capitol City Tours.

Morris nodded at Rory. "The coroner will do an autopsy, but our first guess is that Dr. Walton was poisoned." The group gasped, and Karen Long let out a strangled shriek. "We'd like to interview you all individually about what you observed today."

The police began to take them off individually for questioning, starting with Randall. The rest of the group sat silently sipping their drinks.

When it was Rory's turn, she followed a policeman to a small office in the building. The office was stuffed with books, and there was just enough room for two chairs. According to the sign on the door, the office belonged to Finn Dawson.

Rory sat down across from Officer Morris and started apologizing right away to him. "I feel like I should have done something to protect Mary. This group was my responsibility, and I seem to have brought a murderer to Monticello."

"Any help you can give us would be appreciated, Ms. Adams. But how do you know the murderer was someone in your group?"

"I guess I don't," Rory said. "Not for sure." She continued, "Mary was a know-it-all and seemed to be arguing with someone all the time."

Morris leaned back in his chair with his hands on his stomach. "Do you have any idea of who might have poisoned her?"

Rory told him about Karen and Mary's argument and Karen's version of events. Morris nodded. Karen had already confessed it all to him, and he believed her.

"Someone saw Dr. Dawson serve Mary a plate of tomatoes and then escort her outside the tent," the policeman said.

Rory was shocked. "Dr. Dawson? Why would he want to do such a thing?" Finn Dawson was a well-respected historian who was in charge of a large and influential project. He was at the peak of his career. *Why would he risk everything to kill a cranky horticulturist?* Rory mused.

Rory remembered something Mary had said in the tomato patch, and she wondered now about its significance. She wished she knew more about plants so she could make sense of Mary's comment: "Is there any kind of reference book on tomatoes around?"

They had been sitting in Dr. Dawson's office and had found a book about tomatoes without any difficulty. Rory had flipped to the index and went to the page that had the information she had been looking for. She had not been surprised to find that Mary had been right all along. Mary might have been a blackmailer, but she was undeniably an expert on tomatoes.

"If Finn Dawson claims in all the literature that the gardens here at Monticello are completely historic, then how does he explain the Brandywine tomatoes, bred later in the 1800s by the Amish, and the Soldackis—brought here much later from Poland—that are planted in the tomato patch?" Rory asked.

Officer Morris could not answer the question, so Dr. Dawson was brought down from the house. When Rory posed the question to Finn, his face flushed and he looked angry. "Mary Walton tried to destroy my career and blackmail me over those tomatoes. I have permission to plant whatever I see fit, and no one has ever questioned my choices," Finn said, spluttering with anger.

Mary had apparently blackmailed the wrong person this time, and Finn Dawson had moved quickly to quiet her forever. Rory was quite sure that she would never look at a tomato again without a queasy feeling.

JUSTICE DELAYED

By Maria Hudgins

"IT'S A SHAME. A *damn* shame. Shouldn't happen. Ever."

Judge Maris shifted his weight to the other arm of his big office chair. He and Sheriff Guy Herring were eating a take-out lunch in the judge's chambers on a Saturday. They had unfinished business they found easier to polish off when the courthouse was nearly empty.

"Will he sue the state, do you think?"

"Wouldn't be surprised." Maris scrubbed his face with his big red hands.

"He's been out more than a week, and we haven't heard a peep out of him."

"Don't let that lull you into a false sense of security." Maris peeled the foil wrap from his soft-shell blue crab sandwich and snapped off one of the deep-fried claws dangling out of the bun. Twisting his mouth a little sideways, he crunched it between his back molars.

Herring bundled a sheaf of French fries into his mouth and followed it with a pull on the straw in his paper cup. "No skin off my nose, if he does. My case was solid." He crumpled the foil wrap from his own sandwich, now eaten, and leaned back in the upholstered visitors chair. He swung one foot onto the opposite knee, an impressive feat for one of his age and bulk.

This was the thing about Herring that crawled up Maris's spine. He was always, in his own mind, right. Not just covering his ass either. Herring truly believed he made no errors, and pointing out evidence to the contrary was useless. In this particular case, Herring had probably made an arrest prematurely, followed by biased evidence-gathering on the part of the Commonwealth's Attorney. In the trial, the bite marks on the murder victim's body were identified by a dentist more interested in establishing himself as an expert witness than in any sort of scientific objectivity.

Tony Dyson had been convicted of killing his lover, Victoria Brandywine, *née* Barbara Jones, and the trial had received saturation coverage in the local media. Ms. Brandywine was one of Virginia's most successful writers, with more than forty romance novels. According to the testimony of the married couple who were caretakers at the novelist's house, Dyson was the last person to visit Ms. Brandywine in her bedroom on the night she died. The wife, Anna Goode, found Ms. Brandywine the next morning lying on the floor beside her big, solid brass bed. Her gown ripped, bloody scratches on her face and arms, purple bite marks on her shoulders, she had actually died from asphyxiation. A silk scarf was knotted so tightly it seemed buried in the skin of her neck. Zachary Goode, Anna's husband, testified he'd heard Dyson's BMW peeling out of the drive at about ten o'clock.

Dyson got a life sentence. That was ten years ago.

On the stand, Dyson testified he had been at a hotel in Richmond with another woman, an alibi that couldn't be verified. The woman he named could not be located, the hotel had no record of his being there—at least under his own name. He also got caught in a lie. The story he first told investigators on the day after the murder was that he had been at his own home in Virginia Beach. That was before they told him Victoria was dead.

"He had a hard time in prison," Judge Maris said of Dyson.

"Pretty young boy like that, I'm not surprised," Sheriff Herring added.

Maris clamped his lips together. He felt the blood rising past his shirt collar and flooding his face. He spotted his gavel on the right side of his desk and was seized by an urgent need to crown the old sheriff with it. The conditions that Tony Dyson had to put up with in prison, Maris felt, should never be tolerated in the first place. Sending a young man to prison for theft, for dealing drugs, for too many run-ins with the law was justice. Being raped while serving time was not.

"He spent most of his time in solitary. Mostly for insubordination—minor stuff," the judge said. "Probably went to solitary deliberately, to escape." Herring sucked air through his teeth on one side, with a sort of clicking sound.

"It's despicable," Maris huffed.

"Don't do the crime if you can't do the time," the sheriff countered.

"But he didn't *do* the crime, did he?"

Herring growled.

Maris looked past Herring's shoulder, to the Chesapeake Bay beyond his window. *Calm down*, he told himself. *It's not worth a fight*. His gaze swerved from the window to his citation blue marlin mounted on the wall between two bookcases. In that particular case, the fish had been the biter but also the victim. A biter, he mused, may be the aggressor or the victim. The bitten may be either as well.

Judge Maris drove home that evening with the dregs of this thought still fresh. Tony Dyson had not killed Victoria Brandywine. Evidence that firmly established he was in Richmond at the time of her murder turned up in the offices of the Commonwealth's Attorney and were handed over to the court, *about ten years too late*. Circumstances were such that it was unlikely the crime would ever be pinned on any particular individual. Everything about this case made Maris's gavel hand itch.

Dyson was a free man now, and so was Victoria Brandywine's killer. The case was open again, but ice cold. The new Commonwealth's Attorney would have been in college when Dyson was convicted. The young attorney was out to make a name for herself. What better way than to find and convict a celebrity's real killer? Maris had reread the entire case after evidence of Dyson's innocence was presented to him. The murder was in 1999, when Virginia already had a crack DNA lab and a reputation as one of the best in the nation. Problem was, the forensic team had found no suspicious DNA on the body of the victim. DNA from Dyson, as well as from Anna and Zachary Goode, was found in several places around the bedroom, but that would be expected from the lover, the housekeeper and the handyman, all of whom had been there often and shortly before the murder. *But why was no DNA found in or around the bite mark?* This question gnawed at the judge now as it did during the trial ten years earlier. *How do you bite someone hard enough to leave tooth prints and yet leave no saliva?*

Traffic slowed to a crawl as he drove across one of Tidewater's many bridge-tunnels. It was a hot, clear August night, and he lowered his windows to feel the cool breeze off the water. The Thimble Shoals lighthouse flashed rhythmically on the eastern horizon. The breeze, the lighthouse and Ella Fitzgerald on CD soothed his nerves and calmed his mind. Maris often marveled at how small their community felt despite a population of one and a half million. The home of the late Victoria Brandywine was no more than a mile from his own house. Years ago, before the judge's wife died, he and Mrs. Maris had attended the occasional stupefyingly dull party there at the invitation of the narcissistic and self-promoting author. Ms. Brandywine's house was now occupied by her nephew, a handsome young man named Brett Clark, who inherited her entire estate including the house.

Before Maris realized what he was doing, he had driven past his own house and appeared to be heading for the residence of the late Ms. Brandywine—the site of the murder. He pulled into the gravel drive and around to the front of the Art Deco wonder. Local people had long looked a bit askance at the "modern" house, built in the 1930s, as if it were a harbinger of worse things to come. All stucco and glass, it had porthole windows along one side and one rounded corner lined with tall windows that looked out across the Bay. Having weathered the storms of eighty years, it was close to earning the status of "vintage."

Anna Goode greeted him at the door and ushered him into the living room. Anna and Zachary were a rather sad pair, he thought. Anna and Victoria had taught school together back when Victoria still used her birth name, Barbara. Zach, a gentle, dull soul, was no good with money and managed to dig the Goodes into a deep financial hole at about the same time Victoria's star was rising. She offered them jobs as housekeeper/ cook and caretaker, with room and board included. Having no other reasonable options, the Goodes declared bankruptcy, freed themselves from their mountain of debt and moved in. Anna never overcame the habit of calling her former colleague by her real name, Barbara.

The living room looked much as Maris had remembered: There was off-white furniture, precisely placed, and a floor lamp that consisted of a life-size bronze nude holding a glass light, like a frosted tulip, on her head. Something rather green and metallic loomed up from behind the off-white sofa like a gathering storm. It did seem as if Victoria's nephew had made a few changes, though. The walls were now a manly shade of khaki. The built-in and lighted display case on one wall, once filled with first editions of Victoria Brandywine novels, awards and trophies in the form of hearts, lips and winsome damsels now held an enviable collection of guns.

Anna left the room to let Victoria's heir, Mr. Clark, know he had a visitor. Maris studied the guns in the display case.

"Judge Maris. Pleasant surprise." Brett Clark, in polo shirt and linen slacks, appeared from around the corner, hand extended. Brett could have been a fashion model—impeccably groomed even on this evening when he was at home alone, teeth just slightly crooked, nails manicured. He had a Lotus Europa in the garage. He played at yacht sales as a way of appearing to be employed, but he rarely sold one. "Come in, come in. Have a seat. What will you have to drink?" He turned toward the hall. "Anna?"

"Scotch and soda, if you don't mind," Maris said to Anna, now appearing at the end of the hall, nodding. Anna had gained weight since the last time he'd seen her, her little piggy eyes sunken into the excess flesh around them. He asked about Zachary and, being told he was well and in the kitchen fixing a broken lock, said, "Would you and Zachary join us? I'd like to talk to all three of you."

Brett started slightly, then nodded at her. Turning back to the display case, he pointed out a Civil War-era Colt Dragoon revolver and a pair of English flintlock dueling pistols in a velvet-lined case. "Similar to the ones used in the Hamilton-Burr duel," he said.

"Hopefully, our problem-solving skills have progressed a bit in the last couple hundred years."

"Perhaps. Perhaps not."

Zachary Goode slipped in, as quietly as a ghost, and cleared his throat by way of announcing his arrival. Maris saw that he'd lost as much weight as his wife had gained in the last ten years. He recalled Goode's testimony on the witness stand in Tony Dyson's trial. How his false teeth clacked at the beginning and end of every sentence. He remembered the exact time Dyson's BMW peeled out of the drive, because he was taking pain medication at the time and he had looked at his watch to see if he could take another pill before bedtime. "Ten minutes after ten," he had told the court.

They took seats around the conversation circle in front of

the strange green metal sculpture, Anna sinking into one of the cushy tufted chairs and Zachary perched tentatively on an ottoman.

"Guess you've heard about Tony Dyson being released," Maris said.

Anna snorted, and Zachary didn't react at all.

"You'd have to be living in a cave not to hear about it," Clark said, jiggling the ice in his glass. "It's all over the TV. What's your take on this, Judge Maris? You know more about it than we do."

"I doubt that I do, actually. You were all at the trial same as me. But I must confess that I was never comfortable with the bite-mark testimony."

"Dr. Knox. Wasn't that his name?"

"Ryan Knox. Yes. Coincidentally, he was my wife's dentist," Maris said.

"I heard about your wife's passing," Anna said. "I'm so sorry."

Maris waved away her condolences and went on. "Nice guy, I thought. Good dentist too. Very careful, my wife told me. But I wasn't comfortable with that bite-mark thing. You know? He made a cast of Dyson's teeth, and made impressions on—what was it—a pig carcass or some such. Never heard of such a thing! A pig carcass."

"But he superimposed a photo of those marks over the bruises on Aunt Victoria's shoulder. They matched exactly."

"Depends on your definition of *exactly*. From where I was sitting, they looked mighty damn fuzzy."

"So what are you saying, Judge?" Anna shifted forward in her seat. "Are you saying they didn't match?"

"They obviously didn't match. The forensic man said the bite marks were inflicted *perimortem*." He pronounced the technical term distinctly as if delivering a lecture and listeners should write it down. "At or near the time of death. We now know that Dyson was in Richmond at the time."

"Tony was in her room. I heard them fighting. I heard the

front door slam," Anna said, her tone questioning.

"You called 911 about eight the next morning, right?" Maris asked her. "Forensics showed she couldn't have died any earlier than midnight, at the earliest."

"But they can't tell the time exactly, can they?" Clark leaned forward, elbows on his knees.

Maris noted the rapt attention he now had from all three of his listeners. "Not exactly, but the estimated time of death was three or four in the morning. Long way from ten at night when Dyson left. He checked into the hotel in Richmond at fifteen minutes before midnight. "

"Well, I'm still in the clear," Clark said. "I was at Carlos's Bar until my date poured my sorry ass into the Jeep and drove me home. She spent the night—I know this because she brought me a fistful of aspirin and a Bloody Mary the next morning."

"I recall her testimony," Maris said, not even slightly tempted to feed Clark's ego with a laugh.

"So someone else must have come in during the night," Anna said. Her eyes darted quickly toward her husband, then back to Maris.

"Must have," Maris said.

———————— 🐾 ————————

Driving home, Maris felt depressed. He hadn't made any progress at all. He'd gone in too soon, without a real plan of attack. One or more of those three had been lying, and he should have been crafty enough to force them into a corner. He should have waited, carefully planned what he would say, and then popped in for an unannounced visit. They'd be on their guard now. The time for an ambush was past.

Anna was right, though. Someone could have entered the house in the wee hours. The Goodes' small apartment was on the opposite end of the house from Victoria's bedroom. *Who else* had a motive? How about any of the thousands of writers who might resent her success? Any of the half-dozen agents she had fired? Or one of Tony Dyson's other lovers?

Who benefited from Victoria's death? If money was the motive and it usually was, Maris knew, Brett Clark was the obvious suspect. But the bite marks. Bite marks and scratches and strangulation with a silk scarf made it seem more like a crime of passion. *A premeditated, cold-blooded murder for money? Wouldn't the killer come in armed with something a bit more reliable than teeth, fingernails and a scarf?*

Anna Goode had reason to resent Victoria in spite of her employing the poor couple and giving them a place to live. Anna and Victoria had gone from colleagues—equals—to employee and employer. That must have rankled. *"Yes, Ms. Brandywine. Yes, Barb ... Victoria."*

Zachary's pride, his very manhood, was stripped by a rich bitch who knew his wife. That must have rankled too.

Biting and scratching were more like a woman's style, Maris thought. Plus, he suddenly recalled, Zachary had false teeth. False teeth would hardly be stable enough to make for a good solid chomp.

It must have been Anna. It all fit. Had Dr. Knox made dental casts of anyone other than Tony Dyson? Had he made a cast of Anna's teeth?

Maris recalled again how Zachary's teeth had clacked when he testified. Zachary was taking pain medication on the night of the murder. *Why? Was it because his teeth were hurting him? Might that have resulted in the pulling of all his teeth? Who was his dentist? When did he get his new false teeth?* If they were new at the time of the trial, it would explain the clacking. He might not have been used to them yet. If so, he may have had his natural teeth at the time of the murder and the bite marks on Victoria's shoulder wouldn't have matched any set of teeth still in existence.

But the more he thought about Anna, the more certain he became that it must have been she. The lack of DNA. Anna was a well-educated woman who would have known that DNA could be picked up from saliva, perhaps also from scratch marks. She could have slipped into Victoria's room at any time that night, killed her, and had the rest of the night to clean up the scene. Wash the wounds. Maybe she sneaked in with the objective of *"borrowing"* something. Maybe Victoria woke up and caught her. They fought. *The scarf? Wouldn't the killer's DNA have rubbed off on the scarf? Suppose she wasn't strangled with that particular scarf but with bare hands or a different scarf. Anna could have donned gloves and then tied the silk one around Victoria's lifeless neck.*

The more the judge thought about it, the more sense it made.

Maris pulled into his driveway, tramped straight to the kitchen and looked up Ryan Knox's home phone number. He checked his watch. It wasn't too late to call.

Knox's wife, Phyllis, answered. "He isn't here, Judge Maris. He's out of town—in seclusion, I'm afraid. You've heard about this thing with Tony Dyson, I'm sure."

Maris told her it was the reason for his call.

"It really shook Ryan up, you know. I've never seen him that shaken. He said he had to get away and think, so he's gone to a cabin that belongs to a friend of his—in Montana. No phone, no electricity, and the nearest neighbor lives a half-mile away down a dirt road. But he told me not to worry. He'll be back in a week or so, when he sorts things out."

"How long ago was that?"

"Wednesday a week ago, he left. It's been ten days."

"Doesn't he have a cell phone?"

"I've called it several times, but he must have it turned off."

"Is it like him to go incommunicado like this?"

"No, it isn't. He's such a nervous Nellie, he checks the air pressure in his tires before he goes to the grocery store."

"Maybe he's saving the charge on his phone."

"I'm sure he has his charger with him."

"But no electricity."

"Oh, God. You're right. I hadn't thought of that."

— 🐾 —

The next day Maris drove past Ryan Knox's offices on his way home from Sunday church. No one would be there, of course, so he didn't exactly know why he was doing this. He left the main road and drove around the shopping mall to a small brick building that housed Knox's practice. He parked in front and turned off the motor. The building was dark, with only a yellow security light visible in the foyer beyond the front door.

As much as he didn't care to ever speak to Ryan Knox again, after the erroneous testimony that took ten years of Tony Dyson's life, he needed to talk to him. Knox could tell him how many dental casts were made and of whom. He'd know exactly what had been taken in as evidence. Knox had probably given his receptionist and his hygienists a vacation until he came back to town.

In the sky above the building, several big blackbirds circled. Maris stepped out of his car and walked around to a spot where he could see more of the roof. More blackbirds. Crows? Buzzards? Maris didn't know his birds, but he knew they were there for a reason.

He had a phone with him, but not Knox's number. He called directory assistance, then called Phyllis Knox. "Do you have a key to Ryan's office? I think we need to go in there."

"What's wrong?"

"Maybe nothing. Nothing, I hope. May I come to your house and pick up a key?"

"I'll meet you there in ten minutes."

While Maris waited for Phyllis, he walked around and

checked the roof from several angles. A cylindrical vent punctured a flat portion of the roof, and the birds seemed to be clustered around it.

Phyllis Knox, clad in a pink jogging suit, arrived dangling a ring full of keys and opened the front door. She flipped on an overhead light. Nothing seemed amiss.

"Everything seems all right."

"Let's check around."

In the hall beyond the receptionist's desk, rooms on both sides had been left open, reclining chairs with their overhead lights and cuspidors lurking beyond each door. Each door but one.

"What's this one go to?" Maris asked.

"That's his lab room. It's kept locked."

"Do you have a key?" Maris's gaze sank to the bottom of the door. An electrical wire ran underneath, between the floor and the door, then ran down the hall a few feet where it ended, taped to the wall. "What the hell?"

"I don't know if it's any of these keys, and there are so many. Do you want me to try them all?" Phyllis, absorbed by her keys, hadn't yet noticed the strange wire.

"Wait a minute. I think I see light. Where's the hall light switch, Phyllis? Flip it off."

A band of light now showed clearly at the base of the door.

"If you don't have a key, I'm afraid I must insist we break the door down."

"Why?" Phyllis's eyes widened. "The last person out probably just forgot to turn the light off."

Maris stepped forward and twisted the knob. "It isn't locked."

"Well, go on in." Phyllis sounded impatient, as if Maris shouldn't think he needed permission and they should already be beyond the door.

Maris, however, had a bad feeling. "Go out to my car, Phyllis. Get my car keys. I left them in the ignition, and the door is unlocked. Stupid of me."

Phyllis left, and Maris opened the door. A cloying smell, like rancid lard, hit him squarely in the nose.

On a lab table against the far wall lay a pig carcass—a whole pig, shorn of hair, its feet pointed toward the center of the room. Since the pig was lying directly under a fume hood, it was undoubtedly the reason for the birds on the roof. The aroma of dead pig would be rising up and out the vent directly above.

Ryan Knox lay on the floor, his body curled into a fetal position. Maris knelt and touched his neck, hoping to feel a pulse, but felt nothing. The body was the same temperature as the room, which was quite warm. The air conditioning was off. His vacant eyes still open, Knox had died with a horrible look on his face.

Phyllis stepped through the doorway muttering something about keys, saw her husband lying on the floor, and screamed.

Maris grabbed her by the shoulders and pushed her into the hall. "Call 911 and hurry!" Actually, there was no need to hurry, but if Phyllis thought there was, she'd do as he said.

He found a new T-shirt on the stretch of Formica counter along the right-hand wall. Holding it up, he read the message. "A Bite Mark is as Unique as a Fingerprint."

"Oh, my God," Maris said aloud.

Farther along the countertop, he found a number of dental casts, jumbled, some disarticulated, some not. Maris counted ten sets. Taped to the wall over the array of plaster casts, there were a couple of photographs he recognized. They were photos of Victoria Brandywine's shoulders, taken at autopsy and showing the now infamous tooth prints—fuzzy, yes, but clear enough to show that the biter had a full set of teeth, top and bottom, and the two front teeth weren't perfectly aligned. *Could be my own teeth,* Maris thought. *Mine aren't perfectly aligned either.*

The only other items on the surface were a computer-generated letter and something like a keypad, like the devices in stores where the customer can key in his pin number. Attached to the lower end of this device was the electric wire running down to the floor and under the door. But Maris already knew the wire was attached to absolutely nothing on the other end.

He picked up the letter, hoping he had time to read it before Phyllis came back.

Dr. Knox,

Before we begin, I need to tell you: Don't touch the doorknob! The door you just came through is now locked and wired to a very large explosive device in the broom closet adjacent to this room.

We're going to play a game.

I've left you a jersey to wear. Your team has only one player but then so does mine. I'm wearing a jersey that says, "Bull Shit." Get it? On the table in front of you, please locate the ten plaster casts, one of which (I swear) is of my own pearly whites. Some of the others are casts taken from people the police considered possible suspects until they decided I was their man. I now know that one of these actually was Victoria's killer. Some of the casts are from people who never even met Victoria Brandywine. Each set is labeled in red ink with a four-digit number. Like a pin number, you know. All you have to do is match the correct cast with the bite marks on poor Victoria's shoulders.

I've left a pig on the far table for you. Pigskin is so useful, don't you think? The skin of a dead pig is exactly like that of a living woman. Or so you said in court. You may use the carcass as you see fit.

Now, once you've matched up the bruises on the photograph with the correct set of teeth, all you have to do is key its number into the keypad near the door. You will then see a green light on the keypad and hear the click of the door unlocking. The bomb will now be disarmed. Should you key in the wrong number, you probably won't live long enough to see the red light. Should you attempt to open the door by any other means, the result will be the same as if you had keyed in the wrong number.

Have fun, Dr. Knox. I hope you enjoy our little game as much as I've enjoyed the last ten years.

Yours,

Tony Dyson.

———— 🎭 ————

The pathologist who did the autopsy on Ryan Knox said, "Heart failure."

A colleague of his disagreed and said, "Dehydration."

Phyllis Knox said, "Murder!"

Judge Maris said, "Wicked, yes. But murder? No. There was no bomb, and Knox could have walked out at any time. The door wasn't locked."

Tony Dyson, from the beach on a tiny island in the South Pacific, said, "Justice."

THE CAGED BIRD

By Fiona Quinn

I ALWAYS HATED WALKING this way come nightfall. There's something just shivery about a graveyard when all by one's lonesome. Sometimes when I passed by Old St. John's Church, with its white steeple stabbing a hole in the clouds, I'd harken back to the stories my Grammy told me about all these men and women lying here under their marble slabs. I ran my hand along the black wrought-iron fence, letting my rings jingle-jangle against the metal. Grammy said the ghosts didn't like vibrating sound, so it would keep me safe—the souls wouldn't follow me home. Grammy was full of superstitious ways. I didn't really believe them all, but why take a chance while passing by a graveyard?

As I turned the corner, heading toward my great-auntie's house, I looked in at the tombstones packed tightly together like overcrowded teeth. They jutted this way and that on a rise of land held neatly behind bricks and metal. Everything was locked up tight, keeping the living separated from the dead.

Didn't work out that way for Daddy, though. It was right here in this graveyard that the police found him. He was in the wrong place at the wrong time with the wrong gun still smoking in his hands, and blood spattered all over his brand-new work coveralls. He swears to this day he didn't shoot that gal. I was a newborn at the time. And I guessed my mama didn't like me much 'cause as soon as the doctor gave her the go-ahead, she was out the door. I was left to Grammy, my daddy's mama, to raise up. Grammy was old when she gave birth to Daddy, and my daddy was almost forty when I come along. So it ain't surprising that I have some old-fashioned thoughts in my head.

I stopped in front of the tombstone marking Edgar Allan Poe's mama. She died of consumption when he was only three. Grammy said he was tainted by that death, and every woman he loved after that spit up blood and died. And that's what Daddy said happened right there on Elizabeth Poe's grave. That gal just coughed up blood all over his new work coveralls, then died.

But that story didn't make no sense to no one. And, being poor and all, the only lawyer we could get took our case for free; the judge told him he had to. Grammy said he was a young lawyer fresh out of school. It was his very first case, and the judge made him help someone with felony murder charges. When Grammy got to that part of her tale, she'd cluck her tongue and shake her head. Grammy said the District Attorney ate that boy like he was breakfast then he licked his chops and looked around for a second helping.

Daddy got life. It felt like I did too. Felt like everything I could have been, my future—all of it —got locked up in that jail cell right alongside my daddy. Who's gonna want me around when I got murdering blood in my veins? Bad DNA. I was tainted by that gal's death, just like Poe's women were tainted.

Daddy said that that morning he was just walking to work like always. He was a janitor up at the elementary school, and his job started at five. On my visits with him at the jail, he used to tell me how he loved walking to work under a periwinkle sky. The streetlights, still shining down, made angelic halos above his head. Birds greeted him with their wake-up laughter. But other than that, it was lonely-quiet, and he could think. He said he liked the hush of it.

Daddy was a poet, and he thought up magical, sing-songy words. I have me a whole box of his poems. When I read them over, they made feelings bubble up in my chest. Big feelings. Hurtful feelings. Deep-down honest feelings. Some of those poems he wrote on those periwinkle mornings before my birth.

Those were love words to future-me and to my mama. Then after he killed that woman, his words turned dark and as haunted as this here graveyard.

My great-auntie's house sat kitty-corner to St. John's and seemed to shrink and melt with age, just like she did. I knocked loud on her door and waited. I knew it would take some minutes before she could get up and over to the door and then a bunch more minutes while she undid the nine locks. Nine, according to Grammy, is a magical number that seals out evil. I picked a piece of protective rosemary she had growing and tucked it behind my ear as I watched the sun settle the rest of its way down the hill. I was gonna have to walk home in the dark.

I was surprised that the footsteps came so quick and fell so heavy on the wooden floor. The door swung open. A tall man with a wiry kind of frame held the knob and stepped back. He was wearing a dress shirt with a tie. I looked at him suspiciously. My great-auntie hadn't mentioned company when she asked me to come over.

"It's okay Millie. I'm over here." Aunt Trudy was barely visible under the quilt that she had wrapped around her shoulders. She was sitting at the table with papers spread in front of her. There was a cracked plate with Chips Ahoy cookies on it. They were the same cookies she set out every time someone stopped by. They must be two or three years old now. Everyone knew not to eat her cookies.

I walked over and dropped a kiss on her forehead. Aunt Trudy's skin was paper-thin and spotted with age. I picked up the plate and put the cookies carefully back in their plastic container, the container back on its shelf. The man leaned into the counter and watched this with curiosity in his eyes. But I wasn't gonna explain it to him in front of Aunt Trudy, though he should be thanking me.

He held out his hand for a shake. "I'm Rooster Bowling," he said.

"What kind of name is Rooster?" I asked, sliding my hand into his, feeling anger bubbling up in me like boiling water in a kettle.

He chuckled. "Old family nickname. My real name's Randolph. When I was a kid all I could get out was the Rr Rr Rr."

Everything about him vexed me, or as Grammy would say, "got my hackles up." That feeling made me think of another saying: "Always trust your dog." So if my dog-natured hackles were up, maybe I should be baring my teeth at this man instead of trying to play polite.

"Can I get you something to drink, Mr. Bowling?" I asked, opening the fridge door. The sudden cool air felt good on my over-hot face. The only thing in there was the yellow plastic tray with Aunt Trudy's Meals on Wheels pabulum. I looked over my shoulder to see Mr. Bowling tightening his lips.

"Water would be fine."

I poured the water from the sink faucet into one of the jelly jars that Aunt Trudy used for glasses. She didn't have anything nicer. I thought the man probably wouldn't drink any of it anyway. And sure enough, the first thing he did was push the glass to the side, out of reach. It was rare for us to have someone who had money come in to visit, but when they did, they all seemed to act the same—like we had poor cooties and hard-times was catching.

I sat down across from him and reached over to hold Aunt Trudy's hand protectively.

"I can't make out these words, Millie." Aunt Trudy pushed the papers toward me. "I wanted you to read them to me."

I gathered the papers up. "You're a lawyer then?" I looked over the top of the pages at Mr. Bowling. Why did that name sound distantly familiar to me? Randolph Bowling ...

"I have a law office just around the corner. Your aunt wanted to update her will since her son passed away."

He said it so matter-of-factly, as if he was saying, "Since the sky was cloudy," or, "Since it's May." But it wasn't matter-of-fact at all. Aunt Trudy's son, my "Uncle" Tad, died up at the prison. He wasn't in there for murder though. Uncle Tad was up there doing mission work, trying to save souls. He had a heart attack, fell down the stairs and hit his head. He was dead before the ambulance could get to him. And he was sorely, painfully missed. His being gone left me to look after Grammy and Aunt Trudy all by my lonesome. And to tell the truth, I wasn't sure I was up to it. I missed talking to Uncle Tad. He had a poetic heart like my daddy—but he had turned his poetry toward sermonizing.

I slowly read the words to my auntie. Only half of them made any sense to me. I knew they made even less sense to her. I was going to graduate from high school in a couple more weeks, but Auntie dropped out of school when she was in sixth grade to work as a maid and tend to other people's babies.

I kept stopping and asking Mr. Bowling to explain. He ended up being real patient with us, making sure that everything was clear about her will. But this only made me feel more confused about my junkyard dog feelings. After a while, he even reached out and took a sip from that jelly jar of water I set out for him. So why did he make me feel like I was snakebit and the poison was crawling up my arm?

When we were all done, Aunt Trudy signed the papers, and we left so she could go to bed. It surprised me to find Mr. Bowling keeping apace as I moved down the brick sidewalk. I was running my hand along to jingle-jangle the fence and keep the ghosts away, especially because the night had closed down around us. The clouds hid the moon and the stars. Fog hugged the streetlight selfishly and only let a little bit of the glow reach down to my feet.

"Are you far? I'll walk you home." Mr. Bowling had his briefcase in one hand, the other hand shoved deep in his dress pants pocket.

"I'm just a few blocks more. I'll be fine." I turned the corner onto Broad Street, happy to see the long line of headlights. I felt safer.

"As dark as it is out here, I'd feel better if I saw you home." He looked back over his shoulder, like he had heard someone coming up behind us. I looked too.

Fear tickled over the surface of my skin. My heart was pounding, but I couldn't figure out why. Rooster Bowling had been nothing but nice to Aunt Trudy and me tonight. Just as I was about to say, "Yes, thank you," out of politeness, I saw two boys from school lying across the benches in Triangle Park.

I gestured over to them. "I'm meeting up," I said.

He nodded, turned in the opposite direction, and headed off. When he was gone from sight, I scurried home quick and locked all nine locks.

"You get done with Trudy?" Grammy asked.

"Yes, ma'am."

"Why you looking all flustered like that? Something happen?"

I never could hide much from Grammy. She was half-blind, but she could always see truth.

"Nothing happened. I just got a bad feeling hanging over me."

She patted the couch beside her, and I sat down and told her all about Rooster Bowling. "So you feel like Rooster Bowling and bad things go hand in hand, do you?" Grammy asked. She pushed herself slowly to her feet and worked her way over to the mantel and her box of important papers. If the house was on fire, and I was running to save my life, I had better grab that box on the way out or face Grammy's wooden spoon on my backside. She rifled through the box until she found an old yellowed newspaper article and handed it out to me.

— 🐞 —

I leaned against the beige clapboards, shifting my weight

from foot to foot. I had come here to Mr. Bowling's office instead of going to school today. I was almost done with the year. Shouldn't do no harm. I glanced at my watch. I didn't know what time lawyers got started with their day, but it was already after nine, and I had been standing here an awful long time. My focus was on the tips of my tennis shoes when I saw the four-leaf clover by my right foot. I bent to pick it up, and I tucked it into my bra next to my heart.

Mr. Bowling was fussing with an armful of papers when he climbed out of his beat-up Honda. He startled when he saw me standing there.

"Millie? Is everything okay with Mrs. Nelson?"

"My auntie's fine, thank you. I come to ask you about something else," I said.

He opened the door and gestured me in with his briefcase. I walked through the waiting room and on back to where I saw his desk. His office was dark and felt like a cave, what with the stacks of folders like stalagmites crowding me in. I slid onto a black leather chair as he put his things onto the credenza and sat down to look at me.

On an inhale, I lowered my lashes and hugged my schoolbooks to my chest. "My full name is Mildred Elizabeth Anderson." My voice sounded like I was confessing a sin.

When I peeked up, Mr. Bowling was blank-faced. He was waiting for something more.

"My daddy's name is Lloyd Anderson. He lives in the jail."

Red crept up Mr. Bowling's face, and his lips drooped like an over-watered flower. "Mildred ..." He stopped to cough, then got up and pulled two Diet Cokes from a little fridge on the table behind him, set one in front of me and took a long swig from the one he got for himself. He coughed again.

I pulled the newspaper article from my biology book and laid it out in front of him. "When I got home last night, I asked Grammy who you were. She showed me this article from back when you represented my daddy. I thought I'd heard your name from somewhere."

He put his hands in his pockets and tilted his head to the side.

"I had some questions. I thought that maybe you could help me understand. It says here that my daddy was well respected in the community, that the deacon from the church come and spoke at the trial on his behalf, and the principal from the school where he was working."

Mr. Bowling nodded.

"It says here that the community was all riled up about the case." I was watching Mr. Bowling closely. "It wasn't racial, though. Everyone was white, right?"

He sat heavily down in his chair. "That's right."

"So why were they riled?"

He spread his fingers wide on his desk and looked down at them instead of at me. "Well, Millie, at the time this case seemed to catch peoples' romantic imaginations, the tragedy of it. Sarah Wilson's fiancé had been killed in a car accident just days before, and the family was already grieving that."

"Oh. I thought it might have had something to do with her daddy being a doctor and my daddy being a janitor."

Mr. Bowling slowly nodded his head. "There was that."

I pointed toward the article. "It said that Attorney General Craven was up for election in six months. He wanted to be governor, and this case was causing him problems. It said that Craven sped things up too fast, so he could make it all go away." I inched the paper a little closer to him. "The article said it wasn't only Mr. Craven who wanted things to go fast. Sarah Wilson's daddy wanted to put the tragedy behind them so the family could heal up. Dr. Wilson thought they'd have closure once my daddy was locked behind bars for the rest of his life." Mr. Bowling looked like he'd swallowed a whole glass of rotten milk, but I kept going. "The article said that Dr. Wilson put money behind those words and gave big-time to Craven's campaign fund. The paper said neither thing was fair, and surely an appeal would be filed."

Mr. Bowling looked at me with watery blue eyes and didn't say a word, just pinched his lips between his fingers. I tried again. "Grammy said you didn't file an appeal." I shuffled my feet back and forth in front of me. I didn't want him to feel like I was accusing him of nothing. I just wanted to understand what happened to my daddy.

He looked at me for a long time. Uncomfortably long. "I tried my best at the first trial," he finally said. "Facts are facts. I didn't know how I could make anything any better at a second trial."

I glanced around the cluttered room. "Did you do better by your other clients?" I asked.

He shook his head. "That was my first and only criminal case. I don't have the stomach for it. I can't hold someone's life in my hands that way. Lloyd's case gave me nightmares for years. No. I just do real estate law, wills and advanced directives. Things like that."

"Daddy says he didn't kill that gal." I looked directly into Mr. Bowling's eyes. He stared back at me. I wished he'd blink. It was unnatural the way he held his eyes.

There was a knock at the door, which seemed to wake Mr. Bowling up. I watched over my shoulder as he opened it to a man with a Goldfiend Real Estate jacket on over his polo shirt and khaki pants. Mr. Bowling asked him to sit in the reception area. When he came back into his office, he went to a file cabinet and pulled out a fat three-ring binder. "That's got everything from the trial." He handed it to me and pointed to a door to the left. "Go and look it over. Maybe the answers you want are in there. I have a meeting."

I sat on the floor in the room not much bigger than a closet and opened the cover. It was nice and neat, with tabs marking the different sections. My hand trembled a bit when I picked up the tab that said "photos." I never saw a picture of what Sarah Wilson had looked like. All I knew was that she had been a nursing student up at MCV.

Maybe I shouldn't have opened it up like a can of worms that wriggled their way into my brain and couldn't be shoved back into their container no more. I'd never be able to un-see those photos. These weren't nice pictures—pictures from her yearbook. These were pictures that the coroner took. It said so across the bottom.

I turned through page after page of Sarah Wilson photos. She didn't look much older than me. She was pretty if I looked past the blood all over her mouth. Strange. Not what I thought a nursing student with a wealthy daddy would look like. Her hair was greasy and hugged her head. Her clothes were mismatched. Not the kind of mismatched that I saw in fashion magazines, though. She had bare feet and a flowered skirt. Her shirt was an oversized striped man's shirt with a giant, red-blood flower blooming on her upper chest.

Daddy said that that morning, just as he was turning the corner onto Broad Street, everything came rushing forward in one big explosion from a gunshot. Dogs barking, men shouting, Daddy didn't want to have anything to do with trouble. He ran up the steps to St. John's, where he knew his buddy Jumping Bean would be vacuuming the red carpets in the sanctuary, getting ready for the tourists to stop by and see where Patrick Henry gave his speech about liberty and death. But when Daddy got up there, the door was locked. Sirens were screaming up the road, so Daddy slid to the side yard to hide in the shadows of the gravestones and wait.

That's where he come up on her. She was lying against Liza Poe's gravestone. Daddy saw she was hurt. He knelt beside her to help. Her hands clasped over her chest. He said that when he bent in to talk to her, she coughed up blood. It went all over his face, and he jerked back away from it and wiped his sleeve across his mouth. Then she coughed again, spraying more blood over his coveralls.

He said he watched her fall over with her eyes wide open and unblinking. Daddy knew well enough she was dead. When he looked to the side, he saw a gun and reached over to pick it up. That's when the police came up the sidewalk. They made him lie down and handcuffed him. Then they took my daddy away.

Mr. Bowling cleared his throat at the door. I tilted my head back to look up at him.

"You okay in here?" he asked.

"Why would Sarah Wilson be at St. John's at five in the morning?"

He leaned into the doorframe. "We don't know. Her lawyer suggested it was because she was distraught. She was supposed to get married there at the church the next day, and her fiancé had just died in the accident. By all accounts, she wasn't handling it well."

"Why did they think my daddy wanted to hurt her? Did he know her somehow?"

"They said he wanted to rob her. She had a big diamond engagement ring. It was worth quite a lot of money."

"Oh," I said.

"I'm going out to get some lunch. I'll bring something back for you if you want to keep looking through the binder."

I nodded my head and flipped the page over.

While he was gone, I read the statement that Jumping Bean had given to the police—only they called him David Lawson. Jumping Bean had heard the shot when he was in the sanctuary. He said he locked the door quick and ran to the back to call 911. He was still on the phone with them when the police was arresting Daddy.

"Mr. Bowling?" I asked, reaching up for the brown paper bag he had brought back for me. "It says here that Sarah Wilson had gun residue on her hand."

"It's believed that the gun went off when she was trying to wrestle it away from your father, and she was shot in the chest."

"But it says that my daddy didn't have gun residue on his hands," I said.

Mr. Bowling pulled at his ear. "Because he was wearing gloves."

"Oh. That makes sense. Did you make him try the gloves on in court like they did at the O.J. trial?"

He looked at me funny. "No. They weren't collected as evidence."

"Why's that?" I asked.

He squatted down, pulled the binder from my lap and flipped to the appendix tab at the back. He ran his finger down the evidence list, shook his head, and pushed the book back over to me.

I opened the paper bag and pulled out my sandwich.

"And why didn't they believe my daddy that he come up on her already hurt?"

Mr. Bowling lowered himself so that he sat beside me. Packed tightly into that copy room like that, I felt over-warm with not enough air to breathe in.

"There were three people—Lloyd, Sarah and David—on the church grounds," he explained. "David was inside on the phone with the pastor talking about that morning's sunrise service. He has a rock-solid alibi."

I nodded. I knew that already.

"When the gun went off, the firemen at the station across the way gathered their medical equipment, but protocol said they had to wait for the police to give the all-clear on the scene before they could approach. They were standing at their station watching the entrance to St. John's. They didn't see your father go in, and they didn't see anyone else come out. Only three people were behind that fence. Only your father had the opportunity and motive to kill her. It's a shame, though, that the paramedics had to wait."

"Why's that?" I asked, feeling a little tingle run down my back.

"Sarah was killed by a twenty-two. It shattered her rib and pierced her lung. If help had gotten there a minute or so sooner, they could probably have saved her life."

I turned the page to the photo of a gun lying next to a ruler. It was marked "actual size." "That's the gun? It's itty-bitty."

Mr. Bowling put his finger on the picture. "People call that a pocket gun." He leaned his head back against the doorjamb. "Why are screwing your mouth up like that?"

"Well, my daddy's so big. Has hands are like baseball mitts, is all. Seems to me, a little gun like that would be like a toy in his hands."

"People carry this sized gun for self-defense, Millie. It's meant to be concealed in a purse or a pocket. Your father walked through some pretty bad neighborhoods on his way to work. It would make sense for him to be armed."

I nodded. Mr. Bowling eased up to his feet and went back to his desk.

I was remembering a poem Daddy wrote to my mama right about that time. It was a love poem. No one who read it could think anything but that he was happy. Why would a happy man with a respectable job and a just-born baby follow a distraught girl into the graveyard to steal her ring? I couldn't figure it. I licked sandwich crumbs from my fingers then dried them on my shirt.

I spent the whole afternoon looking and reading. Finally, Mr. Bowling came back into the copying room. "Millie, it's time to go home. You can come back another time and look through the binder."

I shut it and stood up. My muscles were sore from hunkering over for so long. "I'd appreciate that," I said.

He reached out to take the binder from me. "Hey." I stopped

him. "I had another question."

He raised an arched brow.

Putting the album on the table, I opened it back up to the picture of a newspaper clipping that was mostly unreadable because of the blood. I could tell it had been crumpled up and then smoothed back out. "What was that?" I asked.

He came farther into the room and leaned over the table. He rubbed his hand across the back of his neck. "That's the obituary for her fiancé."

"Why's it here? How'd it get all bloody like that?"

"Because she was holding it when she died," he said, closing the binder. He put his hand on my back and moved me through the door. We were almost out of the office when I stalled. "She died with it in her left hand, didn't she?" I asked.

"What?"

"She died with the obituary in her left hand?" I asked, again.

With a sigh, Mr. Bowling opened the binder back up and searched through. "Her left hand, yes," he said. "Why?"

"The gun residue was on her right hand from wrestling the gun away from my daddy. And in her left hand she was gripping the obituary. That doesn't make much sense, now does it? If I thought I was about to die, I'd use both hands to fend off that gun. Wouldn't you?"

I'd read books where all the blood drained from a character's face, but I'd never seen it before. One minute Mr. Bowling was pasty white, the next he was kind of gray and swaying. I was afraid he might be having a stroke like my Aunt Trudy had that one time. I ran through in my head what I should do. Call 911 was all that I come up with, so I moved toward his desk. Mr. Bowling clutched at my arm though, held me there solid. His eyes were a little crazy, and he breathed out, "Suicide."

He pushed past me and grabbed up the phone.

——— 🐞 ———

I walked back toward Broad Street. Grammy would be worried. I should have been home hours ago. I felt bad for that. But she'd be okay once I explained. As I crossed over the street, I caught a glimpse of the wrought-iron fence circling around St. John's like a jail for all them souls. I stopped on the sidewalk and just looked hard at it, wondering as I often did about how life could change all of a sudden—wondering what would have happened on that periwinkle morning if my daddy had been just a block further on down the road. Would he still be listening to the bird's wake-up laughter as he walked up to his job each day?

A big old sob caught in my throat as I thought about a poem my daddy had written to me about feeling like a caged bird unable to fly. That was how I had felt my whole life. Caged up by what happened behind the wrought-iron fence at St. John's. Trapped by circumstance. And now, I had another feeling pressing on my chest—one I hadn't ever felt sitting there ever before. I thought this was probably what people called "hope." I lifted my eyes to see the heavy tangerine sun sliding down the backside of the sky, and breathed in its beauty.

TWENTY-FIVE HEADS ARE BETTER THAN NONE

By Maria Hudgins

I HAD BROUGHT TWENTY-FIVE of my eleventh grade environmental science students to Grandview Beach on the northeast side of Hampton, near the mouth of the Chesapeake Bay. My student teacher from Christopher Newport University, Jason Konrad, was supervising the six kids who were attempting to do a beach transect, while others recorded weather data, analyzed beach sand or darted along the high tide line searching for the items listed on their "scavenger hunt" sheet. Students with me were doing chemical water testing. Each had his own Phosphate Test Kit and each had staked out a position at the edge of the water, softly lapping at the sand.

"Ready? Brendan, grab your marker," I shouted into the wind. "Put this on the phosphate chart."

"Ready, Mrs. McCarthy." Brendan picked up a small whiteboard and a dry-erase marker.

"Lily?"

"Two point O."

"Mike?"

"O point two."

"Casey?"

"O point one."

"Tanisha?"

"O point one."

"Brendan?"

"Huh? Oh. Mine was O point two."

"Okay. Dump the contents of your test tubes in the white bucket and rinse them with the distilled water in the squirt bottle beside the bucket. Then run the same test again at the same spot. We always want to verify our data, don't we?"

Since the Grandview Nature Preserve is a nesting ground of the endangered piping plover, I had scheduled this field trip as late in the spring semester as possible to avoid students traipsing across egg-filled nests. We'd been rewarded with a glorious late-May day. The beach wrack yielded lots of strange flotsam that had washed ashore throughout the winter, and the jellyfish weren't yet big enough to sting.

The beach at Grandview is about as unaltered as any you can find. Unaltered by humans, that is. Saltwater encroachment due to sea level rise and the sinking East Coast has killed off the pines that grew here decades ago, reducing them to desolate, blackened spires poking out of the sand. But as for people, the long walk from Beach Road past bayberry thicket, salt flat and tidal creek keeps out all but the most determined folk and their dogs.

After a long winter wallowing in the overworked-and-underpaid self-pity unique to teachers, I took a deep, liberating breath and looked up the beach at the busy students that I knew so well by this time of year.

And they pay me to do this? I grinned inside.

"Mike, where are your safety glasses?"

Macho Mike, as I sometimes thought of him, found his glasses on the sand behind him. Brendan, who heard a different drummer, squatted a few yards north of Mike, gazing at the sun through the bay water and ascorbic acid in his test tube. Then there was Tanisha the Clown, who'd finally learned to take teasing as well as dish it out, Casey the Mother Hen and lovely little Lily.

Lily wasn't actually little or even lovely, in the standard sense of that word, but she was the new kid in class. Because of her parents' military careers, Lily had attended a long string of schools, and now those parents had separated, leaving her future residence a bit uncertain. To top it all off, her guidance counselor moved her up to college prep classes at mid-term when she noted that the child was making straight A's in the lower level. Lily, I knew, didn't yet feel comfortable with the accelerated academic pace or with her new classmates.

And Lily's reading on that last test had been way off—at least ten times higher than the actual phosphate level in this part of the Bay. I slipped over behind her to see if she was doing the test properly. It looked as if she was.

Lily had taken the southernmost position along the shoreline, near a pile of big timbers that had probably washed up in a winter storm. I hadn't let students go any farther south than that because I needed to keep them all within my sight. Looking north, I saw my assistant, Jason, and his beach transect team heading our way.

"Is everyone finished?" I asked. "Brendan, run back to your data board. Let's get the numbers. Lily?"

"O point two," she said.

Aha. Now that's better. "Casey?"

"O point one."

"Mike?"

"O point one three five six."

"Cut that out, Mike. Brendan, put down O point one."

"Tanisha?"

"O point two."

"Brendan?"

"O point one five. Hey, I swear, Mrs. McCarthy. It was exactly between the point one and the point two, so it's gotta be point one five."

"Whatever."

Lily stood up, knocked sand off her shorts and stumbled sideways, her right hand breaking her fall as she toppled into the pile of driftwood.

"Oh, my Lord! Oh! Oh!" She jumped backward, her hand to

her chest, her throat making strange gurgling noises. Like tacks to a magnet, every student in the class dashed to the spot, most of them getting there before I did.

"Ohh, junk!"

"Holy shit!"

"Miz McCAAARthy!"

It was awful. It wore jeans, a Timberland jacket, work boots, and, judging by its broad shoulders, it appeared to be a man. I would say that he was lying face down, but that wouldn't be quite accurate because he had no face. He had no head.

Reacting instinctively, I spread my arms and pushed back the students within my reach. This was the stuff of nightmares. Mostly sixteen, these kids were of an age to pretend bravado while dissolving on the inside.

To Jason, I yelled, "Call Transportation! Tell them to send us a cheese bus right now!" Yanking my cell phone from my jeans pocket, I dialed 911.

The dispatcher put me through to a policeman. I blurted out my story and emphasized the fact that I was here with twenty-five students.

"Keep them away from the body," the officer said. "Keep them all back. Way back!"

"Do you know how hard that'll be? They're going crazy."

"Keep them away from the body! It's probably a crime scene. It must not be touched."

Helplessly, I looked at Jason, who had migrated to the other side of the body, a cell phone to his ear. "Help me, Jason. Get back, everybody. Now! Police orders."

"Transportation is giving me a rough time, Mrs. McCarthy," Jason said, dashing around to join with me in forming a two-person line of demarcation. "They say we're to be picked up at two-fifteen and they can't come any earlier."

"Give me that phone." The only way to deal with Transportation, I knew, was to act like a bully. They didn't understand polite. "We need a yellow bus at the end of Beach Road, now! We're in the middle of a crime scene, and we have to get these students back to school. Get a bus out here posthaste, or you'll be looking like a fool on the evening news."

The threat of adverse publicity always gets you a bus.

The next hour was a mess. The police seemed torn between wanting us there so they could interview us and wanting us out of the way. Jason and I kept the students in a sort of lump thirty yards or so away from the crime scene tape that the police strung around four iron pegs they jammed into the sand. I sent Macho Mike out to Beach Road to watch for the bus and kept the rest of the class diverted by insinuating that the data we had collected would become a crucial part of the case file, so they'd better double-check it. We might, I suggested, have to testify in court as to how our physical data was collected, and the one clue that would solve the case might already be among the spoils of their scavenger hunt.

Meanwhile, Jason slipped down as close as he could to the yellow tape and picked up bits of the police conversation. He reported back to me, "Looks like he's been dead about twenty-four hours. The guy's head has been hacked off with an ax or something. Not a boat propeller or a shark or anything like that. He was dead before his head was chopped off."

"How do they know that?"

"I don't know. They can't ID the guy either. No wallet, no papers. His pockets are empty."

The cheese bus rattled us back to school at one-fifteen. Our lunch bags lay in a pile on an empty seat, untouched, except by different drummer Brendan who had eaten his peanut butter and jelly sandwich even as some of the kids retched into the beach grass, sickened by the traumatic sight of the headless body. I called ahead to warn the guidance department that counseling would soon be needed.

En route to school, somber conversation floated up to me from the back of the bus:

"So the guy lost his head. So what? They can use his fingerprints to ID him."

"Only if the guy had a record or something. If his prints aren't on file, they're useless."

"So then what? He stays a John Doe forever?"

"They can use dental records. I saw that on CSI."

"Now that's the dumbest—jeez! That's so dumb I'm not even going to tell you *why* it's so dumb."

And from another part of the bus: "No head, no teeth, numbnuts."

———— 🐞 ————

The next time I saw the field trip students was on Monday. I normally devote the next class period to a follow-up and analysis of field trip data and, in preparation for that, I dragged out the data boards, the beach transect diagrams and the collection bags before the first bell.

I saw that the whiteboard on which Brendan had written the phosphate data had been altered. The first test run, station No. 1, now said "0.2," written in a girlish hand. Thinking back, I remembered that was Lily's station and that she had originally called out "two point O." I'd been concerned at the time because the number was too high. Obviously Lily, embarrassed that her reading was so different from the others, had used Brendan's erasable marker and changed it.

I was checking my e-mail when Lily walked in, ten minutes before first bell. She slouched over to the aquarium and studied the water, but it seemed to me that her gaze went through the water rather than to the fish in it. She hugged a black notebook to her chest.

"Mrs. McCarthy, I changed one of my numbers on that chart." Her voice sounded artificially strong, as if she had steeled herself to make that admission.

"Why did you do that?"

"Because the number I got was way too high. I knew it couldn't be right, so I changed it. Over the weekend, I went online and found out about phosphate levels in the Bay. I was way off, but I don't know why. My second test was a two point 0 also. In fact, it was off the chart, so it was really more than two point 0. And I *know* I did it right. It was a simple test."

"Did you ever hear, Lily, that the greatest discoveries aren't made when the scientist says 'Eureka?' It's when she says, 'Gee, that's funny.' I suggest we present this little problem to the class. See what we can come up with when we put all our heads together."

Lily seemed a little nervous about that prospect, so I told her to do one more test. "Grab a test kit and use aquarium water this time," I said. "That will tell us for sure whether it's you or the water."

Jason bustled in with a notebook full of lesson plans. The week before, I had told him to take over Monday's classes, but not this first one. I wanted to handle the field trip discussion myself. "I've talked to a friend on the Hampton Police force, Mrs. McCarthy," he leaned over my shoulder and muttered it softly, so that Lily wouldn't hear.

I pulled him out into the hall where we could talk.

"He says that guy was stabbed in the chest. That's what killed him. If he was in the water at all, it wasn't very long and it was after he was dead. There was no water in the lungs, and his clothes were dry. At least they were dry when we found him."

"Who was he?"

"They don't know. His fingerprints aren't in their file, and he doesn't match up with any of their missing persons. Until they find out who he was, they're stumped."

From inside the classroom came Lily's voice: "Mrs. McCarthy? I got O point one with the aquarium water."

I balanced the portable whiteboard on the chalk tray and explained to the class about the alteration of Lily's numbers. "Lily, when you went online, what did you find was the normal phosphate concentration in the lower Chesapeake Bay?"

"About O point one or two," Lily said, "depending on the time of year."

"So here's the question: How do we explain these high numbers? We know it wasn't Lily's technique."

Silence.

"Where do phosphates come from?"

Tanisha the Clown volunteered, "From land runoff."

"Yes, and why do we find high levels of phosphates in runoff?"

Casey the Mother Hen, raised her hand. "Fertilizers. On farms and lawns."

"Any farms nearby?"

"No, but what about those big homes down around the salt ponds? They've got nice lawns, and the tidewater comes out of there not far from where Lily was sitting."

"Good! I'm impressed, Brendan."

"But would that be enough to make the numbers go up that high? And wouldn't it have at least made the other readings higher than normal too? I mean, the water flows along the shore." This came from a student who'd been scavenger hunting at the critical time.

"If lawn fertilizer can't account for it, what else? What other sources of phosphate can you think of?"

Silence.

"Get out your textbooks and look it up. Go on."

There followed a minute or so of page flipping and muttering, then Tanisha yelled out, "Guano!"

"Bird poop!" added another.

"But why would there have been a high level of guano in that particular spot?" I was, at this point, flying blind, trusting that good old Socrates and his method wouldn't lead us into deep guano.

"Wait! I got it!" Casey nearly bounced out of her seat. "That man. That dead man. His boots were right down at the edge of the water. What if he had bird dookie on this boots?"

"I think it would have already washed off, if he'd been there for twenty-four hours," I cautioned.

"But they didn't say he'd been *there* twenty-four hours," Mike said. "They said he'd been *dead* twenty-four hours."

"How was the tide running when we found him?"

"It was high."

"Right."

"So the water could have been just coming up to his boots," Lily said.

"Where would a man walk around in piles of bird poop?" Tanisha asked.

"Under a heron's nest."

"At the zoo."

"On a chicken farm."

"Like on the Eastern Shore," Brendan said. "My family and I drove up the Delmarva Peninsula last summer, and there's like rows and rows of chicken houses. Zillions of 'em."

I called the police immediately. I would have waited until the bell, but the kids wouldn't let me, so convinced were they that we'd solved the mystery, and they were right.

— 🝮 —

The victim had been an itinerant worker at a chicken farm on the Eastern Shore. He hadn't been reported missing because those men and women, working for brief periods wherever they found a job, fell through the bureaucratic cracks. They lived in a shadow zone between addresses and sometimes carried fake IDs. No one had reported this man missing, but once his identity was known, police quickly nabbed Earl Brooks, the man that a dozen people had seen and heard the John Doe fighting with on that Thursday evening.

SHOPPING FOR MURDER

By Teresa Inge

JANA KARSON TURNED FROM the task of marking sale items at the front counter to face her customer entering the store. "Welcome to Chesapeake Fabrics."

Tucker Boyd slapped a flyer on the counter. "If you don't stop posting sales flyers on my shop window, you'll regret it."

Jana stared at his piercing blue eyes. "I can post flyers anywhere I please in the shopping center." She snapped the cap on the Sharpie and crossed her arms against her chest.

"Says who?"

"Virginia Gentry."

Virginia was the manager of the Great Bridge Shopping Center and had authority over what did, and did not, get posted.

"It's distracting to my customers. They come into my shop to buy bait and tackle, not sissy sewing supplies."

"I'll have you know that several of your customers shop here for supplies. It's less expensive than your high-priced fishing materials." She held her stance.

Tucker's face turned two shades redder than the Sharpie Jana held in her hand. "Is business that bad you have to steal my customers?" Without waiting for a response, he grabbed the flyer and stormed out. She turned to face a customer who sheepishly eased her cart to the counter. "Ignore that man." Jana scanned the items then placed fabric and notions into a bag. After completing the transaction, she said, "Thanks for shopping with us!"

After the customer exited the store, Virginia, a slim, fortyish blonde, walked toward the counter holding a piece of paper.

"Your fabric is ready." Jana grabbed a bolt of fabric by the register.

"Great. But I'm here because Tucker's on the warpath again." She held out the flyer.

"Tell me about it. I thought he was going to blow a gasket."

"Tucker says you're stealing his customers. And I've received complaints from other merchants."

"You said I could post flyers anywhere in the center."

"Yes, but not on merchants' windows." Virginia sighed. "Look. Tucker is serious about this. He started a petition to stop you from posting materials. And he's called a merchants' meeting tomorrow night."

"He can't do that."

"As president of the association, he can call special meetings. And since all merchants are attending, you should as well. But for now I'll have to ask you to only post flyers on your window until this is resolved."

Jana handed Virginia the fabric. "I'll be there."

— 🐾 —

The next day, shoppers flocked to Jana's store to purchase red-tagged fabrics, festive fleece and decorative patterns. It was early November, and sales revenues looked promising for the holidays.

Great Bridge Shopping Center was a strip mall in the center of Chesapeake. As Jana opened boxes of inventory, she heard someone clear their throat.

Colleen Wainwright stood before her in a flirty pink apron, knit pants and low-cut blouse. "I'll have you know I did not sign Tucker's stupid petition." She extended the paper toward Jana and placed her hand on her curvy hip.

Jana stood and faced Colleen. She grabbed the paper and read each signature voting against posting flyers in the complex where she had been a tenant for five years. Jana didn't want to have a big battle, but if she had to, she'd stand up for herself and defeat Tucker, just like the American Troops defeated the British during the Revolutionary War at the Battle of Great Bridge on the land nearby the shopping center. "I really appreciate you not signing this on my behalf," Jana said.

"Oh, girl. It's on *our behalf.* I've thought about doing the same thing since my hair salon is at the end of the strip. I think we should help each other. Plus, anytime I can stick it to lover boy, I'm happy to do so."

Jana's eyebrows shot up.

"And considering how Tucker treated you, I would think you'd want the same."

"What do you mean?"

"Everyone knows he dumped you for Kym Asako from the nail salon."

Jana ignored the comment and the tiny bit of ache left in her heart. "Are you going to the meeting?"

"Wouldn't miss it for the world." Colleen turned toward the door.

"Don't forget the petition." Jana extended the paper.

"Keep it. I made a copy when Tucker was running his mouth about the flyer. Can't wait to see him fired up tomorrow night!"

As Colleen sashayed out the door, Jana glanced at the signatures again. Not everyone had signed the paper. Was there hope her voice would be heard? She stashed the paper under the counter and went back to work.

— 🐾 —

The next evening, Jana entered the conference room in the north end of the center. Merchants stood chatting while waiting for the meeting to begin. She scanned the room for Tucker, hoping to work out their differences before the meeting. She eyed Colleen talking with Larry Marshall, the owner of Great Bridge Barber Shop, and made her way toward them.

"I was wondering if you chickened out." Colleen laughed.

Ignoring the remark, Jana asked, "Where's Tucker?"

"He's in the back kitchen with Kym," Larry said.

Jana headed to the back room. Tucker stood near a window reading a piece of paper.

Kym stepped in front of Jana. "Tucker is prepping for the meeting."

At five foot six, Jana towered over Kym. "You don't need to run interference for Tucker." She pushed past the woman and faced Tucker. "Can we work this out?"

He lowered the paper. "It's a little too late for that, darling." He grinned with a jawline that could chisel granite.

Kym stood next to Tucker, with her arms crossed.

"Look, I was just trying to bring awareness to my business."

"Well, you're not going to get it like that." He placed the paper on the table near a cutting board. "And if you pull any more stunts like that, I'll recommend terminating your lease."

"You can't do that."

"Read the misconduct clause."

Kym clutched Tucker's arm, and they walked away.

Jana started to follow but changed her mind. She turned and snatched a bottled water off the table. After twisting the cap and taking a long sip, she read the notes Tucker left behind. Bullet points detailed Tucker taking a vote to stop her from posting flyers and to discredit her character for stealing his customers.

Colleen approached Jana. "You okay, honey?"

"I'm fine." She set the bottle and paper on the table.

"Don't let him bully you. Besides, you had permission to post the flyers."

Virginia's voice came over the loud speaker. "Thank you for coming this evening. Please take a seat, and we'll get started momentarily."

"Let's sit down." Colleen motioned for Jana to head into the conference room. They sat in the back row.

While Colleen chatted with a neighbor, Jana eased out of her seat. "Be right back. I forgot my water."

As Jana entered the kitchen, Virginia rushed out through the doorway. Tucker turned to greet her, fury lighting his face. Jana grabbed her water and dashed out before he could speak. She didn't want to hear anything he had to say. She returned to her seat and noticed Colleen was no longer there. Moments later, Colleen slipped into the chair and Larry sat down afterward. Jana wondered where Colleen had been and why Larry was so late to sit down.

"Help! Someone help!" Kym screamed from the kitchen.

The crowd turned around and stood up at the cry.

Jana, Colleen and Larry slid out of their chairs and rushed toward Kym.

"Look! It's Tucker," Colleen yelled.

Jana stared at Tucker sitting in a chair in the back of the room with his arms across his chest. At first glance, it appeared he was napping until she saw the blood dripping down the side of his face. She raced to his body, propped between the table and chair.

"Call 911!" Larry hurried to check Tucker's pulse. He shook his head, indicating no heartbeat.

Virginia pushed her way forward next to Larry. "What happened?"

"Blow to the head." He motioned toward a gash.

"She did it!" Kym sobbed and pointed toward Jana.

Jana stood frozen, unable to speak.

"No she didn't. She was with me the entire time," Colleen said.

Moments later, Virginia escorted paramedics into the room.

Jana watched as they checked Tucker's vital signs. She thought of his angry face when she retrieved her water.

Virginia motioned toward the merchants. "Please move back into the conference room."

As Jana made her way back she stopped by Virginia. "Why was Tucker upset earlier?"

"I don't know. I grabbed papers from the table and headed to the podium to start the meeting."

After police conducted interviews, Jana was finally allowed to leave. She headed to her SUV, parked in the back of the store. As she placed her purse in the seat, a thunderous roar distracted her. She spun around. Her brown eyes widened at bright headlights approaching from behind before she dove into the seat. The vehicle ran over a curve, smashed a decorative planter and sped off.

The security guard for the center arrived in a golf cart. "Are you okay?"

Shaken, she slid out of the seat. "I wrenched my back, but I'm okay."

"What happened?"

"A car came barreling at me, and I jumped into my car."

"Did you see the driver?"

"No. I was blinded by the light." She rubbed her lower back.

"It was probably a drunk driver. I'll check the security footage to see if we can identify the car and driver. But as long as you're okay ..." He stepped onto the cart and drove off.

— 🐾 —

Still sore from the incident the next morning, Jana called a coworker to open up the store. That allowed her to take a long, hot shower. She shivered at the thought of Tucker's body. She drove to the shopping center and viewed Larry smoking a cigarette near the accident area. She pulled into a parking space.

"Are you okay?" he asked.

"You heard what happened?"

"Virginia notified the merchants this morning. Did you see the driver?"

"No."

"Somebody's got it in for you." Larry took a long, deep drag.

Jana grabbed a bag from her SUV and glared at him.

"Shame about Tucker."

She shut the hatch and remembered Larry had not signed the petition. "Do they know how it happened?"

"They found blood on a cutting board." He took a final drag, dropped the butt on the ground then stomped it out with his boot before walking away.

Jana looked both ways before crossing the lot. Could someone be after her as Larry said? She shuddered at the thought and headed into the store.

Later than morning, a medium-built man with jet-black hair entered Chesapeake Fabrics.

"I'm looking for Jana Karson."

"I'm Jana. How may I help you?"

"I'm Detective Jack Elliott with the Chesapeake Police Department. I'd like to speak with you about Tucker Boyd."

"I spoke with one of your officers yesterday."

"I have follow-up questions. Is there somewhere private we can talk?"

Jana led the detective to her office in the back of the store. A large display of fabric sample books and sewing accessories lined the sidewall. "Have a seat." She motioned toward a chair.

"Tell me again what happened when Tucker's body was discovered last night." He pulled a small notepad and pen from his pocket.

Jana explained the series of events, trying to erase Tucker's image from her mind.

"Where was Tucker when you retrieved the water?" He clicked the pen and began writing.

"In the kitchen."

"Notice anything unusual?"

"No."

"Why was Tucker upset about the flyer?"

"He claimed I stole his customers."

The detective rubbed his chin. "What about your relationship with Tucker?"

"We dated earlier this year, but it didn't work out."

"Why?"

Jana shifted in the chair. "If you must know, Tucker was incapable of monogamy."

"So he cheated on you?"

"Yes."

Jack leaned forward. "Did you have a grudge against him?"

"No."

"Did you kill him?"

"No!" Jana yelled.

"Do you know who did?"

"No!"

"That's all for now." He reached into his pocket. "Here's my card if you think of anything else."

That afternoon, Jana walked three doors down to the Dollar Store to pick up supplies. Once inside, she spotted Larry in the greeting card section, reading a card.

He turned toward her and placed the card back in the slot. "How did the interview go with the detective?"

Jana glared at him. "How do you know about that?"

"He paid me a visit earlier. Asked a lot of questions about you and Tucker."

"Like what?"

"How long you dated and were you jealous of his new relationship."

Jana placed her hands on her hips. "Did he visit other merchants?"

"Don't know." He shrugged.

After purchasing her supplies, Jana exited the store and noticed Colleen placing a wreath on Tucker's shop door. She walked toward her and viewed a Rest in Peace sign on the doormat.

"Sad, huh?" Colleen pointed toward the sign.

As Jana nodded, she placed her bag on the ground and peeked inside the window. Fishing rods sat in racks against the wall, and bait and tackle supplies bordered the remainder of the store.

She spotted Larry leaving the Dollar Store and turned toward Colleen. "Tell me, did a detective visit you?"

"You mean that good-looking Jack Elliott? Oh, sure. He asked lots of questions."

"Like what?"

"He wanted to know why you and Tucker broke up and if you were still in love with him."

Jana frowned.

"Don't worry. I told him you hated Tucker's guts."

Three days later, Jana and Colleen entered the Great Bridge Chapel on South Battlefield Boulevard, the main highway of the suburban community. After signing the chapel guestbook, Jana and Colleen slipped into a back pew.

"I'm surprised it's an open casket." Colleen craned her neck for a better view. "Do you want to see Tucker?"

"No," Jana said.

"Well, I do. I have this strange curiosity about dead people. Probably because I did hair and makeup on the deceased in funeral homes." Colleen shuffled past Jana and made her way to the front of the chapel.

"I'm surprised to see you here." Kym stood at the end of the pew, dabbing a tissue against her swollen eyes.

"My condolences," Jana said.

"They say the killer always shows up at the funeral."

"Actually it's the scene of the crime."

"Same thing." Kym crossed her arms. "I just hope the police arrest you soon."

"I didn't kill Tucker!"

"Everyone knows you were jealous of our relationship."

"That's not true."

Colleen approached the pew and pushed past Kym. "The service is starting, and the front row is almost full."

Kym hurried up the aisle and squeezed into a seat.

"Don't let her upset you." Colleen patted Jana's leg.

During the ceremony, Jana scanned the chapel. Could the killer be among them as Kym had suggested?

—— 🂠 ——

A week later, Jana reviewed the weekly sales report on her computer. Since the news of Tucker's death, business had slowed considerably, along with holiday sales. She closed the file and thought of Tucker's notes. She decided to visit Kym to discuss it with her.

Once inside the salon, she spotted Kym and Larry chatting at the counter. Jana viewed a romantic greeting card in Kym's hand. It was the same card Larry had held at the Dollar Store. She wondered if something was brewing between Larry and Kym.

"What brings you here?" Kym placed the card on the counter.

"I need to talk to you."

"What about?"

"Why was Tucker planning to discredit me at the meeting?"

"Look, Tucker's pride was as big as the state of Virginia. He wasn't going to let you take business from him."

"It wasn't about that. I just wanted those customers who

shopped at the north end of the center to visit the south side."

"That's not how we see it."

"Let it go, Jana." Larry stood and placed his arm around Kym's waist.

— 🐞 —

That evening after work, Jana walked to the main office to drop her rental check in the after-hours mail slot. Virginia sat at the receptionist's desk, talking on the phone. She motioned Jana to come inside. She cupped her hand over the phone and said, "Have a seat, I'll be right with you."

Jana sat in the chair while Virginia finished her call.

Virginia placed the phone in the cradle. "What can I do for you?"

"You're working late tonight," Jana said.

"The receptionist is sick."

"Here's my check."

"Great." Virginia unlocked the desk drawer and dropped the check inside. "I'm glad you're here. I wanted to talk to you."

Jana sat back in the chair. "Sure."

"You know ... let's go to my office to talk. That way I can show you the finished chairs with the fabric I purchased from you."

Virginia led Jana down the hallway into her office. "Have a seat." She shut the door and locked it.

Jana became uneasy when the lock clicked. She made her way past a bolt of fabric against the wall and sat down. "I told you it was the right choice."

"Detective Elliott came by to see me today," Virginia said.

"Really?"

"He suspects Larry murdered Tucker since Kym was sneaking around with both Tucker and Larry."

"Why would he kill him?"

"Jealousy."

"What do you mean?"

"We all know Tucker was a leech and womanizer. He borrowed twenty-five-thousand dollars and never paid me back. I confronted him at the meeting, and he told me to stop bothering him about it." Virginia's voice became agitated.

"Is that why Tucker was upset?"

"He wanted to get as much money and as many women as possible."

Jana thought Virginia sounded jealous, like she had a good motive for killing Tucker.

Virginia pulled a small handgun from her desk and pointed it toward Jana.

"You killed Tucker?"

"And now I have to kill you since you saw Tucker and me argue when you returned for the bottled water."

"Wait." Jana glanced around the room for a way out.

"Let's go." Virginia waved the gun toward the door. "I knew it was only a matter of time before you realized it was me."

Jana followed since she knew she was dealing with a crazy woman. As she made her way around the desk, Virginia shoved the gun in her side. Jana turned and grabbed Virginia's arm, startling her into dropping the gun. Virginia reached down to grab it, and Jana kicked her arm. Virginia yanked Jana's pant leg, pulling her to the ground. As the women wrestled on top of the fallen bolt of fabric, Virginia choked Jana's neck. Jana struggled for a breath and grabbed the fabric clip that sprang off the bolt and shoved it into Virginia's leg. She rolled the fabric around her like a mummy, tightening the fabric to the point that Virginia's grasp on her began to loosen.

Detective Elliott and the security guard kicked the door in. "We saw Virginia on the security footage trying to run you down with her car," the detective said as he arrested Virginia.

———

Two weeks later, Jana headed toward Colleen's salon for a quick trim. The bruises on her neck were fading, as were her memories of that dreadful day. She waved at Larry and Kym as they entered the sub shop holding hands. She glanced inside Tucker's store to see his son standing behind the counter, flirting with a young woman. She was glad to see his son was able to carry on after his father's tragic murder. It had been an unbelievable ordeal, but now with business back on track in her fabric store, life was good.

OBSESSION

BY LINDA THORNBURG

THE HOUSE SAT HIGH on a hill and had a spectacular view of the Rockfish Valley. Ham Cohen's eye traveled across the land that had once grown tobacco, now covered in trees, shrubs and flowers. Yellow buttercups dotted the grass. In the distance, a cluster of cows grazed peacefully.

Robert Sperry was talking. "Sorry to disappoint. I've done a pretty thorough search on the records for Elk Hill and haven't run across any slave names."

"I didn't really expect to find anything," Ham said.

"How did you come to have a slave ancestor anyway? Seems a bit odd."

Ham shrugged. "Probably not that uncommon. One of my great-grandfathers apparently married a daughter of a slave named Joshua."

"I hope you can find something about him, but it's tough to track down records on slaves."

"It's my cousin who's interested. I'm doing it as a favor."

Sperry nodded. He shifted his weight from one foot to the other. He was a tall man, about seventy. He probably wanted Ham to leave but Ham was enjoying the view and the sense of history he felt at the two-hundred-and-fifty-year-old tobacco farm. "Mind if I just hang out here a minute and take this in?"

"Be my guest," Sperry said. "I've actually got another fellow coming by this morning on a similar quest. Quite a coincidence, since it happens rarely." He said the last as he walked away from the barn structure and toward the farmhouse. "Good luck," he called before he entered the house. The screen door slammed.

Ham wondered what Celia would make of this place. That part of him that contradicted and cautioned, the part that awakened his passion, was missing now that she was gone. Everything was pale gray.

Sperry had showed him the "prizery," the barnlike structure where tobacco had been pressed two-hundred years ago. A huge iron screw that replaced the wooden one that would have turned the press hung above a tobacco hogshead. Sperry said tobacco leaves were cured in another barn and then pressed in the prizery, put into hogsheads and rolled to a wagon where they were delivered to a flat-bottomed boat called a batteau, which would haul them to Richmond and a ship bound for Europe. Alexander Reid first settled the land in the mid-1700s and in 1805, a tobacco farmer named Coleman bought it. In 1850, Nelson County had produced more than one million pounds of tobacco. Of the twelve thousand county residents, half had been slaves. As the tobacco business died out, the farm switched to apples and the prizery was used to pack them.

Ham wondered idly what he would have done for a living in that era. He didn't see himself as a farmer, and he didn't think he could have owned slaves, although some of his employees would probably disagree. He certainly didn't see himself as a slave.

What was it about that view? He enjoyed the sense of openness and majesty so common in central Virginia and loved the lush green and blue, so different from Northern Virginia where he had lived for years. He didn't see why Celia had to leave this area, even if they had argued. She could have stayed and enjoyed the sense of freedom and the exhilaration. Instead she chose to run away. The trip to Elk Hill was a Saturday diversion, a way to keep from thinking about her too much. It wasn't working.

He heard something behind him and turned to see a black man of around his age walking toward the prizery. The man raised his hand in greeting. Curious, Ham walked to the structure to see what he was up to.

"Hello," the stranger said. "Mr. Sperry told me you were also looking for a relative."

Ham nodded. "My cousin asked me to see if I could find anything about a slave called Joshua. The family story is that our great-grandfather married one of his daughters. Joshua worked on a tobacco farm in this area, and it could have been this one, because his last name was Coleman, like the farmer who owned this place. What about you?"

"Same sort of mission. My great-great-grandmother was a slave in the area. Her name was Lally Coleman."

"Had any luck?"

The man shook his head. He extended his hand. "Ronald Wilson."

"Ham Cohen," he said, shaking Wilson's hand.

"That's an interesting handle."

"The short version is that I got the nickname in high school."

"Ah."

There was a silence as they both contemplated the prizery. "I was trying to imagine what sort of life this was," Ham said finally.

"Short and brutish, no doubt."

"For the slaves, yes. For the farmers, maybe more pleasant, but still rough I would guess."

"You would certainly have wanted to be a farmer rather than a slave," Wilson said. "Some of us wouldn't have had any choice."

Ham had never had much of an interest in colonial American history. Most of his relatives had come a generation or two ago from Eastern Europe, where their lives had been filled with the terror of the Holocaust. Joshua was the only ancestor he knew about who had been a slave. Wilson might have had more than one.

"Where are you from?" he asked.

"Pennsylvania. My wife and I run a graphic arts company just outside Philadelphia."

"I run a commercial laundry in this area."

"So we're both businessmen looking for slave ancestors named Coleman."

"Maybe we were fated to meet." Ham said this casually, not really believing it but wanting to entertain the idea. He liked to think about how coincidence brought people together. Or was it really coincidence?

Wilson looked at him with a mildly disconcerting intensity. He seemed to measure every word against some ultimate truth, and Ham had the feeling he fell short.

"You believe in fate?" Wilson asked.

Ham gazed out at the valley below. "I taught physics in college before I took over my dad's laundry, so for me that's a complicated question."

"How did you go from physics professor to running a commercial laundry?"

Ham laughed. "I guess it was fate."

Wilson laughed too. "If that's what you believe."

"You mean fate is only there if you believe in it?"

"Something like that." Wilson gave him another piercing look. "What do you believe is going to happen to this country?"

Ham shrugged. "I haven't got a clue. But it often seems to me like we're in pretty bad shape—environmental catastrophes, health care shortages, aging population, debt crisis, foreign policy crises and polarization in politics. The list goes on."

Wilson wagged a finger at him. "If you're not part of the solution, you're part of the problem, man. I'm willing to bet you don't pay your employees too well, just what you can get away with. I guess most of them are the working poor, aren't they? How many are black?"

Ham shook his head. "I don't have any black employees. It's not because I won't hire black people. They don't want to work for me. Nobody's applied for jobs at my plant."

Wilson snorted. "That you know of," he said.

"That I know of. I've got a lot of Hispanic employees."

"Legal?"

"I hope so."

"So, what's your view on immigration? Are you for more amnesty for illegals or for deporting as many as possible?" Wilson put his hands on his hips.

Ham wasn't sure he wanted to talk about immigration policy with this stranger. He wasn't even sure he had a position. Finally he said, "I see a lot of Hispanics struggling in this country. I know a lot are illegal. They're trying to make some money to send home. They're not bad people, and I think they probably add more to the economy than they take away from it. So I suppose if I had to come down on one side or the other, I would come down on the side of amnesty. My grandfather came to this country and started a laundry, and today I employ more than one hundred people in that business. He was an immigrant who contributed to the U.S. economy. I hope we're still the kind of country where that can happen." He bent down and picked up a small rock and tossed it, watching it sail toward the grass a few yards away.

Wilson bit his lip. "My people were dragged to this country against their will," he said. "They were treated like cattle, worse than cattle—beaten, bought and sold, humiliated after Emancipation, told they were lazy and stupid, and then given affirmative action to make up for it all. But now we have a black president, so I guess that's supposed to show some kind of progress."

Ham nodded.

"Look," Wilson said. "I'm alone here, trying to track Lally down. I'm staying in Charlottesville. Want to get together for dinner and talk about immigration and foreign policy? I'll buy. Help me pass the time."

Ham considered the offer. If he went home he would just think about Celia until Monday morning. He could go bother his dad, but his dad wouldn't give him any sympathy. He thought it was Ham's fault that Celia had taken off. For the first time in a long time, he was at a loss about what to do with himself on a weekend. "OK, but I don't want you buying me dinner. We'll go Dutch."

At seven, they met at the mall at a restaurant called Sandra's. Wilson had gotten there first and had procured a table near the window. The place was packed with locals, most of them from the university. Ham ordered a glass of wine and Wilson had a beer while they studied the menu. After they ordered, Wilson said, "I wasn't sure you'd show up. Why did you anyway? You don't even know me."

"I guess I wanted to hear what you had to say about immigration."

"I believe in deporting illegals. They're taking jobs away from Americans. In this economy that's not good."

"And if that causes a hardship on them and their families back home, because they can't send money anymore?"

"Not my problem," Wilson said, swigging his beer. "They aren't playing by the rules. If they really belong in this country there are legal ways to get in."

"But most of them are desperate and don't have the means or the time to wait."

"Again, not my problem."

"You know what I think," Ham said, articulating a half-baked thought for the first time. "I think if the United States paid more attention to the plight of people in Central and South America and less to countries like Afghanistan and Iran, we'd have better national security, be better neighbors, enhance the economy and be better off generally. I would like to see a more liberal immigration policy coupled with a strategy to form better relationships with all the countries of this hemisphere. Imagine if we could create something like a European Zone in this part of the world. We'd be unstoppable."

"Never happen," Wilson said. "We've got too much invested in Europe. That would require a whole new mindset."

"I guess you're right. But it really makes sense if you think about it."

"Not arguing with that. I've got to use the restroom. Be back in a minute." Wilson got up from the table and started to walk away, but fell instead.

He lay there on the floor, not moving.

"Are you all right?" Ham asked.

The man didn't answer.

"Wilson, are you all right?" Ham stood up to help. A woman at a nearby table screamed. A waiter came and put his head next to Wilson's chest. "No heartbeat," he said.

The restaurant manager came over, took one look and called the paramedics, who, upon arrival, pronounced Wilson dead. Ham stayed at the restaurant until they had taken the body away.

That night, he dreamed about Wilson and Celia. They were having an argument about immigration policy, and Celia told Wilson that he only believed in deportation because he was bitter about being black in a racist country.

In the morning he relived his own real argument with Celia. She had accused him of being a hypocrite because he hadn't followed through on his plans to put on seminars on personal reality and thought, using some new ideas in physics to illustrate the concept that thought influences reality. He insisted that he was too busy at the laundry; he would start the seminars when the time was right. The argument ended after both of them called each other cowards. Celia didn't even say goodbye; she just disappeared.

A couple of days later, Ham got a phone call at work from Wilson's wife.

"Are you the man who was with my husband when he died?"

"Yes, ma'am. I'm so sorry."

"The police told me you were having dinner. What did he say to you during that dinner?"

"We talked about immigration policy. He wanted a stricter policy and I disagreed."

"And your occupation?"

"I run a commercial laundry."

Did he imagine the sigh of relief on the other end of the line?

"He told me he was here tracking down a slave ancestor named Lally," Ham said when the silence became uncomfortable.

"Yes, that's right. I haven't talked to him since last Friday. That's when he called me last. Did he find out anything about her? My children would like to know."

"I don't think so. We met at a place called Elk Hill, looking for evidence of our slave ancestors. Do they know what he died of?"

"I can't get much of an answer. I'm coming down there today. The police want to see me."

"The police? The death is suspicious?"

"Well, he just died, right in front of you, apparently. Of course they think it's suspicious."

They were both silent for a long time.

Finally Mrs. Wilson said, "He mentioned that you had a relative by the name of Coleman."

She hadn't talked to him since Friday but his conversation with Wilson was on Saturday. Ham got off the phone as soon as he could. He called the police. After some waiting, he got a homicide inspector.

"I understand this is being treated as a homicide?"

The inspector confirmed but didn't elaborate.

"What did he die of?"

"Poison."

"This might not be anything," Ham said, "but his wife just called me. She said she hadn't talked to him since last Friday, and then she mentioned something she couldn't have known about on Friday. I didn't even meet the man until Saturday. I saw him at Elk Hill, which was the site of a plantation in Nelson County where we had both gone to track down ancestors. That's how we met."

The detective did not seem enthusiastic about Ham's call. But a few days later he contacted Ham. "We've arrested the wife. He was leaving her because their business was failing, and she wanted to keep pouring money into it. He was going to see a lawyer about a divorce. She's confessed to coming here and poisoning him before his dinner. She put it in a drink and then staged an argument and left again. We wouldn't have been able to break her without the information you gave us, so I owe you."

That night, Ham sat in his living room and listened to a CD of Bessie Smith singing "Down Hearted Blues." He thought about Wilson. What a waste.

GUIDE TO MURDER

By Teresa Inge

"WELCOME TO VIRGINIA BEACH'S Cavalier on the Hill. My name is Connar Randolph. I am the owner of the inn and your tour guide today. By show of hands, how many folks are visiting the hotel for the first time?" Connar flashed her best smile in hopes of securing new guests.

All five hands went up.

"Great. To begin with, please wear the nametag you were given at check-in and stay with the group until we reach our destination. Are there any questions?"

"Is this the original lobby?" a petite woman named Kara asked.

Connar pushed her blond hair off her shoulders and turned toward the woman. "Yes. Construction of the lobby began in 1926. The hotel opened in nineteen twenty-seven under the ownership of my great-grandmother, Helena Randolph."

"Is the chandelier real?" A blonde pointed toward the crystal fixture suspended over the vintage lobby. Light bounced off the chandelier from the ceiling to the checkerboard floor that showered spectacular crystals throughout the room.

Connar viewed the tag on the woman's blouse. "Great question, Sierra. It was donated by a wealthy aristocrat in nineteen twenty-seven. According to family lore, he was taken with my grandmother's beauty and shipped it here as a gift. Today, it's worth a hundred thousand dollars."

Connar watched as Sierra nudged the arm of a middle-age man with the nametag Eddie.

"When was the hotel renovated?" asked a man named

Therian, who repositioned his tag on his stylish shirt.

"Restoration is an ongoing process in maintaining the hotel's elegance and charm."

"Have any celebrities stayed here?" Kara giggled.

"My great-grandmother was the hostess to many celebrities during the Big Band Era, including U.S. Presidents, heads of state and royalty. Please watch your step as we walk to the main dinning room."

Connar led the tour up the lobby stairs and down the checkerboard tile hallway. "The restaurant has a buffet that caters to every taste and mood. As you can see, the original architecture remains."

"These aren't vintage fixtures." Eddie pointed toward reproduction lighting.

Connar glared at him. "As an older structure, some pieces have been replaced over time. But we've been fortunate to preserve many of the inn's original features. Let's head to the indoor pool."

A dozen hotel guests dotted the indoor pool as the tour group gathered by the rail.

"The pool is Olympic size and part of the original construction," Connar noted.

"It's stained and cracked," Eddie complained.

Ignoring the comment, Connar waved her hand in the air. "If you'll follow me to the elevator, we'll head to the rooftop. It's been a popular spot for men to pop the question throughout the years."

The group rode to the top floor.

"How many floors are there?" A woman smoothed out the nametag Ivy on her chic sundress then curled her arm around Therian's waist.

"There are six floors," Connar said. She stepped off the elevator and faced the group. "Repairs from a recent storm are now complete on the roof. Let's take a peek."

She held the door open as the five tourists scaled small steps to the top of the building greeted by sunshine and a salty breeze. "Please watch your head on the low ceiling as you enter through the door. And be careful of construction materials on the far side of the roof." Connar motioned toward a pile of bricks and wood.

"Wow! Check out the ocean view." Sierra leaned against the low wall.

Therian wandered along the rooftop. "Nice restoration. It matches the colonial style building."

"Looks tacky if you ask me." Eddie pointed toward uneven bricks with crumbling mortar.

Connar narrowed her eyes and swallowed her retort.

"I see the Neptune Festival." Ivy waved her hand toward sand sculptures, art displays and food vendors at the boardwalk.

"I see bikinis." Eddie punched Therian's arm and released a belly laugh.

"Look at the rolling hills." Kara pointed toward the front lawn of the grand hotel.

As the group moved about the concrete surface, Eddie's cell phone rang and he stepped away.

"Let's take a group photo so I can remember everyone." Sierra reached into her bag and pulled out her phone. "Can you take it?" she asked Connar.

"Sure."

Everyone gathered in the center for a group shot. Connar snapped the photo and handed the phone to Sierra. "Okay, folks. Let's make our way to a guest suite and the grand ballroom."

The group chatted about the festival while walking toward the suite. Connar led the tour into a renovated room. "Our suites are one-bedroom up through executive suites."

"This is lovely. I could soak forever in a jetted tub." Ivy sat on the corner of the Jacuzzi.

"Take me away!" Sierra laughed.

After visiting the suite, the group rode the elevator to the bottom floor. Ivy walked to the restroom, and Kara headed to the restaurant for bottled water.

"This is the ballroom. We host wedding receptions here," Connar said.

"I love the vintage decor. Is this where the big bands played?" Sierra asked.

"Yes. The room has been host to legendary musicians throughout the hotel's history. Since this concludes the inside tour, let's head outside to view the grounds." Connar led the tour down the lobby hallway and exited near the outdoor patio. She slipped on her sunglasses to shield her eyes from the bright September sun.

"Shuffleboard, lawn croquet and tennis courts are located on the front lawn, just down the hill. Let's go check it out."

Kara rejoined the tour as they strolled along the vintage brick walkway.

"Guests have enjoyed outdoor activities since the hotel opened." Connar waved her hand toward the aged courts.

Sierra gasped then screamed, "Eddie!"

"Oh, my goodness." Kara put her hand over her mouth.

Connar stared at Eddie's twisted body lying upon the Cavalier name, etched in large white letters on the hill.

"Please step back." She knelt, trembling while checking his pulse.

"Is he dead?" Sierra asked.

Connar nodded and called security on her cell phone. She wondered what this would mean for the inn.

Ivy walked up the pathway and stood behind Therian.

"What took you so long?" he whispered.

"I don't feel well." She rubbed her stomach. "What happened to him?"

"Don't know. We got here, and there he was, just lying there."

Moments later, a hotel security guard arrived, followed by the rescue squad and police. While paramedics checked the body, a police officer secured the area. Connar escorted the group to the indoor patio per police instructions.

After a long wait, a handsome man gripping a black case and wearing a holstered gun on his belt approached Connar. "Detective Tate Barley."

"Connar Randolph. I'm the owner of the inn."

"Can you tell me what you saw?" He set the case on the tile floor.

"We toured the inn then went outside to the shuffleboard court. That's when we found Eddie." Connar stared at the small crowd gathered near the body. "How long will he be there?"

"The body will be taken to the medical examiner to determine cause of death when our investigation here is complete."

"How did this happen?"

"That's what I'm trying to determine."

"The police are upsetting my guests," Connar snapped.

"Look. I don't plan to be here any longer than needed." He grabbed a notebook and pen from the case. "Where was the last place you saw Eddie alive?"

"The rooftop."

He clicked the pen and began writing. "Anything unusual occur?"

Connar shook her head.

"Anyone with Eddie?"

"Sierra Russell. She's sitting with the others."

"Do you have surveillance cameras?"

"Yes."

"I need to see the video."

Connar led the detective to the security office just inside the patio.

"Whatcha got?" Tate asked the guard.

"Footage from the front cameras." He ran video of Eddie standing near the roof's edge talking on his cell phone.

"Is there audio?"

"No. But look at this." A piece of wood slammed against Eddie's head, propelling him and the cell phone over the side.

Tate leaned toward the screen. "Zoom in closer."

The guard enlarged the image. "We can't see the full picture. The camera didn't capture the entire rooftop."

Tate turned toward Connar. "Anyone on the tour have access to a board?"

She viewed the screen. "Yes. Construction materials are on the roof."

"Did anyone leave the tour?"

Connar rubbed her forehead. "Eddie stayed behind to finish his call. Ivy went to the restroom. Kara walked to the restaurant."

"I need a list of each tour member and a room to interview them."

Connar led Tate to her office and grabbed the list. "This has all the pertinent information." She extended the paper toward him.

"And the interview room?"

"Follow me. It's just down the hall."

He placed the case and list on the desk, retrieved a laptop and plugged the cord in the outlet. He then spoke into a microphone attached to his shoulder strap, calling Officer Jonathan Tyler.

"Anything else? I need to check on my staff." Connar frowned.

"Look. I know you're worried, but like I said before, we'll be out of here soon."

A few minutes later, Officer Tyler stood in the doorway.

"I need a statement from each person." Tate handed papers to the officer.

"Sure thing."

Tate conducted background checks on the victim and each tour member, using his laptop.

An hour later, the officer plopped statements onto the desk. "How's the research going?"

"Victim's known as Fast Eddie Moretti. A forty-eight-year-old land developer who's had run-ins with other developers."

"Any leads?"

"Not yet."

"Let me know if you need anything." He exited the room.

After completing his research, Tate spoke into the microphone requesting the officer send in Sierra Russell.

Sierra entered the room moments later, her eyes red and swollen.

"Tell me about your relationship with Eddie."

"I'm his assistant," she said in a shaky voice.

"How long did you work for him?"

"Three years." She dabbed a tissue against her eyes.

"What brings you to the inn?"

"Eddie found out the hotel was struggling, so he met with Connar to make an offer."

"And?"

"She said it's not for sale."

"Then why go on the tour?"

"Eddie was relentless. Figured he would nitpick the hotel, flash some cash and buy it out from under her."

"According to your statement, nothing unusual happened on the tower."

"That's true. We walked around the rooftop and checked out the view."

"Was Eddie with you when you left the roof?"

"No. He was on the phone, as usual. Said he would meet me downstairs after the call."

"That's all for now. Please have a seat with the others."

He summoned Therian and Ivy Prescott into the office.

"What brings you down from Richmond?"

"The Neptune Festival." Therian grabbed Ivy's hand.

"According to your statement, you're a land developer."

"Yes."

"Working on any projects now?"

"I always have projects in the works."

"Does that include purchasing this property?"

"The hotel is not for sale."

"Rumor has it Connar is having difficulty keeping it going, and it might go up for auction."

Therian released his wife's hand.

"Have you had any past encounters with Eddie?"

"Fast Eddie was a piece of work," Therian said.

"How so?"

"He would outbid developers, buy the properties and laugh about it. So I'm not surprised he was sniffing around the inn."

"Did he do this to you?"

"Yes."

"Did you have a grudge against Eddie?"

Therian wiped his forehead with a folded white handkerchief he had pulled from his pocket. "No. Just because I didn't like him doesn't mean I killed him."

Tate stroked his chin with the thumb of his right hand. "That's all the questions I have."

The officer escorted Kara Marciano into the office.

"What brings you up from the Outer Banks?"

"A getaway weekend."

"Seems you would be tired of the beach, living near it and all."

"I love visiting Virginia Beach." She sipped her bottled water.

The detective viewed his paper. "You're widowed with two grown children?"

"Yes."

"What did your husband do for a living?"

"He owned a bait and tackle shop in Nags Head. Why?"

"According to my research, Eddie spent a lot of time fishing in the Outer Banks. Ever cross paths with him?"

"No."

"Notice anything unusual during the tour?"

"Just one thing. Eddie and Connar had an argument before touring the roof. I couldn't hear the conversation, but she appeared upset."

Tate tapped his pen against the desk. "I have no further questions."

Moments later, Connar entered the room and handed the detective a bottled water.

He leaned back in his chair and twisted the cap off the bottle. "Tell me about your conversation with Eddie before the tour."

"He made a ridiculous offer on the inn. I told him it's not for sale."

"Is the hotel in financial trouble?" He sipped the water.

She lowered her head. "Yes."

"What did you and Eddie argue about before visiting the roof?"

She crossed her arms over her chest. "He badmouthed the inn during the tour, so I asked him to stop."

"And?"

"He refused."

"Then what?"

"He threatened to post negative reviews about the inn on the Internet if I didn't sell. I asked him to leave the premises."

"Why did he want to purchase it?"

"To tear it down and build condos. I'll do whatever I can to stop that."

"Include killing Eddie?"

"No! But I did watch the video again."

Tate's eyebrows shot up. "And?"

"I noticed a quick flash of yellow material."

"Go ahead."

"Then I took a long hard look at the tour group, but could not match the pattern."

"And?"

"That's when I remembered taking a picture of the tour with

Sierra's phone. I distracted her and grabbed it from her bag." Connar waggled the phone at the detective and retrieved the photo. Tate leaned in to get a good look.

Connar said, "Kara has a pullover on now that she didn't have on when I took this picture. See the yellow underneath?" She pointed toward the photo.

He bolted from his seat. "Let's go!"

They ran toward the patio. "Where's Kara?" Tate asked the officer and security guard in the hallway.

"The restroom," the officer said.

"Secure the entrance," he ordered.

The officer and guard took off down the hallway.

Connar and Tate raced toward the bathroom.

"Virginia Beach Police." He entered the room, kicking in one stall at a time with his gun drawn.

"Out here," Connar yelled.

Connar and Tate raced back to the patio to find Kara pointing a semi-automatic at Sierra. Therian and Ivy stood nearby.

"Stand back," Kara said.

"Put down the gun. We can work this out," Tate said.

"Like hell we can. He ripped off my husband in a business deal. Tony never recovered financially and then he died. Eddie was a piece of dirt, and he killed my husband. He deserved to die."

"Let's talk this through."

"There's nothing to talk about. She deserves to die just like Eddie."

"She had nothing to do with it."

As Kara repositioned the gun, Sierra bit her arm. The gun dropped to the floor. Tate lunged for Kara. She kicked the detective in the groin and reached for the weapon. Sierra elbowed Kara in the stomach and pushed her down. Connar pinned Kara to the floor. Kara began screaming obscenities. Sierra ripped her nametag off her blouse and slapped it across Kara's mouth.

"Thanks for shutting her up." Therian grabbed the gun and helped the detective to his feet. The officer and security guard entered the room and handcuffed Kara.

A short while later, Kara was placed in a police car.

Therian and Ivy approached Connar. "This is for you." He handed Connar a check.

Connar stared at the six digits. "What's this?"

"Despite the crazy day here, the hotel is a landmark and should be enjoyed by all. I want you to start a foundation for the preservation of the hotel."

Connar wiped a tear off her cheek and reflected on Kara. Although it had been an awful day, she was glad Kara would pay for her crime.

Therian winked. "Call it the Fast Eddie Foundation."

A TRI-ING DAY

By Smita Harish Jain

PATRICK SWANN STRUTTED UP to the packet pickup table as if the race were a foregone conclusion.

"Swann, Patrick," he said, before the volunteer manning the registration table could ask. "Invited athlete."

She moved her forefinger down a column of names. "Here you are, Patrick, number twenty-nine." She riffled through a box of manila packets and pulled out the one that matched his number.

"Driver's license and USA Triathlon membership card?" she asked, required to verify each racer's identity, age group and credentials.

Patrick had them ready and dropped them in front of her.

She looked at Patrick then at the ID cards. Satisfied, she handed him the envelope containing his race number, decals and course information.

"Timing chip?" he asked. She inhaled deeply, with barely a lift to her shoulders, reached into a box and handed him the chip. Were it not for the simultaneous closing of her eyes, I might not have noticed the effect Patrick had on her, the same intimidating effect he's always had on me.

Patrick made his way to the body marking station, next to the covered picnic tables clustered in the middle of the large grassy area flanking the beach. He lifted his left T-shirt sleeve and flexed his muscles.

"You'll need to relax your arm, sir," the teenage volunteer instructed.

Patrick gave her a toothy grin. "If you say so," he said, and made a production of extending both arms over his head in an exaggerated stretch with both biceps flexed. The young girl smiled and turned her head, rolling her eyes and coughing to cover it up. When she turned back, the marker cap was off, and she started outlining the number twenty-nine on Patrick's left tricep.

He left his shirt sleeve rolled up as he walked toward the next pre-race stop—the bike transition area. Hundreds of Kestrels, Cervélos and Felts crowded in the seventy-five-by-two hundred foot space, rack after rack lined up in succession. Patrick wheeled his tri bike to a stall, added numbered decals to his bike frame and helmet, and made one last check of his equipment. Next stop,the bar for his customary pre-race Dewar's. That's where I found him, just as I had planned.

"Patrick," I started and sidled up next to him. He was sitting alone at the bar, and I waited for him to ask me to join him. First, I would have to wait for him to recognize me. *Bastard.*

"Hey, yeah, Jimmy Parker."

"James," I said, under my breath.

"You ready for tomorrow?" I asked through my forced smile.

"Born ready, my man!" He bared his teeth in an aggravating grin and slapped me on the shoulder.

"Twenty-nine, huh?" I said, pointing to the black numbers written in permanent marker on his left upper arm. All the racers got their race numbers written on their left arm and left calf, to make them easy to identify as they passed certain checkpoints. I hadn't gotten my number, fifty-two, put on yet. I didn't want anyone to know I was so anxious to be in this race that I signed up right after all the pros and the invited racers were given their slots.

Patrick flexed his arm and gripped the muscle that formed.

"Tomorrow, this will be a number one," he said and waggled his eyebrows.

He would leave me standing forever—if I didn't make the first move.

"Hey, why don't I get that for you?" I said as the bartender placed a highball of whiskey in front of him. "For old times' sake."

Patrick tossed its contents back. "Why don't you get the second one too?" he asked, laughing at his own attempt at cleverness. He tapped the bottom edge of the empty glass on the bar in front of the bartender and motioned with a nod of his head for her to refill it.

The bartender looked at me, and I nodded that it was okay. "Bring me one too, please."

"So, you still riding that Gary Fisher, or did you finally spring for a big-boy bike?" he asked.

Yeah, sure, I sprung for the new Specialized Shiv Pro Tri with the salary I make, you prick.

I reached into my pocket and fisted three long yellow tablets. "Yes, still the Gary Fisher," I said, turning away so he wouldn't see my lips twisting into a grimace.

The bartender returned with our drinks. I placed my hand on top of my glass and dragged it toward me, letting the Percocet fall in. I had gotten the prescription a year ago, when an injury in the Colonial Beach Olympic Triathlon had left me with a twisted ankle from a spill on my bike that had sent me skittering across the road and over a short embankment. My foot lodged in the spokes the entire way. The drug was standard issue for athletes and wouldn't seem out of place when they found it in Patrick's bloodstream.

I needed a distraction and called the bartender to bring us some menus.

"I haven't eaten since lunch," I lied. I needed to keep him there long enough for the Percocet to work. "You hungry?"

"You buying?" he asked, and grabbed a menu out of the bartender's hands. She pulled her hand back and curled her lip in disdain. Patrick was already behind the menu, creating his order, and didn't see it. She moved away, leaving me free to slide my drink next to his and slide his over to me.

He reached around his menu and pulled his drink behind it. Two swallows, and the entire contents of the glass were gone. By the time the bartender returned to take our orders, Patrick's eyelids were drooping. When she looked at me, I looked at the empty drink glass in front of Patrick and raised my eyebrows, suggesting he'd had a few too many. She took our orders and left, shaking her head the whole way.

Long before our Supreme Nachos and Reubens arrived, the Percocet had kicked in. The bartender, probably assuming Patrick was drunk, smiled when I half-carried, half-dragged him out of the restaurant's bar.

I put him into the back of my van. The sun had gone down, and most of the racers and their families had either retired for the evening or were still finishing up their meals inside one of the many chain restaurants in the Aquia Marketplace shopping area.

Once in my room, I stepped into the bathroom where the lighted mirror made it easier for me to write the number twenty-nine on the back of my left upper arm. I did the same on my left calf. In the morning, I'd take the van—with Patrick inside, my bike and a few other things—to the wooded area near the spur off the bike course.

Let the games begin, I thought, and pulled the covers to my chin.

———— 🐾 ————

The Battle of Aquia Creek Sesquicentennial Half Ironman commemorated the anniversary of the 1861 fight between the

Union Navy and the Confederate shore battalions to keep the Union forces from advancing down the Chesapeake River and to protect the railroad terminal situated in Aquia Landing, the point where the Aquia Creek empties into the Potomac River and one of Stafford County's most-visited historical landmarks. Today, the site would commemorate an anniversary of a different kind: ten years since the day I decided to kill Patrick Swann.

It was so cliché, it was pathetic. Patrick Swann had beaten me at everything: He stole my high school sweetheart; he attended an Ivy League college; he graduated from one of the best MBA programs in the world; and he started a company that skyrocketed to $200 million in annual revenue, and he was making well into the six figures.

What did I do? I worked for him, for less than half of what he made.

Race day was everything it should be during May in Virginia—a bald eagle sailing through the air; a family of ducks riding the gentle tides swirling the water into a brackish mix; pieces of driftwood and clumps of seaweed gathering in the one-hundred-foot C-shaped coves making up the border between the shore and that portion of the Potomac River; the temperature, holding at a triathlon-perfect sixty-five degrees.

The crowds had started to gather. The gravel parking lot was filled with the cars of the event organizers and the invited athletes. The rest of us had to be bussed in from the parking lot of Spotswood, the local high school. Event photographers mingled with the crowds. Some set up their tripods in strategic locations, where they could catch each athlete coming and going. Families and other spectators staked out their patches of grass with lawn chairs and umbrellas for shade. Blankets were spread for babies to snooze on and toddlers to run around.

The older children charged across the grass and over the riprap lining the shore and splashed in the water lapping on the beach, in a sort of mini-triathlon of their own. Porta Potties, fifteen to a row, three rows deep, lined the second transition area where athletes changed from their biking gear to their running gear. Baby strollers sat empty or held the day's snacks. Some of the participants would be out for ten or twelve hours, and their families would have to stay at the race site because the shuttles into town ran infrequently. By the end of the day, the portable toilets would be disgusting.

I made my way to the waiting area for the swim start. I walked alone, distracted by the sound of a cargo train going over a railroad trestle on the other side of Aquia Creek.

"A full wet suit? Man, you're going to cook out there."

I turned to see another racer, in a Speedo, jogging up next to me.

"Bad circulation," I said, by way of explanation.

"Whatever, man," he said as he continued jogging to the timing mat.

I joined several other swimmers under the arch designating the site of the first timing mat, and we walked across it together. The mat would record the number of swimmers who started and, at the end, verify that the same number came out of the water. Our actual start time would be determined by the start time of the group in which we were racing. For me, that was Men ages forty to forty-four.

I got some more questioning looks for wearing a full suit on such a warm day; the age sixty-five-plus racers and I were the only ones wearing them. Once the race got started, I expected people would forget about me, and my full wet suit. For now, it was the only way I could cover up the two timing chips I was wearing on my ankle—Patrick's and mine. As long as I made sure to go across each timing mat with a group of racers, no one would notice two identical times.

I watched the parade of swimmers move under the arch and across the timing mat, big black numbers drawn on their arms and calves. They marched in practical silence, reminding me more of concentration camp prisoners than elite athletes.

The announcer's voice boomed: "All you swimmers getting acclimated to the water, come on in. We're about to begin."

The small packs of yellow swim caps, pink, blue, green, and others, stayed congregated in their clusters, out in the water.

"Or ignore me," the announcer said.

Slowly, the swimmers made their way to shore. The spectators, squinting into the sun rising in the east, lined the outside of the swim start. The athletes were gathered between two lines of red and white pennants strung along a nylon rope, separating them from the cheering fans. The yellow caps, the professional triathletes, moved right to the front; the newbies hovered near the back; the rest of us jockeyed for position, as close to the yellow caps as we could get.

Once the horn blew, eight hundred or so racers would run into the water, one group at a time, the spotters in the kayaks trying their best to make sure all the heads that went under came back up.

The announcer continued, "Your swim course today is a triangle marked by two buoys. You'll swim out to the first buoy, the large blow-up of the Confederate soldier."

The spectators and swimmers looked in the direction he had indicated, and a small roll of laughter moved through the crowd. It was not unusual for triathlon organizers to break up the monotony of the seventy-mile race with whimsy, and what better to have as buoys than something marking the event being commemorated by the race.

"Along the way, you'll see orange tetrahedrons you can use for sighting. You can go on either side of them, but you must keep the buoys on your right. All turns are made to your right. Once you round the second buoy, the Union soldier, you'll see the big dancing man we've inflated to help you find your way to the Swim In."

The audience followed along with the announcer and looked at the various blow-ups set up for the swimmers. The laughter grew louder then subsided when the announcer addressed the athletes for the final time before the race.

"Good luck, swimmers!"

The crowd erupted again. It could be annoying to have so much screaming throughout the race, but most of the athletes used it to propel them through the next few miles.

"Ninety seconds, yellow caps. Say your goodbyes to your loved ones."

The yellow caps don't bring loved ones; they're focused on winning, nothing else.

"Forty-five seconds."

The spectators were jumping up and down, applauding, screaming.

"Fifteen seconds, yellow caps. Green caps, you're next."

The yellow caps all but had their toes in the water. The horn blew, and the race was underway. Every three minutes, the announcer sent out another group: Men twenty to twenty-four, Men twenty-five to twenty-nine, Men thirty to thirty-four, and so on. He did the same with the women. Then, finally, he released the Clydesdales and the Athenas, the large male and female competitors, weighing between one hundred and eighty-five and two hundred and twenty-five pounds. There were no limitations from the county about when people had to be out of the water, so the event organizers didn't have to let the slow swimmers go first.

I should have waited at the back of my group, so I wouldn't get kicked and submerged and elbowed in the middle of the eighty-three people in my category, but I had to make sure I stayed with a group. The two timing chips on my ankle would stand out less, if they beeped as part of a larger set of beeps.

I turned at the Union soldier buoy and made my way to the big inflated dancing man. I wasn't tired, like I normally was at the end of a one-mile swim; the adrenaline was keeping me alert. I sped up to catch the pack of five or six men swimming ahead of me and closed ranks even further, once we were on shore. The seven of us ran across the timing mat in unison.

I ran past a set of crying twins, confined to their blanket prison surrounded by a sea of crushed goldfish. I stripped my wet suit off to my waist as I ran to the first transition area, the nondescript, gray tri suit I was wearing underneath letting me blend into the background.

I counted my strokes, focused on my technique, varied my breathing—anything to keep my pace with the group of men I was following. I moved along the rows of bikes in Transition One, all the way to the other end. The bikes were corralled in order, so twenty-nine was in the first row. No one paid attention to which bike you got on, as long as the number on your arm and calf matched the one on the bike. My bike slot was in the row right behind Patrick's, and it was empty.

The announcer informed anyone listening through the din of cheering spectators and noisy vendors about the order of finishers. "The first of the gals is coming in; Tracy Miller, two-time bronze medalist in the Olympics, is looking strong. Over on the men's side, we have Matt Benzer leading the baggy shorts division. How does that guy swim in those things? It might explain why he's coming in with the ladies. A close second behind Tracy is newly turned pro Susie Vanderpool, giving the Olympian a run for her money ... or should I say, a swim." He laughed at his own bad joke.

I peeled off the rest of the wet suit, dried my feet with the waiting towel Patrick had left near his bike and put on the socks he had also left there. Like any experienced triathlete, Patrick had made sure to have everything organized for a quick transition to the bike. I attached my race number to my race belt and grabbed two packets of goo. I shoved one into the elastic loop on the belt and sucked the contents out of the other. The shot of caffeine added to my already adrenaline-fueled energy. This was happening. Finally, I would have what I'd been waiting years for. I caught my breath, let the smile cover my face, and for a few seconds imagined what my life would be like when the race was over.

I picked up the bike and ran it to the mount line in only my socked feet. I had been careful to pull the socks up over the timing chips. Patrick wore ankle-length athletic socks, so I had to push the strap with the timing chips on it down below my anklebones. It would hurt like hell by the time I got them off. Patrick had left his shoes clipped on to his pedals. I would slip my feet in, once I started the bike course. We didn't wear the same size, but I wouldn't be on the bike long enough that it would matter.

Even more spectators lined the bike path than were at the swim. Cowbells made a racket. Horns went off for every biker. Every manner of inspirational song—"Eye of the Tiger," "Let's Get the Party Started," "We Are the Champions," "We Will Rock You"—blasted from speakers along the way.

One of the volunteers lining the bike path handed me a flat Coke, standard fare to give athletes a boost of energy during the race. It was better than the lukewarm chicken soup. I tossed it back, not needing the energy it was giving me; the adrenaline was taking care of that. I grabbed another two and made sure the guys I was riding with saw it.

"You better slow down, or you'll be taking a leak," one of them said.

"Or piss on yourself. They don't have showers here; it's only a half," another one cautioned.

"You'll be smelling yourself the whole way!" the first one came back and laughed.

The practice, in full triathlons, of urinating on yourself to save time was known to the racers. In a Half Ironman, though, it wouldn't be unusual for a racer to pull off the course to go to the bathroom, especially if a portable john wasn't available.

"Rough night, man. Got to," I replied. I lifted my left arm and stretched it in an exaggerated gesture, hoping the rider next to me would see the number on my arm. I left it there for an awkwardly long fifteen or twenty seconds. Then, for good measure, I said, "Only twelve miles in, and I already gotta take a leak." This should be enough to establish that Patrick was alive during the start of the bike portion, I thought.

"You're gonna kill your time, twenty-nine," one of them said before pulling away from me and taking the rest of the pack with him. They were probably glad to have one less person to have to beat, especially if that person was an invited athlete.

"It's not my time I'm killing," I mumbled to myself, unable to keep the smile from spreading across my face.

I veered right and off the bike course. The area was lightly wooded, and no one would be able to see me unless they stopped in that exact spot. The path I took to get there was not paved or even trodden, and it was deep enough into the woods that no one would waste valuable race time to come to it. I moved fast.

I had parked my van on a service road that was closed to traffic because of the race. I had made sure to get the van—with Patrick's body, my bike, rubbing alcohol, a black magic marker, and the syringe full of potassium chloride, into a thicket of trees, where someone had abandoned an old sailboat, now overgrown with wild grasses and dried leaves. From the look of things, no one had been here in years.

I dragged Patrick's body to the spot where his bike lay in the woods. He was still unconscious, thanks to the Percocet. The time of death had to show during the race, so no one who saw me with Patrick last night would be able to connect me with this. I pulled out the syringe and injected the potassium chloride directly into Patrick's heart. I thought about injecting the extract—so easy to make with drugstore ingredients and Internet directions—into his left arm, under the thick black twenty-nine. The number would more than cover the puncture mark, but potassium chloride in the heart was a sure thing. It would look like he crashed into a tree because his heart gave out. I dissolved some potassium chloride tablets in his water bottles and slid them into their holders on the bike, to make it appear as if he were drugging during the race to use the potassium chloride to feed his muscles. If anyone ever found the body and autopsied it, it would look like the physical exertion of the race, coupled with an overdose of potassium chloride, had killed him.

I slipped his timing chip back on to his ankle strap and transferred his shoes and socks from my feet to his. I got on my bike and used the service road to connect with the back of the bike pack. I made my reentry through another spur along the path, and anyone who saw me would assume I had just taken a leak. The number on my arm and calf now read "52."

I crossed the timing mat at Bike In and again at Run Out, this time with just one timing chip on. Only a thirteen-mile run, and I'd be done with this race, with Patrick Swann, and, maybe, even have a shot at his grieving widow again.

I made it through the second transition, the one between the bike portion and the run, with no difficulty. I put my bike in its spot, changed socks and shoes, and started down the run course. It didn't matter anymore if I ran with a group or by myself. Patrick's times were no longer being recorded.

I finished with the first seventy-five or so racers in just over five and a half hours—a personal best for me for a Half Ironman. My time would probably put me in contention for an age-group win. The day was getting better and better.

I waited for the race results in the food tent set up for the competitors, enjoying my complimentary slice of pizza, cookie and bottle of water. After about twenty minutes, finishers started moving toward a stand-alone bulletin board, which normally gave visitors park hours and rules. I joined them.

The results of the race were posted there, alongside pictures of the athletes at various points in the race. There were pictures of everyone, everywhere—one of the moneymaking opportunities for the race organizers. There were even some pictures of me coming out of the swim, coming out of the bike and at the finish. I looked good, strong, like a winner.

I scanned the list of finishers until I saw my name. I went back and counted how many men in my age group finished ahead of me. Only two. I was third in my age group, my best finish ever! Granted, I took a short cut on the service road, but only I knew that.

I made my way to the announcer's canopy, where the awards would be given. I talked to the other participants, accepted their congratulations on my place and gave out congratulations of my own. Today was a day to celebrate.

Thirty minutes later, the event organizers still hadn't arrived with the plaques and envelopes of one hundred dollar cash for the age group and overall winners. In front of the scoreboard, a crowd had gathered. One man, who looked to be around my age, was waving his arms about frantically, pointing to the scoreboard and then to the officials. One of the officials turned in the direction of the announcer's canopy and scanned the small group of winners looking for someone. He looked back to where the agitated racer was pointing on the board and then squinted directly at me. He crooked his finger, motioning me over.

"Sir, this gentleman is claiming you ran as two different people. He wants you disqualified because the rules say, one racer, one finish."

I looked where he was pointing. Under the winners in each category was a picture of them in each of the three events. There I was, in my crowd of six other swimmers, the number twenty-nine easily visible on my left arm. There I was again, coming out of the first transition, the number twenty-nine still on my arm.

There I was at the finish, the number fifty-two announcing the change in my identity. Shit!

"Where is twenty-nine in the finish pictures?" the flailing-arms man asked. "This man cheated," he said, pointing directly at me. "His time is only seconds shorter than mine, but he cheated. I got fourth; I should have gotten third! There is no twenty-nine anywhere at the finish."

This guy had no idea. I decided just to give up my third-place age group and leave. Who cared if they thought I cheated? I never had to do another triathlon again. I got what I had come for.

"Look, I don't want any trouble. I'll DQ myself. I'm disqualified, OK?" I said.

The man was still angry, but he looked appeased. I started to walk away, when one of the volunteers loped over to the race official standing by the scoreboard.

"Twenty-nine never got off the bike course, sir. Everyone else has," he said.

"But this man is twenty-nine." The race official looked at me, the wheels in his head clearly spinning. He ran his fingers down the columns of results. He checked finishing times, event splits, even transition times. He looked from the results to the photos and back again.

"There are seven men in this Swim Out photo, including you, but eight chip times." Then, he dragged his right index finger to the next photo. "There are three riders in this shot coming off the Bike Out timing mat—again, you are one of them," he said, and with his left hand, dragged his index finger down the column of results, "but four times are recorded." He did the same thing with the Run Out and said, "But here," pointing to the picture of me crossing the timing mat before the start of the run, "there are four people and four times. You are one of the men, but the number on your arm has changed." Now he was looking only at me.

"Check the bike path, all of it," he said to the race volunteer. "Find number twenty-nine." He motioned to someone behind me, and, before I knew it, both of my elbows were in the vise of a burly security guard, and I was being dragged away to the race officials' tent.

It was only a matter of time before they figured the whole thing out.

Patrick had beaten me again.

A NOT SO GENTEEL MURDER

By Maggie King

"DO YOU BELIEVE THE gall of that jerk? Here I invited him as *my* date and he shows up with that, that *slut!*" Olivia Thompson punctuated her tirade with furious drags on her cigarette.

I didn't point out that Olivia hadn't exactly *invited* Sherwood Aimsley to be her date, rather had taken the coy route of mentioning the party on his Facebook page and suggesting that he drop by, saying how great it would be to finally meet him in person. From that he was supposed to have intuited that he was to be her date. But the nonintuitive Sherwood appeared with one Carmen Minton on his arm. When my cousin Agnes Murphy made the introductions, Olivia, initially stunned, had rallied and decided that Sherwood and his escort were father and daughter. The woman was no more than thirty, if that old.

"I can see the resemblance." Olivia claimed in a playful tone. "You're *definitely* your father's daughter." I resisted the urge to roll my eyes. There wasn't an iota of resemblance between the two of them.

Carmen and Sherwood looked at each other and burst out laughing. Then Sherwood put his arm around Carmen and gave her a tender kiss on the lips. "No, I just met this lovely lady a week ago."

I didn't dare look at Olivia when I asked, "How did you meet?"

"In a bar," Carmen said sweetly, adding a wink.

Olivia gave a half-laugh before excusing herself, dragging me along with her. Her face flushed with fury, she'd exclaimed,

"Sharon, I simply *must* have a cigarette." And so I found myself standing in front of the Kent-Valentine House, breathing secondhand smoke and listening to Olivia wail about her lost opportunity to snare Sherwood.

"We'll find you someone else, Olivia. Let's go back inside." But Olivia, lighting another cigarette, gave me a sour look and stood planted on the sidewalk in heels that no sixty-something woman should be able to wear. My own two-inch heels felt more than high enough.

Olivia Thompson had long been a thorn in my side. Over the past four decades, she'd had a string of affairs with her friends' husbands, Agnes Murphy and I being two of those many friends. Agnes had been especially upset about her late husband's succumbing to Olivia's charms.

My own husband, Andrew Taylor, fell hard for Olivia, so hard that before I knew what was happening he was asking for a divorce. He expected Olivia to follow suit so they could marry and live happily ever after. But Olivia got cold feet about the divorce and, by the time Andrew got the final decree, she was already fooling around with someone else. That left Andrew brokenhearted over Olivia and me brokenhearted over Andrew.

Olivia got her comeuppance just six months before, when her own long-suffering spouse left her for a much younger woman.

When Agnes read an article about how refusing to forgive could jeopardize one's health, the two of us told Olivia we wanted to let bygones be bygones and, further extending the olive branch, invited her to lunch. When Olivia launched into a lament about her ungrateful husband's defection, Agnes and I looked at each other and smiled. Agnes told Olivia about Sherwood Aimsley, a widower who Agnes knew somehow. When Agnes offered to connect the two of them on Facebook, Olivia lost no time registering on the social networking site, using a post-facelift photo for her profile. Agnes had assured her that Sherwood looked exactly like his photo, not like some who posted decades-old pictures. His Colgate smile and peppered hair had prompted Olivia's sort-of invitation to a party at the Kent-Valentine house—an invitation that hadn't met Olivia's expectations.

While Olivia fumed and smoked, I regarded the imposing Kent-Valentine House, headquarters of the Garden Club of Virginia. Majestic magnolia trees flanked the antebellum mansion in downtown Richmond. Ionic columns supported a veranda crowned by a wrought-iron balcony. Maybe I had the Ionic part wrong, but it was close enough. When I'd toured the house during Historic Garden Week with my son, Ray, Agnes Murphy had bombarded us with details, most of which had gone right out of my head. While Ray and I had munched cookies and sipped lemonade, Agnes had given us a very thorough tour of the premises, including the third floor and basement, areas not usually included. But perhaps she'd been bored since the flower-hatted Garden Club matrons were out touring historic gardens, leaving us as her sole audience. And as a member in good standing of the Garden Club, she'd had the run of the house.

That was two weeks before, and tonight I was back at the house for Deb Carnachan's sixtieth birthday party. Ever since Deb had attended some do here years before, she'd vowed to celebrate her next milestone at the imposing mansion just steps away from the Jefferson Hotel.

This was my first social event in the two years since I'd lost two key people in my life. The first loss was when my ex-husband's injuries from a skiing accident proved fatal. Though I saw Andrew from time to time over the years, mainly because of our two children, we'd maintained a distance. Neither of us remarried and I never stopped loving him, but pride kept me from admitting that. After his accident, I found myself regretting that decision. To my surprise, he left his estate to me. Olivia, his former lover-cum-fiancée, didn't attend his funeral or even send a card.

The second event that cut like a knife was the suicide of Renee, my estranged daughter. Renee had stopped speaking to me some years before her death after one too many conflicts over drugs and her ill-advised choice of husbands. I like to think we would have eventually reunited had it not been for her fourth, and last, husband, an abusive control freak who wouldn't let her have anything to do with her family. But my son, Ray, managed to see his sister on the sly when he visited from New York. As Renee's husband wouldn't even let her have a cell phone, Ray gave his sister a prepaid one in his name with instructions to call anytime she needed him.

Unfortunately, she didn't call him before she took her life with her husband's gun.

Renee was cremated. There was no mention in the paper, no funeral, and the family wasn't notified. But Agnes Murphy was neighbors with Beverly Livingston, the medical examiner. Beverly, knowing that Agnes was Renee's godmother, made a condolence call to a shocked Agnes. We held a memorial service, not inviting the husband. What he did with Renee's ashes was anyone's guess. Ray and I had become closer since the tragedy and he visited more often, even though he didn't feel as free to practice his alternative lifestyle in Richmond.

Growing weary of standing outside on East Franklin Street, I repeated my suggestion of going inside, adding, "There're lots of attractive men at the party, and you look fabulous." Along with her post-divorce facelift, liposuction and butt lift, Olivia had splurged on honey-blond highlights and a black sequined dress that created a slimming illusion. I felt downright dowdy standing next to her in a drab navy number that did nothing to disguise the pounds that had crept up on me.

"Okay," Olivia moaned. She squashed her Virginia Slim under a strappy sandal and said, "Let's go."

Deb Carnachan, the birthday girl and hostess for the event, had gone all-out for the occasion. Sprays of flowers in primary colors complemented the eighteenth and nineteenth century antiques that furnished the Kent-Valentine House. As I recalled from Agnes's tour, the house was built in 1845 for Horace Kent, a wholesale dry goods merchant. In the early 1900s, the house was sold to the Granville Valentine family, who added the beautiful east wing and third floor. The Colonial Revival style of the new wing blended beautifully with the Gothic Revival one designed for the Kents.

In 1971, the Garden Club of Virginia purchased the house and transformed the residence into a functional space. In 1995, they completely restored the house to its original design, complete with tiered chandeliers and ornate fireplaces. During this restoration, a tower wing was added to the east side of the house that included an elevator, allowing the house to be handicapped accessible.

At least a hundred guests filled the parlors, and Olivia and I had to squeeze past groups of people balancing drinks and food-laden plates. We saw many friends who looked especially good for the occasion. I almost didn't recognize Julie Barnes with makeup. I wanted to suggest that she always wear it, but feared it would sound insulting. Terrell May's facelift took twenty years off her age.

Agnes Murphy had tried—sort of. Shoe-polish black replaced her usually colorless gray hair, and a couple of patches of red rouge adorned her cheeks, a red slash across her lips. As usual, black-framed glasses sat on her nose at a crooked angle. I complimented her on her curls, an improvement over her usual hastily assembled bun. Her old-lady shoes were probably a lot more comfortable than mine or Olivia's, but still. Bless her heart!

Many of us lived in the same neighborhood, belonged to the same bridge and book groups, and had gone to high school together. Agnes was a notable exception, having grown up in the wealthy part of Richmond, attending private schools, marrying well. I was her "poor relation." But she and I had remained close and would do anything for each other.

"Where have you two been?" Deb the birthday girl looked smashing in lots of diaphanous ruffles and silver jewelry. Not waiting for an answer, she asked, "Have you tried the salmon?" before flashing a smile at the couple behind us.

In the dining room I picked up a plate and walked around the table. What did I want to try first? Everything, I decided. What a spread—crabmeat-stuffed mushrooms, bite-sized filet mignon wrapped in bacon, salmon, chicken satay, potato bruschetta, fresh fruit, vegetable crudité, the works.

As I nibbled on a canapé topped with spinach and a cream cheese spread, Olivia dug blood-red talons into my arm and whispered, "Look, by the salmon." Indeed, Sherwood and Carmen were heaping salmon on their plates. He wore a custom-made Italian suit, flashing teeth that were whiter than Joe Biden's. The quilted bag Carmen had looped over her shoulder was a duplicate of the one Olivia carried.

I had to admit that the blonde and statuesque Carmen was lovely in her form-fitting black tulip dress. Kohl-rimmed blue eyes and the kind of full red lips that grace glossy magazine ads—what man could resist her? Looking at her, Kim Novak and Grace Kelly came to mind. As Olivia and I were roughly the same age, I'm sure she was making the same comparison, even if she'd prefer to confer slut status on Carmen.

Carmen whispered something in Sherwood's ear, and he gave her a look that I could only call lascivious. I hoped Olivia had missed this interaction, but no such luck. I felt those nails digging into my arm again.

Balancing his plate and drink, Sherwood boomed, "Olivia, thanks so much for inviting us. This is quite an event. Lots of buzz."

Olivia managed a painful smile.

Not wanting to make another trip outside while Olivia puffed on multiple cigarettes, I excused myself and Olivia, saying I'd just spotted a man who especially wanted to meet her. I emphasized "especially" for Sherwood's benefit. I pulled Olivia along with me and introduced her to Deb's brother, down from Northern Virginia for the occasion. Then I said, "Be back in a minute," and went in the direction of the restroom and stood in the inevitable line, listening to complaints about the loudness of the music. Agnes had suggested this group to Deb, but I wasn't sure if she'd actually heard them play. A guitarist, bass guitarist and drummer had set up in the back parlor. They formed a small group, but with a big sound—too big for this venue.

When I finally came out, I spotted Olivia in the front parlor with some of our book group. Apparently she hadn't hit it off with Deb's brother. From her arm waving and angry expression, I took it she was regaling them with the Sherwood-Carmen drama. As for the now infamous couple, I found them in the dining room with Agnes and Terrell May. Sherwood guffawed while Carmen looked bored.

Eventually, Deb's birthday cake was presented with lots of fanfare. It seemed like each person who spoke lovingly of Deb did so at length—husband, daughter, son, grandchildren, in-laws. Speeches over, the enormous sheet cake, a strawberry concoction smothered in whipped cream and adorned with more strawberries, was served. Deb had requested no presents, so we were spared having to ooh and ah over them.

As I ate my cake, I looked around for Sherwood and Carmen but didn't see them. Perhaps they'd gone off to indulge their lust. I didn't see Olivia either—she was probably bending someone's ear about Sherwood's "betrayal." The band was on a break so I could pick up scraps of conversations. A petite woman with a Minnie Mouse voice proclaimed that every woman needed a gun for self-defense. Her words echoed ones I'd recently heard from Olivia.

Along with her physical overhaul, Olivia had decided that, as a single woman, she needed protection and so had acquired a gun, something she could carry in her purse. She'd e-mailed the book group all the information on her selection, some Smith & Wesson model, hoping she could get us to follow in her footsteps. With my luck, I'd wind up shooting myself.

Just then Olivia appeared. How did I get stuck babysitting such a drama queen? I eyed her bag hanging from her shoulder, wondering if she had her gun in there.

She looked around and asked, "Where's Sherwood?"

"I think they left. Let's go upstairs. There's an exhibit of bird and botanical prints on the third floor." Apparently such prints didn't motivate Olivia, but my promise that she could smoke upstairs got her moving.

Agnes sat in front of a desk on the second floor, texting. The desk overlooked a wrought-iron balcony. I imagined Eva Perón standing on it while she belted out "Don't Cry for Me, Argentina."

Agnes looked up and gazed at us. "How's it going, ladies?"

"Pretty good. I'm so happy for Deb. This is such a great party." I turned to Olivia. "Don't you think so, Olivia?"

"It would be if it wasn't for that Sherwood. He actually thanked me for inviting them to the party. *Them*." She crossed her arms and shook her head. "I don't recall inviting the bimbo."

I rolled my eyes at Agnes. She smiled and pushed her glasses up on her nose.

"Let's take a look at the library, Olivia." The library was my favorite room in the house. The rest of the second floor functioned as office space for the Garden Club of Virginia staff, but the library was an oasis, holding floor-to-ceiling shelves of books on gardening, historic gardens and flower arranging. Tall windows looked out on East Franklin Street.

Agnes asked, "Did you see the exhibit upstairs?"

"Not yet. We're headed there next."

"You don't want to miss it. But you'd better go that way." Agnes pointed in the direction of the newest addition to the house, known as the Tower. "You don't want to let Sophia catch you going up there." Sophia was the housekeeper and staff representative for parties at the Kent-Valentine House. She ran a tight ship and didn't take to people wandering about the house unsupervised.

Olivia and I bypassed the main staircase and walked down the hall through a door that took us to the Tower wing and another set of stairs that ascended to the third floor.

Olivia opened her purse to get a cigarette, and I saw a metal item that could only be a gun. No doubt about it.

"You brought your gun to a birthday party?" I asked.

"You better believe it. I don't go anywhere without it. You know who I'd like to use it on right now, don't you?" I considered the question rhetorical, so didn't bother responding.

The band had started up again, but the music was slightly muted on the top floor. "The exhibit's in there," I said, waving my hand toward a large meeting room on our left.

I stopped. "I hear a phone. Is it mine or yours?" I asked.

"I didn't hear anything."

We both checked our phones, but had no incoming calls or messages. I heard something like Beethoven's Fifth, but the sound was faint. Was my imagination going into overdrive?

"Is your ring tone Beethoven's Fifth?"

"Huh?"

"Never mind."

Then I heard other strange sounds. Moans, cries. I traced the noises to a closed door that likely was a restroom. Someone having a quickie. Restrooms didn't strike me as the most comfortable of places for a tryst. But there was the adventure factor, especially in the bastion of gentility that was the Kent-Valentine House. I wondered if the daring lovers were Sherwood and Carmen.

Olivia had the same thought. "I bet it's that asshole, Sherwood. And his *slut*." She pounded on the door and yelled, "Couldn't keep it in your pants, could you Sherwood? You have to copulate like animals, in public."

Dying of mortification, I slipped into the large meeting room that housed the collection of prints by eighteenth century naturalist Mark Catesby. "Olivia, please come away from that door," I pleaded as I searched for a wall switch. "You don't even know who it is in there."

Just then I heard a shot. And another one. Or was it the drums? No, it came from the restroom. By the time I got to the meeting room door, Carmen was running through the door that led to the tower. Olivia was standing in the hall, her smoldering cigarette lying forgotten on the floor.

She and I looked at each other in shock and disbelief. Light poured out of the restroom. I stepped into the hall and stamped out the cigarette. I knew I should run, but I couldn't resist peering into the restroom. I gasped when I saw Sherwood on the floor, pants around his ankles, private parts on display. And blood—lots of it.

I looked at Olivia in horror. "Olivia, did you ... did you ... shoot—"

"Of course not, you idiot!" She shrieked and pointed toward the tower. "The slut did it."

Olivia continued to shriek.

I ran.

— 🐞 —

Ten minutes later, I slowed my Prius to pick up a tall young man at the corner of Grace and Foushee Streets. We rode in silence for a few moments.

When I pulled over on the Lee Bridge, the young man got out of the car. He heaved a king-sized pillowcase into the James

River. I knew what the pillow case contained: the gun that had killed Sherwood Aimsley, a black tulip dress, blond wig, a pair of sky-high heels and a quilted shoulder bag. Oh, and the phone with the Beethoven's Fifth ringtone—Agnes's daughter Sylvia had donated that item to the cause. I also knew he'd stashed his own clothes, a sweatshirt and jeans, in the basement, where he'd made a quick change from the Carmen getup before sprinting out the back door, not stopping until he'd reached our prearranged meeting spot.

The young man got back in the car and I continued driving. We didn't speak until I drove into the crowded parking lot of Crossroads Coffee and Ice Cream on Forest Hill Avenue. He turned to me, blue eyes still smudged with kohl, lips still red, hair now black and short and sticking up in tufts.

"There's some makeup remover and tissues in the glove compartment. And here, take my compact." We thought it too risky to use the lighted mirror in the sun visor, but the parking lot's lights were sufficient.

As he tended to his face, I drew a deep breath. "So ... is he really dead?"

"He's dead all right."

"Good. I hope Sherwood Aimsley rots in hell."

"Do you think anyone heard the shot?"

"I doubt it, not with that loud music. Agnes suggested that group for their volume. I was surprised I could hear Beethoven's Fifth when I dialed Sylvia's cell phone. It was faint but I heard the ringing in the restroom."

When the young man, finished with his makeup removal, wondered aloud if the police were already swarming around at the Kent-Valentine House, I said, "Probably. I'm sure Olivia went tearing downstairs, screaming her fool head off all the way. Someone would have called the police." I laughed and said, "Those genteel Garden Club ladies won't be happy when they hear about this not so genteel murder."

The young man chuckled. "Wait until they discover that Olivia has a gun, the same model that killed Sherwood."

I told the young man about spotting the gun in Olivia's purse. "All her promotion of that gun wound up backfiring on her, no pun intended." When Olivia had e-mailed the book group telling of her purchase of a Smith & Wesson M&P, caliber 9 x 19 mm, 3.5" compact, perfect for "us girls," I doubted that she anticipated one of us, meaning yours truly, would acquire the same model and use it to frame her in a murder. "And she told anyone who would listen how angry she was at Sherwood for bringing that slut Carmen to the party." As Olivia had, at one time or another, bedded the husbands of any number of the women at the party, they surely wouldn't hesitate to mention her anger to the police. "Of course, it will turn out not to be the gun that shot Sherwood anyway. But it will make her sweat a bit to be questioned—small payback for not only stealing my husband but for dumping him to boot. Not to mention her affair with Agnes's husband."

The young man said, "One thing's for sure: We can never repay Agnes. She gave us that tour of the house so we knew the layout top to bottom."

"We may need her help yet again once the police discover that Sherwood was my late son-in-law. Thankfully, she isn't averse to offering sizable bribes to the police or politicians from either party. Agnes would do anything to protect her family." I laughed when I remembered how Agnes, wanting to meet Sherwood and start our plan of revenge, hosted a Facebook party at her home and invited the recently widowed and divorced. Everyone not already on Facebook was invited to register. Sherwood all too happily complied.

I said, "Plus Agnes was the one who suggested that Olivia 'friend' Sherwood on Facebook. And all the verbal cues she gave me when we went upstairs. 'Did you see the exhibit yet?' meant it was safe to go up to the third floor. Otherwise, if someone was up there, she'd have suggested we look around in the library until she issued the all clear."

"Yeah, Olivia sure fell into our plans—Facebook, the gun. Any problems getting her upstairs?"

I shook my head. "Piece of cake. You can get the woman to do anything if you tell her she can smoke."

The young man laughed. "Yeah, everything went off without a hitch for me. Meeting Sherwood in the bar, luring him over to the Kent-Valentine House. Luring him upstairs. Child's play."

"How could he resist you as Carmen?"

His expression turned rueful when he said, "Unfortunately, I had to do a few things I didn't care for ..."

I put my hand up like a traffic cop. "Please." The less I knew about the sexual aspect, the better.

We didn't speak for a few minutes, just watched people entering and leaving Crossroads, a funky gas station turned café. I sighed. "Unfortunately, it doesn't bring back Renee. But we did avenge her death." It still seemed strange that, until just hours before, I'd never met my daughter's scumbag husband who had led her to take her own life.

A note of worry crept into the young man's voice. "Do you think they'll ever find me?"

"No. They'll be looking for Carmen. And she doesn't exist." I did worry that the police might find out about the young man's transvestite lifestyle in New York and put two and two together. Yet another opportunity for us to lean on Agnes and her deep pockets.

I took a deep breath, smiled and said, "Let's go inside and get some ice cream."

"Sounds good."

"I love you, Ray."

"I love you too, Mom."

BIRDSEED

By May Layne

"I FORGOT TO PICK up the birdseed I promised Beulah. Now she'll think I don't love her. That I'm having a fling with someone and I got distracted."

Freddie put his head in his hands, then lifted it and stared out the train window. Stoplights and houses and strange faces flashed by.

"Maybe you should go back," said Matt.

"Maybe I should come up with some story why I couldn't get it."

"Better tell the truth."

"That would never work."

"Tell her you were still thinking about work, and how glad you were to be done for the day, going to see her." Matt pushed his glasses up.

"That's laying it on a bit thick. She'd never buy that."

"Why? Aren't you looking forward to seeing her?"

Freddie sat with his mouth open. Had he been looking forward to seeing her? Or had he been thinking of Christie, the new girl, who wore her skirts a little shorter, a little tighter than the dragons in the office? "They'll eat her up and spit her out," he said.

"Who?" asked Matt.

"The dragons." Freddie made a roaring sound and did a zombielike thing with his hands.

Matt knew about the dragons. Though they didn't work together, Freddie had told him enough stories. "Eat who up?" he asked.

"The new girl, Christie."

"Oh. There's a new girl? Hot?"

"Very."

"You'd better go back and get that birdseed."

Freddie descended at the next stop and waited on the platform for forty-five minutes. An accident at one of the intersections tied things up. At last, the white flash of the light rail train, known as "The Tide" in Norfolk, rounded the corner and pulled to a smooth stop.

Freddie got off at the end of the line and walked nine blocks to the home improvement center, where he purchased a forty pound sack of songbird feed, hefted it onto his shoulder, and walked the nine blocks back to the station, achieving a sort of alternating balance, listing left awhile, then shifting the bag with a grunt then listing right awhile. He only had to wait ten minutes for the next train.

At last he arrived at Beulah's building and climbed the four flights of stairs to her flat. He set the bag down with a huff and knocked.

No answer.

Knocked again.

He leaned against the wall, a long flappy breath escaping his lips. Then he left, leaving the heroically acquired bag of birdseed behind.

He stopped in a deli for a sandwich, moistened by ripe tomatoes, which he ate in the street. The red juice dripped to the heel of his hand then off, causing him to jerk his foot back to keep his shoe clean.

He went home, watched a little TV, and then went to bed. He never heard the phone ring—slept right through it. But in his dreams he heard it, and he dreamed he and Beulah had broken up. He feared the voice on the other end, afraid it was Beulah, calling to give him another chance. He woke, pulsing and nauseated.

Next morning, he got through all his Saturday chores by noon, and then he glanced at his answering machine and there was a message. He ignored it for three more hours by playing war games on his Wii. At last he listened. Beulah thanked him for the birdseed. She said the bag was too heavy and asked him to come over and help her with it. She'd be home all day. Freddie wished he lived across town instead of only six blocks away.

He went over and knocked, and Beulah opened the door, her long brown hair swirling around her head as she spun back into her apartment. He carried in the birdseed, and she pointed to the linen closet. He set it on the floor inside. She snipped off a corner and used a spoon to scoop up a little bit then opened her screen and sprinkled it across the windowsill for the pigeons.

They made up. Freddie's insides were at war with his outsides.

"I'm going to visit my mom," she said.

"When do you leave?" asked Freddie.

"Tomorrow morning. Would you water my plants?"

"Sure, of course."

"And feed the pigeons?"

"Happy to. How long will you be gone?"

"Two weeks."

Freddie kissed her goodbye and left her to pack. An odd feeling lifted him to his toes and rocketed to his fingertips, making his arms swing up in an arc around him. People stared, but he only laughed.

That evening, he called Christie, and they met for dinner then decided to see a movie. Since she lived across town and it was late, she stayed at his place.

For almost two weeks, Freddie spent time with Christie, and he forgot all about Beulah's plants and pigeons until Saturday, the day before she was due back. Then he remembered and told Christie he'd have to run over there.

"Don't go anywhere," he said.

She ate a chocolate-covered strawberry and smiled.

He walked the six blocks and four flights of stairs to Beulah's place. When he got to her door, he thought he could hear noises on the other side, and after some internal debate, afraid she was home, he knocked. The sounds ceased, then increased, then ceased. He knocked again. He used his key and opened the door.

The first thing he saw was a mass of stuffing from the couch all over the floor. Next he saw black pellets everywhere. He took one step in and saw a hole in the linen closet door and birdseed spilling under the door and out into the room. Then he saw beady eyes staring at him through the hole, and he felt a chill down his spine. He saw a dark nose and light whiskers peering from under the couch. Then he saw a big rat run from behind the couch to the closet, where it jumped through the hole in the door and was greeted with unearthly squeaks.

Freddie backed out the door, closed it and locked the deadbolt. Some plants, he thought, can do without water for months.

For the next week, Freddie waited for the hysterical phone call from Beulah, the one when she'd cuss him out. But it didn't come. He continued to spend time with Christie, and on days when he didn't see her, he called her at least four times. Another week passed, and then another, and Christie stopped taking his calls. When she dumped him, it took all of three minutes.

"I don't want to hang out with you anymore," she said. They sat across from each other at Starbucks. She finished her skinny latte. "Goodbye," she said all chipper, like a flight attendant waving the latest batch of passengers off the plane. She left. He stayed behind with his mocha frappe, making slurping noises with his straw.

He walked the streets, head bowed, feet kicking at the sidewalk then he found himself approaching Beulah's building. Six marked police cars cluttered the street outside along with two unmarked. A black van blocked the sidewalk, rear doors wide open. Freddie sidled up to one of the neighbors.

"What's going on?" he asked.

"Dead woman," the neighbor answered.

"Who?"

"Beulah something," he said.

Freddie's mouth dried to cinders, or dust, or maybe sand. In any case, it made him cough.

The neighbor looked at him. "Aren't you the boyfriend?"

"No. No. I'm not," Freddie said, rasping the words.

The neighbor waved a patrolman over. "Here's the boyfriend," he said.

"That right," said the officer. "Let me get your information."

Freddie provided his essentials. "What happened to her?" he asked. The officer ignored him and walked away. A few moments later, he returned with a guy in a suit and tie.

"You the boyfriend?" asked the suit.

"I was, but it's been more than a month," Freddie said.

"That right," said the guy who introduced himself as Detective somebody or other.

"What happened to her?" Freddie asked.

"Won't know that until the medical's done." The detective stared at Freddie. "But there appears to be a head injury."

The neighbor said, "And there sure are some fat and happy rats around."

Freddie's stomach turned inside out with the inevitable result. The detective, quick on his feet, got out of the way. Freddie, however, ruined his shoes.

DEATH COMES TO HOLLYWOOD CEMETERY

By Vivian Lawry

"C'MON, BEAU." I USED my purring kitten voice. "He won't let anybody in without an introduction, and I'd love to see those five thousand birds. I've heard he has a tame finch that sings on command. Is that true?" We were in my room at The Blue Moon in Ashland, right on Railroad Avenue.

Beau—one of my regulars—looked me up and down. "I suppose I might take you." He grinned. "You're as fine a specimen of a soiled dove as I've ever seen, Clara. Uncle George should like you just fine!"

"Oh, thank you, Beau!" He laughed at my excitement, and I proceeded to show my appreciation in the style he liked best. Afterward, we went dancing.

Ashland, a resort town where Richmonders escaped the heat of the city, was booming as a result of the War for Southern Independence. Soldiers joined civilians patronizing the saloons, dance halls and pleasure houses lining Railroad Avenue. A nearby racecourse drew crowds. We hit all the high spots. As we parted I said, "Don't forget about your uncle!"

The following week, Beau introduced me to his uncle.

Colonel George Levereaux—a veteran of the Mexican War— was an albino, very small, with poor eyesight, a head too large for his body, and a peculiar little beard. When we met on what he called "my little farm" in Hanover County, he wore three-inch heels and a feather boa.

He took my arm in his bony grip. "Come, Clara, let me show you my collections." He'd dyed all the pigeons in his dovecotes various pastel shades. When disturbed, they flew into the air like a cloud of confetti. I laughed and clapped, which pleased the colonel mightily. As we finished the tour, he said, "You seem like a sporting lass. I propose a wager: twenty geese and twenty turkeys to run a ten-mile course. Your choice of birds. If one of yours wins, you may have a brooch from my collection. If one of mine wins, you will stay here with me for a week."

I surveyed his property and considered the odds. A brooch might be valuable. Could I convert it to cash in the midst of this damned war? A week away from The Blue Moon would be mighty welcome, and who knows what else might come of that week? Turkeys have never been known for stamina. "I'll take the turkeys." The last one dropped out after three miles, while more than half the geese were still going strong.

The Colonel provided a lavish dinner that night. Though he ate nothing but dumplings, he urged the rarest delicacies on me. I could scarcely eat a bite for gawking. He had a pet goose that waited at the table with a napkin under its wing. Cages of songbirds serenaded us. We shared a bottle of port and played cribbage before retiring.

I had an apartment next to the Colonel's. As I removed my chemise, the Colonel stepped out of my wardrobe, naked and painfully thin, looking like a nicely polished skeleton. He carried a pot of chocolate in one hand and a clutch of goose feathers in the other. He said, "Beau tells me you are liberal minded in these matters."

Dipping the feathers into the warm chocolate, I painted his entire body. I expected to do much more, but discovered that the Colonel's idea of a good time was to crack the cooled chocolate from his body and feed the chips to me.

The week passed in great fun. The Colonel invited friends to dinner every night. One brought a trunk full of jewelry. He said, "I'm very fond of having beautiful young women wear my gems," and for dinner decorated me with hairpins, necklaces, brooches, rings, watches and bracelets. Each piece glittered in the candlelight. No earrings. I have an aversion to earrings. And an absolute revulsion for pearls in any form.

I awoke in the night to find him standing over my bed. He asked me to strip naked then covered me with gems, which he stroked and patted till dawn, exciting himself immensely. "The jewels become worried if I don't give them enough attention." When he repacked his trunk, he gave me a fine emerald ring.

Another of the Colonel's guests arrived with his face painted chalk-white, a circle of rouge on each cheek, penciled-in eyebrows, and a jet-black wig. I complimented his banter lavishly, as the Colonel expected me to do. After dinner, the guest accompanied me to my apartment. He snuffed the candles to remove his hairpiece unseen and applied so much solvent to the glue affixing it to his bald head that he reeked of fumes the rest of the night. Apart from the makeup, smell and his absolute aversion to touching anyone else's hair, our time together was unremarkable.

One guest's greatest pleasure was to wedge his backside into a waste-paper basket and roll around on the floor barking like a dog. All I had to do was clap and squeal.

My last night at the house, the Colonel said, "Clara, you should ply your trade with the Butterfly League. Butterflies have special needs, and a beautiful young woman such as yourself—a woman who bathes regularly, who still has all her teeth, and who understands our—proclivities—well, our members would pay top dollar." I made up my mind faster than a blink.

— 🦋 —

One of my regulars at The Blue Moon, a real artist, tattooed a red heart pierced by a long blue arrow on my right buttock to advertise the general nature of my trade. Another regular made up my *carte-de-visite*. He photographed me, naked, facing a blank wall on which I was drawing a picture of a butterfly—the coded advertisement for my new specialty trade. He mounted the photo on thin, square-cornered cardboard, two inches by three inches, with a gold border. I gave dozens to the Colonel, for members of the League to present by way of introduction. I'd been in the trade long enough to know caution.

My new line flourished. Except for insisting for the health of all, that my gentlemen wear French letters, I was accommodating. I made house calls. For one gentleman, I sat naked astride a horse in his drawing room while he painted pictures of me. With a musician and composer, I walked on high window ledges and slept naked atop or beneath his piano. He commissioned several life-size papier-maché models of me to fill the seats in his private auditorium. One Butterfly had a system of washing which involved dividing the body into twenty-four washable sections. Each required an individual bowl, pitcher, soap dish, soap and towel. We bathed each other before performing the act. I shared mud baths and gave enemas dressed as a nursemaid. I immersed myself in ice so a Butterfly could make love to my cold, seemingly lifeless body.

One young man, wild and brandy-sodden, asked to be flogged with a steel-tipped whip. "Please," he said. "It's from my school days. Eton is notorious for birchings. The headmaster knew our backsides better than our faces. Now I need it." He called his scars his blue roses. That one, I refused.

My new clients included a dapper, middle-aged bachelor named Charlie who lay with me in his rosewood coffin. "I want to make sure it will be comfortable." It swung from his bedroom ceiling by long chains and rocked like a cradle all night long. We had a standing appointment for Thursdays.

When I arrived at Charlie's house in Richmond as usual, just at dusk, he said, "Tonight we're going to celebrate."

With Charlie, it was always something. I laughed. "Celebrate what?"

"Whatever you like. Stonewall Jackson pushing the Union forces back across the Potomac. The full moon. Being alive." He rubbed his hands together, eyes sparkling. "Tonight we'll have a special romp."

He handed me into his carriage. The horse clip-clopped through empty streets. I had no idea where we were going, even when Charlie stopped on Cherry Street. A scudding cloud uncovered the moon, revealing the gates to Hollywood Cemetery.

"We can't go in there after dark."

"Who's to know?" Charlie jumped from the carriage more nimbly than I expected and took my hand. "Come see the family mausoleum. My sarcophagus is quite spacious—more so than my casket." He waggled his eyebrows.

At that I tumbled to the action. What a lark—turning a trick in a cemetery, at night. "Lead the way!"

Moonlight bright as dawn bathed the paths, rendering Charlie's lantern almost unnecessary. In spite of the smell of freshly turned earth—so many soldiers being buried every day—I was excited. Charlie skipped a step or two. He led me to a marble mausoleum, white as eggshells. Greek columns bracketed the doors. I glimpsed clusters of grapes, draped urns and an arch with a laurel wreath. Charlie pulled a huge iron key from his pocket and swung wide the door. Three sides of the mausoleum held drawers of his relatives. In the middle of the floor sat a rectangular marble box, covered by carvings I couldn't quite see in the dim lantern light. He said, "We shall tryst in my final resting place."

I giggled. "Let's tour the famous people first!"

We meandered from one marker to another until we came to James Monroe's grave. I loved the cast-iron monument there. It reminded me of a fancy birdcage. But the grass beside the monument looked mottled and scuffed. I felt a chill. Perhaps walking among the dead plucked a nerve. I said, "We've dawdled long enough. Catch me if you can!" With that I darted off, dodging and hiding among the trees and gravestones, sometimes calling out when he strayed too far in the wrong direction.

I twined my way to his mausoleum through moonlight-dappled shadows. As I slipped through the door, someone grabbed me from behind. How did Charlie get ahead of me? A rough hand covered my mouth. Writhing against the hard body, scrabbling at the coarse material of a sleeve, inhaling strong chemical fumes, I knew it wasn't Charlie. He lifted me like a feather and dropped me into Charlie's sarcophagus. Struggling to right myself, I felt lumpy cloth, arms, a face. I screamed forever, it seemed, before Charlie peered over the rim of the sarcophagus, lantern high.

I grabbed his arm and hauled myself out, tumbling both of us to the marble floor. "There's a body," I sobbed. "It's still warm!"

"A body?" We scrambled to our feet and peered in. Charlie said, "Let's go. Now."

Even in that light, I knew the man in the sarcophagus: Stevenson, one of my Butterflies. "We can't just leave him. We must tell the sheriff."

"How would I explain my presence here at night—with you? I'll come back in the morning, tell the sheriff I discovered the body then."

"What if my attacker returns? Or some resurrectionist takes the body tonight? I've heard they're great opportunists."

Charlie hesitated, worrying his side whiskers. Finally he said, "We'll go now. When you are safely away, I'll send an anonymous note to the sheriff's office."

— 🦋 —

The sheriff summoned me the next morning, Friday the thirteenth. I thought both of those things boded ill. And I wondered, for I knew Charlie would never have mentioned my name. I dressed in lady clothes and went forthwith. I sat in his office, a bland smile fixed firmly in place. "Why ever would you want to see little ol' me?"

"Now, Clara, you can just turn off the charm. I've got a body from Hollywood Cemetery." I gasped but said nothing. "The doc tells me the corpse was wearing pink satin undies. Naturally I thought he might be one of yours. Come take a look."

"I don't much like dead bodies."

"Just look at his face." He smirked. "Or whatever body part you're most likely to recognize." He pulled me to my feet and down the hall.

Walking back to the sheriff's office, I marshaled my thoughts.

Sheriff Coltrain dropped into his chair, propped his elbows on the armrests, tented his fingers under his chin and swiveled back and forth. "So what can you tell me?"

"Well, now, Eli—Sheriff—my trade depends on discretion."

"And don't I just appreciate that discretion! But I've got a dead man here. You're gonna tell me what you know or the law's gonna land on your ... activities ... like a duck on a June bug."

I did not doubt he meant it. How little could I say? "We met awhile back. He was exceedingly fond of women's underwear, paid extra to wear mine while we ... enjoyed pleasures. I knew him only as Stevenson."

The sheriff peered from under bushy brows and waggled his fingers in a give-me-more gesture. "What else?"

I took in all the air my lungs would hold then exhaled slowly. "Some weeks ago I went to one of Jefferson Davis's open houses. Just for a lark, you know?" His wide-eyed surprise irritated me. "You think I don't have friends with connections? And I can look and act as ladylike as anybody! Stevenson was there. Very noticeable, over six feet tall, broad-chested and very handsome in his uniform. I thought he might avoid me. But he strode right up, offered to fetch a cup of punch for me. I asked about his cane—new since last I'd seen him. He whispered, 'My fellow surgeon extracted the bullet. No need to explain my lavender bloomers, chemise and corset to a stranger.' So I guessed Stevenson was a doctor."

Coltrain drummed his fingers on his desk. "The anatomical man denies knowing anything about the body but says he saw a man and woman going into Hollywood. What do you know about that?"

"Why would I know anything about that?" I made my eyes round and tried to look sincere. "I've told you all I know. Really."

The sheriff looked hard at me, pinching his chin, saying nothing for so long I felt heat rising in my face. Eventually he said, "It may be all you know, but it ain't all you can find out if you want to stay on the right side of the law in this town." He stood. "I'll get what I can on any Army doctor named Stevenson. You find out who knew about his underwear and anything else about his pastimes that might have led to his murder." As I gathered my reticule, he added, "And if I find out it was you in the cemetery, up to something with Stevenson that went mighty wrong ... you just better be leveling with me, Clara."

I hesitated. Charlie could clear me. But if I revealed Charlie to the sheriff, I'd never set eyes on a Butterfly again. I had to find another way. I nodded and left.

I made my way to the anatomy building at the medical college and strode up to the janitor as if I belonged. He was a tall, muscular black man, but he slouched, ducked his head and turned his cap in his hands. "What's your name?"

"Jefferson Baker, ma'am. What for you be askin'?"

I stepped closer and a strong chemical smell assailed me: formaldehyde. The smell. His size and build. Suddenly, I knew I was facing my attacker. "What were you doing in Hollywood

Cemetery Thursday night?"

His deep bass gave way to a higher-pitched whine. "Ever time somethin' happen in a graveyard, ever'body look at the anatomical man. First the sheriff and now you. I tol' him and now I'm tellin' you: I ain't been diggin' up no bodies in Hollywood Cemetery. Them be rich folks—white folks. I got no call to be doin' that. So what you be wantin' wif me?"

"I know you were there. You tell me everything or you'll rot in jail till you're too old to lift a shovel!"

"You got nuffin says I was dere."

"Being freeborn won't do you one jot of good. It's your word against mine. Who do you think the sheriff will believe?" I felt bad threatening him, but my own freedom might depend on it.

Eventually he mumbled, "I got a knock on my door that night. Jus' a voice through the door tellin' me there be a fresh body in Hollywood. I says, 'I ain't diggin' up no body there. They be important folks, soldiers an' all—I could get a heap uh trouble.' An he say there weren't no diggin' about it. He say, 'You know President Monroe's grave? You jus' go there an' you'll find a dead man. Not buried.' I think that ain't so bad, so I went along wif my bag, and I find de man, dead fur sure. So I be takin' him out, thinkin' how dem medical students' tip me fur dis one, when I hears laughin' and sees a lantern bobbin' round."

"Then what?"

Baker shifted from foot to foot. "There's this little house for dead people. Comin' in, I seen it, the door open. I dropped the body in a box in dere an' skedaddled."

"And? Out with it!"

"Before I could get outta dat dead house, a woman come in. I put her in wif de body." He cut a look at me. "I guess maybe dat was you?"

I arched one eyebrow. "If you don't say anything, neither will I." I caught the ghost of a smile before he nodded.

———— ✺ ————

I dipped the goose feather into the pot of chocolate and painted another stripe on Colonel Levereaux's belly. "Please. Pretty please with sugar on top? I really need your help."

"Now, Clara, you aren't here to talk murder. You just tend to business. I'll think about it." He rolled over so I could paint his backside.

Two days later I sat at the Colonel's table with half a dozen members of the Butterfly League. After the expected exchanges of banter, compliments and suggestive double entendres, I said, "You're all such sweethearts to help. The sheriff positively ordered me to find out about Stevenson. Who knew about his underwear? Who knew he was a Butterfly?"

The Colonel said, "Only other Butterflies knew he was a Butterfly—and you, of course. We swear secrecy on that."

The musician Butterfly said, "But pretty much anyone could know about the underwear. We were in a saloon once when he took a tiny pair of pink doll's knickers from a pouch in his pants pocket, slipped them over his fingers and walked them across the bar for the amusement of anybody who happened to see."

The Butterfly who liked gems added, "And all his comrades knew. He sometimes came to staff meetings wearing a gray satin wrapper and a lace nightcap with pink ribbons. So what if he was womanish, liked to wrap himself in angora and such? He was very brave for all of that."

The Colonel said, "As I can testify. We served together in the Mexican War. He worried more about the effects of sun and the dust of battle on his appearance than about getting shot. He sometimes confused the enemy by turning up on the battlefield painted, powdered, covered in ribbons and ruffles. But no hat." The others chuckled knowingly. The Colonel turned to me. "He refused to wear a hat for fear it might ruin the lie of his curls."

I looked around the table. "If he made no attempt to hide

his preferences, perhaps he exposed himself to the wrong person. Someone intolerant of differences or a religious fanatic perhaps?"

"There might be something there." The Colonel scratched his thin goatee. "He's been married for years, but he was known to seduce his male aides upon occasion."

After the others left, the Colonel took my arm. "There's one thing more, Clara. I didn't want to say in front of the others—didn't want to besmirch the character of a dead man—but a former comrade told me charges of official misconduct were pending against Stevenson, for treating patients in his private time."

— 🝓 —

I plied my fan, stirring the hot air in Sheriff Coltrain's office. "So, Eli, in a nutshell, anybody and everybody could have known about his undies. Nobody seemed to care. Perhaps there is something in these charges of official misconduct."

The Sheriff shook his head. "I know all about that. Stevenson claimed he was working hard, gratuitously visiting the hospital on Main Street near Third, as well as treating people in private residences. He claimed he was guilty only of poor judgment. Those charges were being dismissed."

"But I told you everything. So we're square now?"

"Far from it. You're still my best bet for how Stevenson got there."

I considered giving him Baker. But I'd promised. And Baker could give him me. "I'll try to learn more."

— 🝓 —

By fall, the Seven Days Battles, Harper's Ferry and Antietam had made clear that the war would be bloody and probably long. Troops and munitions rode the rails through Ashland. I felt it my duty to service the soldiers, Butterflies or not. So I showed myself to the lonely boys, rentable for riding. By then I was getting five dollars a go. I made lots of money nature's way, sometimes presenting a soldier with a bill for forty dollars or more—nearly four months' wages, but usually they paid—and I sewed the coins into the hems of my petticoats. But I lost my taste for the whoring trade, for being ketched and squeezed, poked and slobbered over by any man with money in his pocket. I longed for the war to be over, to focus again on the jolly Butterflies.

Among my soldier clients was one I liked, though—a farm boy, young and lonely. Mostly he talked. He bemoaned wormy hardtack and leaky boots. He talked about his sergeant and the wounded soldier who turned out to be a woman. He reminisced about brothers and sisters and home. He recalled the antics of his mother's goats. He said, "Goats need companionship to be happy. They're mighty sociable animals, and if they don't have a herd, they'll follow a sheep or a cow or a child. But not a chicken. A chicken just don't cut it." He made me laugh.

During one visit, he paced my room, all het up over an article in the *Richmond Dispatch* about a doctor selling military deferments and discharges. "What kind of son of a bitch would do that? The cause needs every able-bodied man we can muster." He crumpled the paper and threw it at the wastebasket. "If I ever got my hands on a skunk like that, I'd break his neck."

His outburst got me thinking about Stevenson. By then the sheriff had dropped Stevenson's death, except that every time he called on me, he said I was still under suspicion. And I always said he could have his pleasures for free. Now I had an idea.

The next morning I called in at Old Dominion Bank. "Macklin Tierney, as I live and breathe! How are you?" I got through the pleasantries as quickly as I could. "I have such a big favor to ask. I know it's unusual, but I believe my friend Dr. Stevenson did business here. And I just want to know whether you could answer a couple of questions."

Macklin leaned back in his chair. "You know customer information is private."

"Oh, I don't want anything private, just one tiny piece of information." I batted my lashes at him. "Couldn't you do that for little ol' me, sugar?" Macklin's special pleasure was for me to sprinkle sugar over his body and then lick it off. I figured it didn't hurt to remind him of that.

He turned red as beet juice and rose to close the door. He sat again. "Exactly what is your question?"

"Just whether Dr. Stevenson had money coming in from sources other than his Army pay?" I looked at him wide-eyed. "I don't want to know amounts, or where it came from, or whether it was cash or bank drafts. Just whether there was any. That's all."

Macklin hesitated so long, I felt sure he would refuse me. "It's highly irregular. But being that he's already dead and all ..." He went to the safe and opened a huge leather-bound ledger. I could see that a letter of the alphabet headed each page of inked entries. He paused, skimmed an "S" page then snapped the book shut. "I can confirm that he made irregular deposits of varying amounts."

"Thank you. I'm ever so grateful." I rose to leave. "Will I see you soon?"

He blushed furiously and nodded. "Just don't tell anybody I told you."

—— 🦋 ——

I wormed information from Butterflies, contacts in the military, merchants and hospital workers. Stevenson wasn't just seeing private patients, he took money from them. Some whispered that the money was for medical discharges or deferments. I gathered names. My queries eventually turned up the name of Jacob Barber. His brother, Jedediah Barber, was a corporal assigned to guard the Tredegar Iron Works. I invited him to my room at The Blue Moon. Jedediah didn't want to talk about it, but I plied him with port and a soft embrace. Finally he said, "My brother—" and burst into tears.

I patted his back and made shushing noises. "Sometimes talking helps."

"It ain't a proud thing for my family. After he was wounded, my brother couldn't face going back to war. In the hospital, he heard this Stevenson could be bought. Stevenson said Jake didn't have enough money, but he would take it out in trade. So they agreed to meet. My brother wasn't that kind of man, but he did it. Stevenson was getting dressed when Jake saw the underwear. He said, 'I did it with a pervert who wears pink satin undies. I think I'm gonna puke.' Then he spit tobacco juice on Stevenson's boots. That's when Stevenson hit him. It was a pretty mean fight. Stevenson ended up dead. Jake came and got me, told me what I just told you. I helped him dump the body in Hollywood Cemetery then went 'round to the medical college to tell the resurrectionist where to find it. We thought, you know, Stevenson would just disappear."

"Where's your brother now?"

At this, more tears poured from Jed's eyes. "That's the hell of it—Beg pardon for the language. Stevenson was dead before he recommended Jake's discharge. Jake died at the Second Battle of Bull Run."

I drew him to me again. "You poor thing. But time will make it better." All that night, he clung to me like a heartbroken child.

— 🎭 —

The next day, I again made my way to Sheriff Coltrain's office. I told him Jed's story about Stevenson.

"Selling deferments and discharges? That's a disgusting blot on Southern honor!"

"Don't work yourself up, Eli. The Yankees must have the same, or worse. Folks are folks."

The sheriff huffed and puffed and demanded to talk with my source. I claimed I didn't know the brothers' names. What good would come of heaping trouble on Jed?

"You expect me to believe he didn't tell you his name?"

"I surely do. He was just one of my charity cases, a lonely boy with a few hours in Ashland before going back to the lines. All it took was a warm body and a willing ear for him to unburden himself." I tilted a smile at the sheriff. "Have you ever known me to lie to you, Eli?"

"Known? No. But why would you treat me different from any other man?" He chuckled. "I suppose now you expect me to go back to paying full freight?"

"I surely do." I smiled. "And you'll still enjoy the same discretion I give all my clients."

Back at The Blue Moon, I brushed my hair and dressed for the evening, pretty pleased with myself. I'd solved the mystery of Stevenson's murder and gotten the sheriff off my back while protecting Charlie, the anatomical man, the Barber brothers, and the Butterflies. Leaning close to the mirror, I saw the faintest beginnings of lines at the corners of my eyes. My appeal to the Butterflies wouldn't fade anytime soon. But just maybe a career as a detective was in my future.

WHERE HEAVEN FINDS YOU WAITING

By Michael McGowan

MEMORY. I GRAB MY notebook and pencil.

There's a coffee shop two blocks from Sadira's apartment, a renovated house on Colley Avenue in Norfolk. We climb the stairs to the second floor loft and sit in easy chairs in the corner. Across from us sits a kid in an ODU sweatshirt with his netbook plugged into a power strip. An Espresso machine grinds in the background.

"I want to show you something." Sadira leans over the armrest of her chair and smooths out a piece of paper—a shattered windshield of creases—across my lap. "Go ahead, read it."

She smiles.

Memory. Grab my notebook and pencil. Dark-brown eyes. Chestnut hair. Complexion like a late evening sunset.

I look at her paper. The first line reads, "If you say you love me then you're a fool."

Close the notebook.

— 🏵 —

"Who are we waiting for?" Sadira asks.

I don't turn to look at her as I reply, "Trevor. We're waiting on Trevor."

"Why do you keep writing in that notebook?"

She's never asked that before, but she's seen me do it plenty of times.

Memory. Christmas when I got my first ten-speed bike. Grab my notebook and pencil. Memory. Graduation. My mother gone, my father there, just on the incapable side of holding back tears. Grab my notebook and pencil.

Memory. When I first saw Sadira on the steps outside the student center, eating an egg salad sandwich with her nose buried in a book on the romantic poets.

Grab my notebook and pencil.

I'm not a chronicler. I don't write biographies or memoirs. Memory is who we are, all we will ever be, and it's designed to be damaged. To fade.

We're all designed to lose our soul slowly as we live. Some much faster than others.

This is rescue. This is triage. This is the man grabbing for precious mementos as the house burns down around him.

"I always thought there were things people wouldn't *want* to remember," Sadira once said. "At least you lose the bad with the good."

I didn't answer. She wouldn't have understood.

We sit in an overflow lot of the middle school along Colley Avenue. I try not to take my eyes off the street, even when I see the canvas tarp draped over the patio of the restaurant across the road. Memory. Our first date. Summertime when the patio was open air. She wasn't courageous enough yet to read any of her poetry. I gave her a lecture on story arc, how everyone's life has to get a lot worse before it gets better.

I start to grab my notebook and pencil, but stop. Walking in the direction from the restaurant is a bulbous man with beige spiked hair and a blue and gray jacket. He walks past a woman with a dog on a leash, stops, bends and pets the mutt a time or two. She smiles. He smiles.

"That's him," Sadira says.

That's him. I've heard her voice like this before. Shed of the confidence, of the pleasantness, of the life. A voice skating on the rails of desperation.

"Don't worry," is all I can say to her as I step out from the car. It's a typical February night, air icy still and you can't breathe without shooting out jets of vapor. I keep my face tilted low as I move up the walk to the corner. I glance up. Trevor's in front of the video store. He opens the door.

Trevor's become a ghost, that spoken of but unseen force in our lives. I hadn't even heard his name until three months ago.

— 🎎 —

Memory. It's after one in the morning, and Sadira calls and screams and cries through the phone at the same time.

She tells me she's bleeding.

She tells me she can't breathe.

It's all because of him.

Trevor.

I call 911 and direct the paramedics to Sadira's rented apartment near the campus. I get there a hair behind them and tail them to the hospital. She's admitted to the ER before I can see her, and two hours later a doctor comes out to tell me they're going to patch her up and send her home.

"Patch her up?"

The doctor gives me a cockeyed look. "The bleeding," he says. There was a glass on the sink where Sadira and her roommate kept their toothbrushes.

Sadira had picked it up and smashed it against the side of her head.

I don't know what to say.

He does.

"You know she's done this before, right?"

— 🎎 —

I wait for a break in the traffic and cross Colley. When I get to the picture window with the buzzing neon sign reading Naro Video, I see Trevor plain as day, leaning against the counter. There's a girl working the counter, blonde, about Sadira's age or maybe a bit younger. She smiles and laughs at something he says.

He smiles back and reaches into his coat pocket and takes out his wallet. Opens it and fishes out a wad of money. I can't tell the denominations from where I'm standing, but it's not for a rental.

One bill. Two. Three. Four. Trevor presses them on the counter one after another like a game show host. When he's finished, he pushes the wad in the blonde's direction. She's got that happily surprised mouth "O" shape and pantomimes a polite refusal.

Trevor waves her off and picks up the money. Takes one of her hands, making an effort to be gentle, and presses the money into it. Curls her fingers around it. Final ink on the deal.

This is how it starts. Gentle. Friendly. My hands ball into fists, and before I realize it I've pounded them against the window. There's enough sound that Trevor and the girl at the counter turn their attention in my direction. The girl's money hand disappears behind the counter. Trevor makes his way to the door.

I retreat, backtracking toward the corner.

"Hey, hey you!"

I turn. Trevor's coat is open, his hands spread out wide. "You got a problem?"

I think about the distance between the two of us. Not enough for him to throw a punch, but enough for a hulk like him to cover fast if he thinks things are on. There's a cold burning in my gut. An impulse at the same time pushing me and denying me.

I once-over him one more time then turn away and round the corner.

I hear him shout, "Yeah, you better run."

His back is to me when I peer around the corner. He's going in the opposite direction, walking under the marquee overhang for the Naro theater. He stops at the ticket booth. I think for a moment he's going to glance back and to the sides to see if anyone is still clocking him, but he doesn't. His wallet comes out again. He buys a ticket and goes inside.

In my wallet, I have just enough money for one ticket.

Memory. Grab a pencil and notebook.

— 🂡 —

Two days before Christmas. Same night we were in the coffee shop.

If you say you love me, then you're a fool ...

Christmas double feature at the theater. We climb the stairs to the balcony level and manage to find two seats together in the middle.

"Wouldn't it be awesome," Sadira says, "if we were the only ones in here? How would you like to make love up here during a movie?"

There's a slight, unnerving vibration every time someone gets to their feet to move.

"We might bring the whole thing crashing down," I say, then draw her close.

"What a way to go."

Then her phone rings.

I feel it spread all over her. Tense. Rigid. Even before she gets a look at who is calling. She shuts off the phone in a flurry and stuffs it into her purse. When she gets close again, the need to be held is gone and she's crying.

"He won't stop," she says.

"Who won't?"

"Trevor."

It wasn't bad at first, she says. He called, at most, once a week. Then twice. Then every day. Now he alternates between shouted threats and just breathing when she picks up.

I hold her, try to reassure her, but it's more anesthetic than a cure. She stays stiff as the first movie, *A Christmas Story*, starts. She's that way all the way into *It's a Wonderful Life*. Jimmy

Stewart grabs and kisses Donna Reed, and I hear Sadira squeal "Oh, God ..."

"What's wrong?"

"It's *him*."

"Who?"

"*Trevor*."

She points, keeping her hand low.

"Front row."

Truth is, the front row is packed, and there are a lot of people who could be who she's talking about. But I don't labor things by asking her to be more specific.

"Get me out of here ..." Her voice is so sharp, it's like a knife blade running across glass.

As I help her to her feet, I look to see if anyone watches us. No one turns, no one notices, and I help her to the stairs.

In the lobby, she completely falls apart and ends up on her knees, a roar of furious anxiety pouring out of her to the point she can't breathe.

Someone calls the paramedics. And we're back at the hospital again.

Déjà vu. Nurses can't pinpoint a reason for her attack. There's an issue about payment, bills from previous visits still outstanding.

And I drive her home.

"Did you mean it?" I ask.

"Mean what?" Her eyes are dead and defeated and don't leave the road.

"That I can't say I love you."

"Please ..."

"I'm serious."

"So am I."

"So what's the problem? Don't you feel the same way?"

"That's not the point."

"Then what is? You want me to be honest, you want me to say what I feel, so why can't I say ..."

"Don't you dare—"

"Why can't I—"

"Don't you *fucking* dare."

"Why?"

"Because then we're fucked!" she screams, finally turning her face to me. Her eyes are blood red and raw, her cheeks puffy. "Because when two people say they love each other, they're saying that they've reached the pinnacle of what they are to each other, that there's no place else for them to go, and the only thing, the *only* thing they have left is to lose each other."

I'm dumbfounded. "You're not going to lose me."

"Yes I will. Remember what you said about story arcs?"

I do. Any good narrative has the same thing. Things have to get worse before they get better. If they get better at all.

"He's going to kill me," she says. "I had bills from the hospital, I couldn't keep up, so I borrowed money from him. Now I can't pay it back, and he's going to kill me."

— 🎭 —

I buy the ticket and head to the balcony. Not like Christmas—the place is almost dead.

The kind of night where we *could* have made love up here.

Except there is one person. Trevor sits alone, iPod buds in his ears, front row.

The lights go down. I hear the metallic squeal of pulleys as the curtains below open.

I get up from my seat, negotiate down the row to the side, trying to stay out of his peripheral vision.

Sadira *did* eventually show me her poem, and as I make my way forward, she whispers it in my ear:

If you say you love me, then you're a fool

Because in our light, neither you or I can remain

I sidestep my way down the second row.

Ashes to impermanent ashes, dust to temporal dust

This beauty between us is meant to wither and die

I take my time. Trevor is still transfixed on the screen, not moving a muscle.

I'm meant to leave you, cast you aside in the realm of the living

Leave you as nothing more than fading afterglow

Out of my pocket I pull a length of clothesline rope, twisted and turned on itself. I take a breath, fast loop it around Trevor's neck, twist and *pull*, bracing one foot against the back of his chair and letting the rest of my body weight fall backward.

But don't despair, because all is not ended

What we have can never be truly killed

When you strangle someone, your first fear is them grabbing back for you, getting a hold of the rope or you. But people are creatures of fear and habit, and Trevor uses every moment he has left and every bit of strength trying to pry the rope from around his neck.

I twist it more and fall back further and hear something snap.

And even though we have to part, one day I will come

Suddenly the air is pungent as Trevor's bowels release. His head rolls onto his shoulders.

Where heaven finds you waiting

When I get back to the car, Sadira is gone and I'm alone.

Memory. Grab a notebook and pencil.

Two weeks ago, right after that last night in the hospital, Sadira stopped going to class. Got nothing but her voicemail when I called her.

A week ago, I got a call from her parents. Her car was found at a motel in Chesapeake. She was inside a room, pharmacy bag on the nightstand with a receipt for fifty dollars worth of sleeping pills.

She'd been there a couple of days, the police said.

I finish writing, close the notebook and lay it and the pencil on the seat next to me.

I'm not a chronicler. I don't write biographies or memoirs. Memory is who we are, all we will ever be. This act is over, things getting worse before they get better, and I'm leaving this for whoever finds it. So they know who I am. Why I did what I did.

Out from under my seat, I pull a small revolver and position it against my temple. I look at myself in the rearview mirror and say one thing before I pull the trigger.

"If you say you love me, then you're a fool."

— 🐞 —

"So what do you think?" I ask.

The coffee shop two blocks from the apartment. A renovated house on Colley. Across from us, there's a kid in an ODU sweatshirt with his netbook plugged into a power strip.

"What does it all mean?" Sadira rocks forward in her chair. "And why do I have to die at the end?"

I smile, nervous. I tell her about story structure. Tell her about arc. About how things have to get worse before they get better.

She looks cross, face etched out of stone, and I think she's about to go off … and then she laughs. Hard.

"So when do they get better?" she asks as she recovers.

I shrug. I tell her I don't know, I haven't figured out how to end it yet.

Memory.

I put away my notebook and pencil. I want to try holding on to this.

"Forget it. I want to show you something," she says, and flattens a piece of paper out on my lap.

"Go ahead. Read it."

BEST FRIENDS HELP YOU MOVE THE BODY

By Jayne Ormerod

"THE CAPE HENRY LIGHTHOUSE silently guards the entryway into the Chesapeake Bay. Standing near the 'First Landing' site of the Jamestown settlers where in 1607 Captain Newport raised a cross to offer thanks for their safe crossing of the Atlantic, the Lighthouse has stood sentinel since it was completed in 1792." ~ *Preservation Virginia*

"I could kill Stella Edwards by pushing her down these stairs." Courtney Danvers's voice echoed down to me from her position above. She was about a dozen feet higher on the iron steps circling around the inside of the Old Cape Henry Lighthouse in Virginia Beach.

I'd known Courtney long enough not to be alarmed. Since she'd read her first *Nancy Drew* book in fifth grade, she'd aspired to be a mystery writer and was always looking for unusual or creative ways to dispatch her characters. For twenty years she'd been all talk and no action. But since learning her position as a government contractor would be throttled back on account of the sequestration furloughs, Courtney decided now was a good time to investigate other sources of income. Hence her recent commitment to put fingers to keyboard. In true Courtney fashion, she'd developed a business plan, the first step of which was to scout an interesting place to knock off her victim, the beautiful yet diabolical Stella Edwards.

"The way this old iron staircase spirals down," Courtney continued her fictional murder planning, "Stella would tumble ass over teakettle for a long time. All it would take is one smash of her head against these iron steps or a bash against this metal handrail or good hard slam against those old bricks and she'd be a goner. Not a single landing to slow momentum, just one long spiraling fall, ninety feet downward into the abyss." Courtney let out an excited squeal. "Look here, a steep ladder. One misstep and it's sayonara, Stella! I love it!"

I suppose I should mention that Stella is not purely a figment of Courtney's imagination. Oh no. Stella is based—right down to the last blond curl tucked behind a multi-pierced ear—on Courtney's childhood nemesis, Stacy Evans. This literary murder is payback for Stacy's close encounter of the sexual kind with Courtney's boyfriend. I should also mention this happened back in high school. I suppose Courtney offing Stacy in a book is cheaper than therapy.

Still climbing, I rounded the curve just in time to see my friend's Nike-clad feet disappear through the opening over my head. Her "steep ladder" comment wasn't an understatement. It was at least twelve feet high, practically vertical, with the risers being a mere three inches deep. Up I climbed, slowly and carefully, holding tight to the iron railings so as not to prove out Courtney's deathly tumble theorem.

After another short circular staircase, I found myself at the top of the lighthouse, a glass-enclosed landing offering views that took my breath away. Well, what little breath I had after that one-hundred-ninety-step climb. A few hundred yards away stood the conical black-and-white structure of the New Cape Henry Lighthouse surrounded at its base by a smattering of quaint Coast Guard houses. Buildings that supported the Fort Story military base dotted the sand dunes along the coast, and off to the south you could see the high-rise hotels of the Virginia Beach oceanfront, an area we locals call Tourist Central. Beyond the buildings a blue summer sky met shimmering green waters where the Chesapeake Bay joined the Atlantic Ocean. A few deep-sea fishing excursions sped between the large, ponderous tankers heading into port. Their destinations would be Norfolk,

Newport News or Baltimore, Maryland about two hundred miles farther up the bay.

"Isn't this view amazing?" Courtney asked.

I had to agree. This was one of those picture-perfect days in Tidewater, Virginia. Even though I'd lived here for three years, I'd been a slave to my job and too tired to battle the tourist crowds on the weekends. But as Courtney had pointed out in her plea for me to play hooky from work and join her today, there were fewer tourists on the weekdays, and it was too nice of a day to be holed up in the kitchen design showroom where I worked.

"My parents would love this place." Courtney stopped to snap a few pictures for her writing journal. "I'll bring them down next time they visit. Mom won't be able to make the climb so she'll have to wait in the car, but dad will just eat all this history up with a spoon. Listen to this ..."

I listened with half an ear about how the lighthouse had been commissioned at the first session of the U.S. Congress in 1789, and was constructed of Aquia Creek sandstone from the same quarry as the stones that were used to build Mount Vernon, the U.S. Capitol and The White House. The other half of my thoughts were focused on the next research item on our agenda, A Day at the Beach. No, we weren't going to spread our towels on the sandy shore (then I would *really* feel guilty for skipping a day of work). A Day at the Beach was the hottest new drink in town. It consisted of four of my favorite things: coconut rum, amaretto, orange juice and grenadine. It had to be good, right? Courtney wanted me to take it out for a test drive. All in the name of writing research, of course. She hoped to do for A Day at the Beach what *Sex in the City* had done for cosmopolitans. Who was I to refuse?

Courtney snapped enough pictures to fill a dozen writing journals then we headed back down the spiral steps.

"Next stop, Twillager's Tavern for beach beverages," Courtney announced. "Then we'll rent bikes and ride along the boardwalk."

"Can we make a pit stop so I can get a Band-Aid first?" I asked. "These new shoes are giving me blisters." *Note to self: don't break in new leather sandals when playing tourist with Courtney.*

"I've got a first-aid kit in my trunk. Here." She tossed me her keys. "Doctor yourself up while I run back and ask the docent if there have been any deaths in the lighthouse. Won't it be fabulous if I can layer my mystery with stories of it being haunted? I could scare the bejesus out of Stacy—I mean Stella—before I knock her off. Oh man, this is going to be the best mystery ever written."

It would be interesting, that's for sure.

I used the key to pop the trunk of Courtney's Hyundai Accent. The smell of death hit me in the face just before the sight of a contorted, lifeless body. The sound of a woman screaming like a banshee pounded my eardrums. *But wait!* The body in the trunk was incapable of screaming; therefore the mournful shrieks must be coming from somewhere else. A moment later, I realized they were coming from me. And yet, I couldn't stop.

Courtney pushed me to the side and peered into her trunk. "Holy guacamole! A real dead body! In my car! This is the luckiest day of my life!"

— 🐞 —

"That is so cool you knew the vic," Courtney said. A mere six hours spent in the company of police and she was already proficient in cop talk.

"Not cool," I said as I inserted my key into the deadbolt on my townhome. "While I may not have particularly liked the vic, I mean victim, Desiree didn't deserve to be bashed on her head and then stuffed in your trunk."

"You're right. I apologize." Courtney slipped past me into the entryway then continued down the hall to the kitchen.

I tossed my keys in the starfish-shaped bowl I kept on a table by the door for just such a purpose, and then used my hands to massage my temples. Our day of mystery-writing research had turned out to be more than I bargained for—an actual interrogation by a police detective and a ride home in the back of a squad car, since they'd impounded Courtney's Hyundai for evidence. While standing in the entryway, I toyed with the idea of going straight upstairs to bed, but one look at my own spiraling staircase reminded me of our trip to the lighthouse. Funny how the twisting steps had seemed quaint until Courtney had put the thought of murder into my mind.

At the sound of ice dispensing into a glass, I decided what I needed was a good stiff drink. I hauled my tired self down the hallway and planted my rear end on a counter stool. A smile tugged at my mouth, the first since discovering Desiree's body, as Courtney reenacted a scene from *Cocktail*. She mixed up a batch of Tropical Storms—rum, banana liqueur, orange and pineapple juices, a splash of grenadine and a banana, which made them a healthy option. She then poured the beverage into a tumbler and slid it down the counter to me. I lifted the glass, raised it in her honor, then took a long, sweet swallow. The drink was heavy on the rum. Yum.

Courtney picked up her cell phone. "You look like you're in a mushroom-chicken-and-onion-pizza kinda mood," she said then called for delivery.

Sometimes it was eerie the way Courtney could read my mind.

As soon as the pizza had been ordered, Courtney dropped her phone on the counter, grabbed her drink then slipped onto the counter stool next to me. "Wanna tell me about Desiree?" she asked.

"No," I said.

There was a heartbeat of silence before she responded. "Okay, let me rephrase that. You need to tell me about Desiree."

I took another long sip of my drink. Again, yum. "What, one Psych one-o-one class in college makes you a shrink?"

"I didn't pass that one, remember? So I'm not trying to help you through your grief, here. I'm asking because I wanna get the details right for my story. I'm thinking Desiree's murder might make the perfect debut novel. And who better to write it than the person into whose trunk she had been stuffed? And who better to help me than the person who knew the vic?" Courtney grabbed her purse off the counter and fished around inside, eventually pulling out a small voice recorder. She pushed some buttons then set it on the counter. "With your permission, I'd like to tape our conversation."

"I would rather not be in your true-crime article, if you don't mind."

"It's not gonna be true crime. I'm gonna fictionalize it. You know, change the names and location and stuff." Courtney slid off her chair and went to fetch the pitcher of drinks.

"I'd love to help further your literary career, but I really don't want to talk about Desiree Pierson." At the mention of her name, my mind flashed to the image of her lying in the trunk of the car, those cold lifeless eyes staring at me. That was going to haunt me the rest of my life.

I polished off my drink and signaled for another round. Courtney complied.

As she poured more Tropical Storm into my glass, she said, "How about I make Desiree short and homely, with no fashion sense whatsoever, and you'll be the blonde beach babe who kicks ass?"

I swirled my drink then took a fortifying swig.

"And I promise to hold out for Channing Tatum to play your love interest in the movie version."

Courtney could always make me smile. And rum would always make me chatty.

After another fortifying sip of my drink, I rattled off the

Cliffs Notes version of Desiree Pierson's life history as I knew it.

Desiree was one of those pulled-herself-up-by-her-stiletto-straps success stories. The daughter of a crack-whore mother and hard-drinking father currently in jail for killing his brother, Desiree's life changed when she'd been paired up with Vondra Scott, a mentor through the Big Sisters program. Thanks to Vondra's friendship, encouragement and life-skills lessons, Desiree graduated high school with honors and received a full academic scholarship to Old Dominion University. Desiree lived up to her name and was beautiful, popular and smart, and had gone on to make a small fortune flipping houses during the real estate boom. But when the bottom dropped out of the market, she'd been left holding a lot of expensive property.

One financial albatross was a strip of seven townhomes in a fifty-unit complex along the Chesapeake Bay. What had once been a highly desirable place to live now had more abandoned properties than occupied ones. Desiree struggled to keep her financial head above water.

I'd met Desiree three years ago when I first arrived in the area and rented this townhome from her. It was rather small and hopelessly outdated, but it had a nice view of the water. We'd hit it off instantly, and she would often stop by for a drink after showing other properties in the 'hood. That's how I learned her life story. Eventually our friendship progressed to business associates when she asked me to design some kitchen remodels on homes she was flipping. On weekends, I snuck into my office at a local design firm and used their equipment to draw up plans, and Desiree paid me under the table. It was win-win, and all was well, until Desiree stopped paying me for my work. That was about three months ago, and we hadn't spoken since. My lease was up next month, and I'd given her thirty-days' notice a week ago Monday. That afternoon, I'd become the focus of her rants on Facebook and Twitter. Since then she'd added more friends and business acquaintances to her hit list.

The calm, savvy, even-keeled businesswoman had turned into a venomous, raging lunatic.

And now she was dead.

—— 🐾 ——

Courtney ran out of bananas long before the pizza arrived, so we were forced to give up on the Tropical Storms. Still in need of something to take the edge off the nervy state, I suggested we switch to RNDCs (Rum 'n Diet Coke), heavy on the rum. Yum.

By the time the pizza arrived I could barely feel my tongue, let alone offer a coherent argument against one of Courtney's harebrained ideas.

"I think we should try to solve the murder," she said.

I gave her my best *Are you goofed on skunkweed?* look.

"In the fictional sense. For my book. You know the vic so you can help propagate the list of suspects. I've read all the Nancy Drew books and watched every single episode of *Castle*, so I know how to puzzle out who the killer is. We're a perfect team. And think of the publicity this will bring! I'll be famous! And move to L.A. And you can visit me. And we can shop on Rodeo Drive and rub elbows with the stars."

Did I ever mention that Courtney enjoys a rich fantasy life?

"And how's this? I hold out for Katherine Heigl to play you in the movie version."

"I loooovvveee Katherine Heigl," I said in a rather sloppy drunk kind of way.

"Great. So let's get to work."

One pizza and God only knows how many RNDCs later, we had ourselves a list of potential suspects.

Top of the list was Desiree's father, who had recently been released from jail. Since he'd killed his brother, he'd proven himself capable of murder.

Next came Desiree's mother, often high on cocaine and

Oxycontin and capable of anything.

Desiree had one sister and two brothers, who never made it out of the old neighborhood and were always coming around asking for money. The last time I saw her brother Jared, it looked like he had a gun tucked under his jacket.

Then there were all the coworkers and friends whom she'd slammed on social networking—to include her Big Sister Vondra, which I thought was kind of tacky—along with a few sorority sisters she hadn't parted on good terms with after college.

Trying to keep all the names straight made my head hurt. "Your novel is getting confusing," I said.

"They're called red herrings. It leads the reader off on the wrong trail. The more the better. Now, didn't you tell me riding to the 7-Eleven with Desiree took a few years off your life?"

"Yup. She's ooonnneeee crazy driver."

"Good. Every mystery needs to consider a random act of violence. Say a case of road rage." She scribbled down some notes. "Anyone else?"

"Only the most obvious: You." Courtney flashed me a hurt-puzzled look, so I expounded on my theory. "Only because the body was found in the trunk of your car."

"Yeah, but I don't even know the chick. Besides, the police say it was a coincidence."

Courtney had left her Hyundai parked and unlocked in downtown Norfolk overnight. She'd gone out to party with her coworkers and didn't pick her car up until almost nine this morning. She'd come to my house to clean up then we'd gone off to play tourist. Since Desiree lived and worked in Norfolk, the police had determined the body being stuffed in Courtney's trunk was a case of the Hyundai being at the wrong place at the right time.

"And you know me," Courtney continued her defense. "I can't even squish a bug, so there's no way I would be able to take a human life."

Courtney tossed her pen down on the table and leaned back in her chair. She raked her fingers through her long hair then twirled it up into a chignon before releasing it to fall down about her shoulders. "You know, it would be a real twist in the end if you, I mean your character, turned out to be the killer. After all, you have motive, since she'd slandered you on social media, and you have means, being six inches taller and fifty pounds heavier."

"Forty pounds," I corrected her.

"Thank goodness you don't have opportunity, or I'd feel honor bound to call the police right now."

We laughed hysterically at the idea.

— 🜨 —

Unfortunately, the police weren't laughing.

My name was added to the suspects list when Desiree's BMW was found parked at the end of our condo complex. Further investigation found a puddle of blood—Desiree's blood—at the bottom of the spiral staircase in one of her vacant units two down from mine. Somehow they unearthed the Twitter war between Desiree and me. Did I have an alibi for eight in the morning of her death? No. I was alone in my apartment reading *The Virginian-Pilot* local newspaper while drinking coffee. So, to quote Detective Sanchez, *Voila*! I now had the trifecta of suspicion—means, motive and opportunity—hanging over my head.

I'd been dragged down to the police station twice. Sanchez had a lot of questions. So many questions and suppositions and scenarios I began to think I *had* killed Desiree and just blocked the event from my mind. Sanchez didn't have a shred of evidence against me, though. Hence, no official charges of murder in the first degree. Yet.

I tried not to worry. I mean, they never send the *wrong*

person to jail for murder, do they?

About a week after Desiree's death, I came home to my empty apartment, trying to decide what to fix for dinner, which would determine which bottle of wine I opened for Happy Hour. I'd been drinking a lot since Desiree had turned up dead. Tonight I felt the need for comfort wine. What goes well with a nice Merlot? Nathan's hot dogs cut up and mixed in with blue-box macaroni and cheese sounded perfect. I was just sitting down to eat when my cell phone buzzed. Courtney.

"Hello," I said into the phone with as much enthusiasm as I could muster.

"I know how I can prove you had nothing to do with Desiree's death."

"How?"

"A little test of your body-moving skills. I'll be there in an hour, so get ready." She disconnected.

As I said previously, I'd known Courtney long enough to not be alarmed by statements like that.

I finished my dinner, cleaned up the kitchen, then polished off the bottle of wine. When the doorbell rang, I answered it to find my best friend standing there, but I hardly recognized her, dressed as she was. Her black jeans matched her black T-shirt, which was printed with large white letters, "YOU CAN GET MUCH FARTHER WITH A KIND WORD AND A GUN THAN YOU CAN WITH A KIND WORD ALONE. ~ AL CAPONE."

Despite the unseasonably warm temperature, she had heavy work boots, thick work gloves and a bandana tied around her head. "I told you to be ready," she said, giving a disgusted appraisal of my lightweight batik skirt, beige camisole and bare feet. "How do you expect to move a dead body dressed like that?"

"A dead body?" I didn't like the sound of that. Not one bit.

"Yup."

"We're seriously going to move a dead body?" I asked.

"Not we. You. In the name of proving your innocence, that is.

And it's not a real dead body, just a fake one. Go change."

I was game for anything that would provide me a get-out-of-jail-free card, so I did as asked. I mimicked Courtney's attire as best I could, only my T-shirt read, "PRACTICE RANDOM ACTS OF KINDNESS AND SELFLESS ACTS OF GIVING." And it was hot pink.

I joined Courtney in the driveway. She was lifting something heavy and unwieldy out of her trunk and onto a flatbed cart the condo complex kept for people moving in or out. The bundle could best be described as a scarecrow made out of white pillow cases that appeared to be filled with sand then sewn in sections that resembled jointed arms, legs, torso and head. It was "dressed" in a cute sundress that I recognized from Courtney's college days.

"I figure Desiree weighed about one-twenty," Courtney said as she slammed the trunk of her Hyundai.

"That's about right." I was still curious and dare I say slightly nervous as to where this little field test was leading.

"Come on." Courtney rolled the cart to the front door of unit 13B, stopping just short of the yellow crime scene tape. She dumped the body on the front steps then pulled a small tube of red paint from her pocket and smeared some on the back of the scarecrow's head. "That's blood," she said. Then from under her shirt she pulled a stopwatch hanging on a string, pushed a button and said "Go!"

"Go where?" I asked.

"Go drag this body from here to my trunk," she answered. "I'm timing you to see how long it takes."

I grabbed the life-sized Desiree doll by the non-painted end and started to drag.

"No, no, no," Courtney said. "The police used Luminal and determined there was only blood inside the house and in the trunk of my car. You're gonna have to get it there without the head touching the ground."

After a few fumbling attempts to lift the scarecrow into a fireman's carry, I gave up and started dragging it by the head to load it on the pushcart.

Courtney shoved the cart out of reach. "I talked to the manager and confirmed the cart was locked in the office and wouldn't have been available when Desiree was killed," she told me. "You're gonna have to get it there on your own."

I learned one very important thing: Moving dead weight is harder than it looks. By the time I reached Courtney's car, I was covered in "blood" from head to toe and feeling weak from the effort.

I deposited the body in the trunk and slammed it shut.

Courtney clicked a button on the stopwatch and announced, "Sixteen minutes and forty-seven seconds. That just might qualify you for the Guinness Book of World Records."

"But how does that prove my innocence?"

"Easy. It's all in the timeline. The police figure Desiree's body had been stuffed in your trunk while my car was parked here. I got to your house at nine that morning. You were talking to someone when I arrived."

"Yes, I was. Vondra Scott, Desiree's Big Sis. She was showing one of the unit's to prospective tenants because Desiree was tied up at a real estate closing or something."

"So Vondra can vouch that you were not covered in blood at the time. As can I."

I nodded my head.

"I left my car parked next to yours, unlocked again. I really need to stop doing that. Then we walked into your townhome together. I went to grab a much needed shower after a night on the town. We were in my car by nine-twenty and seated at The Sandfiddler Restaurant at nine-thirty. We'd talked to the waitress quite a bit, and I'm sure she'll remember us."

"I don't get where this is going."

"We just proved it took you sixteen minutes to move the

body, and it left you covered in blood. So if someone saw you clean at nine a.m. and I saw you clean, and in the same clothes I might add, twenty minutes later, and we were at a restaurant ten minutes after that, how would you ever have had time move a bloody body and then clean up? *Voila*, proof you are innocent."

If Courtney's fictional mystery were half as clever, it was sure to be a bestseller.

"So the question now is," she asked while tapping a crimson-painted fingernail against her upper lip, "who could have put that body in the trunk of my car while it sat in front of your home at nine last Friday morning?"

I settled my backside on the hood of Courtney's Hyundai and ran my toes through the grass. I mentally flipped through the list of suspects we'd compiled. It still could be any of the ones we'd come up with, to include a random act of violence.

When my toe scraped across something hard in the grass, I looked down to see a small object reflecting sunshine. Thinking it a shard of glass and not wanting any barefoot person—mainly me—cutting their foot, I bent down to pick it up. Only it wasn't a shard of glass, but a diamond encrusted pendant in the shape of a V. I held it up for Courtney to see, and asked, "Are you thinking what I'm thinking?"

"If you're thinking the killer left this souvenir behind, and that our only suspect with a V in their name is Vondra, then that's proof that best friends think alike."

Two nights later, Courtney and I celebrated the arrest of Vondra Scott in the brutal killing of Desiree Pierson. The thing that broke the case wide open was Courtney's dead-body-moving exercise, which, in turn, led to my finding the V pendant.

According to the morning's paper, Desiree had given the necklace to Vondra for Christmas. It was more than a token of friendship, it was an amulet of guilt, since Desiree had been sneaking around with Vondra's husband. Vondra had caught them in bed together the night before the murder.

The murder hadn't been premeditated. Vondra had followed Desiree to unit 13B, the empty townhome near mine. Desiree was scheduled to show it that morning and wanted to touch up a few things first. When confronted by Vondra, Desiree had gone freakin' crazy and a fight had ensued. They'd been standing at the top of the spiral staircase. Vondra had shoved Desiree, who had tumbled down the steps, hitting her head numerous times on the iron railing on her way down.

Vondra had been leaving the scene of the crime when I'd flagged her down to talk. Then when Courtney left her car unlocked and with nobody was around, Vondra disposed of the body in Courtney's car.

She just might have gotten away with it too, had Courtney and I not been on the case.

Tonight we were enjoying a celebratory dinner at Twillager's Tavern, toasting the outcome.

"How's the book coming?" I asked.

"It's gonna make me rich and famous," Courtney said without a hint of modesty.

"Do you have a title yet?"

"I'm thinking about calling it *Friends Help You Move, but Best Friends Help You Move the Body.*"

I offered up a toast. "To best friends writing best-sellers!"

"And to Katherine Heigl playing you in the movie."

We clinked glasses. I took a big sip of my A Day At the Beach cocktail, heavy on the rum. Yum!

KEY TO A CRIME

By Fiona Quinn

OFFICER COOPER WAS DONE for the day, his mind already at home. He drove down Route 288, smack dab through the middle of Virginia, counting off the last few minutes of his shift, when he pulled parallel to a powder-blue minivan, turned his head and saw her face. Never in his fifteen years as a state trooper had he felt such a kick-in-the-gut reaction to a face. When Cooper saw her, every hair follicle on his body stood at attention, like a soldier ready to go into battle, and he knew his day was shot to hell.

At first glance, the woman looked like any other suburban mom. But her hands clamped tightly on the steering wheel. Her body jutted stiffly forward as if she pushed the van down the highway with her mind instead of using the engine. She looked over at him. Her eyes stretched so wide that it looked like her irises floated in pools of white sclera. Her jaw clenched so tightly he thought she'd dislodge her teeth.

He let her move ahead of him. Going forty-five on a sixty-five-mile-an-hour stretch of highway was officially reason enough to pull her over—something beyond the look on her face. He eased in behind her and flipped on his blue lights. Slowing immediately, she pulled far off the roadway into the grass, her car tilting at an uncomfortable angle on the embankment.

Cooper tapped the usual information into his MDT computer, grabbed his hat from the passenger-seat hook and made his way to her window. He left the requisite fingerprints on her brake light as he strode by—just in case.

Usually by the time Cooper had made his way up to a woman

driver's door, she would have the window down, ready to greet him with a flirtatious smile. That, or tears of indignation. This woman did neither. She hunkered down, scribbling red lipstick across a ripped open McDonald's bag.

Cooper rapped at the window. Instead of rolling it down, the woman plastered the bag against the glass for him to read. "HELP! He has my daughter. Listening on phone and scanner. Body in back." *Yup. This day is shot to hell.*

Keeping one hand on his gun, he cupped the other against the windshield to block out the mid-afternoon sun and peered in. The woman held up her phone. Her lips were colorless and stretched tightly over her teeth. She wasn't blinking. Cooper wondered what kind of drugs she might be on. She shook harder than that boy he'd pulled out of the half-frozen pond two days ago when the idiot had been texting his girlfriend and skid off the side of the road. Up until this minute, Cooper thought he had seen just about everything in the course of his duty, but he had a feeling that this was beyond—way beyond—anything he'd ever dealt with before.

Cooper looked past the woman. Kid debris filled the car: paper, toys, a small jacket, a running shoe and what looked like a red high-heeled pump wedged onto a human foot, sticking up at an improbable angle behind the woman's seat.

Jeezis. His hand still on his gun, Cooper moved to his safety angle, positioning himself with rigid vigilance to the right of her door, and knocked again. This time the window came down, and with it came the smell—cloying sweetness, wild animal, feces, copper penny—the unmistakable smell of a ripe corpse. "Body in back," the note said. No kidding.

"Ma'am, I need your license and registration, please."

The woman nodded and reached for her purse. She breathed in raggedy gasps as if she were searching the air around her for extra oxygen. Unable to master the closure on the wallet, she thrust the whole thing at him.

"Ma'am, I'm going to need you to step out of your vehicle and come back to my car while I run your information."

Again, she wiggled her phone at him.

"Please leave your phone and purse on the seat and get out of your car." Cooper reached up to his radio and depressed the button. "Richmond, send a second vehicle."

The woman's hands came up rigidly, swiping at the air as if to erase his action. She pointed at her phone and thrust the bag at him with emphasis. Something darkly red had dried on her hands, crusted on her forearms and smeared on the front of her modestly buttoned butter-yellow blouse. Cooper focused on her hands. They were badly scratched and bruised. The webbing on her left thumb lay jagged from a deep gash. It was black with coagulated blood.

Cooper pulled his gun from its holster and took a single step backward. The woman opened the door and leaned out to vomit.

Cooper had been puked on many times over the years. He had developed a pretty good reflex for jumping out of the way, but she still spattered his shiny black shoes with what looked like only partially digested hamburger and fries.

"Ma'am, are you sick? Do you need an ambulance?" She shook her head. She still hadn't said a word. Her jaw clenched shut again. She pointed back to the phone then at Cooper with pleading eyes, and his body reacted with cold prickles across his skin. He didn't like that. Cooper was always professionally distant, but this woman was radiating horror, and his body absorbed the waves.

Cooper put his gun back in the holster and pulled out his cuffs.

"For your safety, ma'am, I'm going to put these on you, and then we're going to walk back to my car while I run your information." The woman turned to look at her phone. Her hands fastened back on the steering wheel. She focused down the road, and Cooper thought she might make a run for it.

"Ma'am, you can cooperate, or I can use force." The moment passed, and she quietly held out her hands with a short nod.

———— ✿ ————

Mrs. Patricia Arlene Clark. Home-schooling mom. Brownie troop leader. Sunday school teacher. Housewife. Patty had started the day, like she started every day, by opening the back door to let Cocoa out into the yard. This morning the surprise of spring weather greeted her. The cold snap was over. The blissfully warm air held the fragrance of burgeoning green. Patty decided it was the perfect day to get out of the house with the kids and enjoy nature. They would go letterboxing in Henricus Park—a little history lesson, a little reading-direction-following exercise, a little fun.

As her family wound through the reconstructed historical site, Patty felt somewhat guilty, knowing that the public school kids were sitting at their desks, looking longingly out the windows. The Clarks watched the interpreters, dressed in period garb, cooking over the outside firepit and digging in the garden. A militia of three elderly, potbellied men ran musket drills over by the log walls. Patty and her kids followed the clues on the letterbox instruction sheet that she had pulled off the Internet before leaving home. They moved slowly from the thatched huts to the river.

There, in the hollow of an ancient oak, lay the Tupperware box of victory. It held an inkpad for leaving the families' stamps, a booklet and pen if someone wanted to leave a message, and a little token to take. Usually, they'd find a plastic key chain or fast food toy. This time, they found a golden locket nestled next to the notebook, probably bought for a dime at a yard sale. Pretty though. Ginny jumped up and down, claiming the unexpected treasure as hers. Pete kicked the ground with his Captain America sneakers in disgust.

"It's okay, Pete. We'll let your sister have the locket, and we'll get lunch at McDonald's. You can have both of the kids' meal prizes." That seemed to appease the sibling rivalry. *Well done. This is turning out to be a wonderful day!* Patty told herself. But then her hand poised over the notebook that lay opened in her lap to stamp their family symbol. She read the sentence from someone who had come before them and her stomach knotted. Something wasn't right here.

"Ginny, let Mommy see that necklace for a second." Patty's seven-year-old reluctantly pulled the chain over her head, catching it briefly in the honey-blond tangle of curls that spilled halfway down her back. Patty opened the locket to find a small key, but no photograph. Patty pocketed the key and gave the locket back to her daughter.

— 🜚 —

"Mrs. Patricia A. Clark. Is that your correct name? Are you still at this address?" Cooper held Patty's license in his left hand and typed rapidly into his MDT computer with his right. Even though his brain was abuzz with a thousand questions, he went methodically by the book. Patty nodded in affirmation.

"Ma'am, have you been drinking? Or doing any drugs today? Anything recreational? Anything prescription?"

Patty twitched her head back and forth, mechanically. Her eyes stayed fixed on her hands, secured in the cuffs. They glazed over; she looked like a trauma victim going into shock. Cooper typed in a request for an EMT.

A semi barreled past them. The wind shook the car and seemed to rouse Patty from her stupor. She shifted her eyes to Cooper.

"Do you know the name of the deceased in your van?" he asked. In the rearview mirror, Cooper saw his backup coming up the road.

"No." Patty's voice snapped like a dog protecting a piece of meat.

"Ma'am, do you know who has your daughter?"

"I think it's the man from the park."

"Your daughter was taken from you at the park?"

"No, from McDonald's."

"Which McDonald's?"

"Up the street from Henricus on Route 1." Officer Cooper typed in the McDonald's information and a request that dispatch send someone from Chesterfield over to check on a possible kidnapping. Backup pulled in behind them. Cooper stepped out of his car to let Officer Davis know that he had just put a foot into a rattlesnake nest. Davis walked forward to look at the dead body. Cooper sat back in his driver's seat.

"Mrs. Clark, I need you to start at the beginning, so I can understand what's going on here. How many children do you have?"

"Two. Two children. Pete is six and Ginny is seven."

"Why aren't they in school today, ma'am?"

"We home-school."

"Why aren't your children with you right now, Mrs. Clark?"

High pitched and rapid-fire, her words were almost unintelligible.

"When we were leaving Henricus Park to get lunch, my son, Pete, caught a dog that had run off and returned it to an older couple. My daughter, Ginny, showed them the golden locket she found when we were letterboxing. When she held it up, I felt someone staring at us over my left shoulder. There was a man standing there, focused on Ginny. I didn't like the way he was looking at her, so I hustled the kids into the minivan and we left."

"Can you tell me anything about the man?" Cooper asked. Officer Davis hovered by the cruiser, listening.

"Short, skinny, thin gray hair pulled into a ponytail, drinking coffee from a 7-Eleven cup."

"What was he wearing?"

"A dirty white T-shirt, ripped blue jeans, work boots."

"And he was just standing there, looking at you?"

"He was leaning against his work van, smoking."

"How do you know it was a work van? Can you describe it? Did it have a logo?"

"I didn't pay that much attention." Patty's eyes rolled up in her head. Cooper wondered if she was thinking hard or having trouble controlling their movements. He had seen a lot of craziness in his day, but nothing like this.

"It was green, windowless ... no, I don't remember anything else."

"Did you see him follow you?"

"No."

His brows knitted together, forming a single line. "Then why do you think this man has your daughter?"

"Because the voice telling me what to do sounds like the kind of voice that man would have. And because I'm a mom."

Cooper blinked. He thought about the course he had just taken on how to deal with mentally impaired citizens and the words "delusional," "psychosis" and "schizophrenia" bubbled up.

"You heard a voice, ma'am?"

"Yes. When I was in McDonald's, I was talking to my friend Heather when I got a call from a number I didn't recognize. It was my daughter, Ginny. She said 'Mommy?' and then a man's voice came on the phone. He said, 'I have your girl. If you want her alive, you'll do what I say.' So I've been doing what he says."

"Your daughter was on the phone? I thought she was with you at McDonald's."

"She was. While we ate our lunch, my son spilled his soda ..." Her eyelids quivered. She blanched and slid to the side.

"And you didn't call 911 immediately?"

Cooper's bark snapped Patty to attention and she steadied again. "He said not to!"

Cooper did a mental eye roll. This story stank from more than the corpse. This woman was obviously unstable, and he needed to make sure the children were safe. Cooper decided to play along. "What did he tell you to do, ma'am?"

"He told me not to hang up ... to go to some address, drive around back and park by the shed."

"So where is your son?" Davis asked, joining the questioning.

"I asked Heather to watch Pete. I said I had a family emergency."

"What's Heather's phone number? I'll give her a call and check on Pete for you." Davis smiled encouragingly.

"I don't know her number off the top of my head."

"So how were you going to get your son back?" Davis asked.

"She lives two doors down from me. I'll get him when this is over."

Cooper abruptly redirected the conversation. "You drove to a house?"

"I drove to the address the man told me. I used the key that I found in the locket to open the padlock. Like he told me to do." Patty's voice wavered off.

"You were just following directions. You went to the shed. Is that when you killed the woman?" asked Davis.

"Me? No. Barney already had the package wrapped."

"Who is Barney, Mrs. Clark?" asked Davis.

"I don't know." Her voice came out singsong and distant.

"You said Barney had the package wrapped. Are you referring to the body?" asked Cooper.

Patty stared vacantly at Officer Cooper. He glanced at his rearview mirror, hoping the EMT would show up quick. He tried again. "Are you taking the body to Barney?"

"No. Barney killed the woman and left the body wrapped in a tarp for the man on the phone. The man who took Ginny. Then when I found the key, the ponytailed man said I should take care of it for him. Keep his hands clean."

Cooper looked down at Patty's hands, caked in dirt and blood. "How did you meet Barney?" he asked.

"I never met Barney. I'm telling you what the man on the phone said to me."

"If Barney is the one who killed the woman, why is there a body in your van?"

"The man on the phone wants me to dump it at Pocahontas Park for him."

"Why didn't Barney do that himself instead of leaving the body in the shed?"

Patty's eyes sharpened momentarily. "Now how would I know that?"

Cooper tried to hide his frustration. He kept pecking at the story, hoping for a grain of truth. "Okay. What happened at the shed? How did the body get into your van?"

"It was lying on a tarp. So I dragged it."

"You were able to do that all by yourself?" Officer Davis asked, his eyebrows stretching to the brim of his hat. "The body looks pretty heavy, and you're pretty petite."

"Dragging it wasn't hard, but I couldn't get it to bend. I even took out one of my van seats and left it behind. But the legs were all stretched out wide, and I couldn't get them through the sliding door."

"Well, she's in your van now, ma'am. If no one helped you, how'd you get her in?" Cooper was using the soothing voice he had developed for emergency calls with very small children. He resisted the urge to go back to his trunk to get her a stuffed bear he had there.

Patty spoke with her eyes squeezed tight. "I had to use the sledgehammer from the shed."

Cooper's eyebrows shot straight up. Of all the things he had heard so far, this was the hardest one to swallow. The idea of this hundred-pound woman sledgehammering the knees of a corpse so she could stuff it into the back of her minivan was mind twisting. Davis had seen the body and would have seen the sledgehammered legs. Cooper sent him a questioning look. Davis nodded in affirmation.

"How did you know how to find the shed?" Cooper worked the surprise out of his expression.

"He told me the address, and I put it into my GPS."

"Why didn't you call the police when you saw that there was a body in the shed? That was a crime scene."

"He said not to. He said he'd make Ginny disappear, and I'd never know what happened to her. He said I couldn't hang up!" Tears made slow rivulets down Patty's cheeks, but she didn't wipe at them. Her hands in their cuffs stretched out in front of her as if suspended from invisible strings.

Officer Davis stood at the open window of the cruiser, shaking his head. "This story is sounding pretty far out there, ma'am."

Cooper gave Davis a warning glance. He was pretty sure this woman's hold on sanity was sliver-thin, and he meant to get every piece of information he could before she snapped.

Patty sat rigidly, looking straight ahead as if she hadn't even heard him, or maybe she realized she had no defense.

"Did you kill the woman, Mrs. Clark?" Cooper asked again in his comforting voice. Patty's shackled hands thumped up and down as she pounded on her knees.

"No! She was dead. It didn't hurt at all when I hit her. If I broke her legs, it didn't matter." Sobs roiled the air, followed by a moment of silence.

"What did you do with your children, Mrs. Clark? Where are your children?" Cooper modulated his voice to show his care and support, to let Patty know it was safe to tell the truth. He had a bad feeling about those kids.

"Where are my children?" Patty repeated flatly.

"What about your husband, ma'am? Where is he?" Cooper asked.

"Chicago. Business."

Officer Davis was short on patience. "Where's this shed?" he snapped.

"I put the address into my GPS. Would you listen to me already? *Please*, you have to find my daughter!" Patty shot out both hands and dug her nails into Cooper's arm. Normally, Cooper would have restrained her with the seatbelt, but nothing seemed normal right now. And frankly, he was afraid she was about to throw up in his front seat.

"You're supposed to be helping me! You're supposed to be helping my baby!"

"We're doing our best, ma'am. We've sent Chesterfield Police to the McDonald's." Cooper clenched his jaw and worked on keeping his gaze impassive.

—— 🐱 ——

The EMT team moved Patty from Cooper's car to the back of the ambulance. A paramedic checked her vitals as she sat on the platform, her feet dangling above the gravel. Patty pinched the cloth of Officer Cooper's uniform shirt between her thumb and fingers. It was an odd thing to do. Cooper looked down at her hand when she first made the gesture, surprised by how infantile it felt to him. He decided to tolerate the intrusion on his personal space.

Traffic moved to the left-hand side and slowed as people looked to see what was going on and to give the rescue workers the required free lane. Davis stood at the back of the ambulance, leaning against the door.

"Mrs. Clark, what does your daughter look like?" Cooper asked.

"I have pictures of her in my wallet."

"I can't send a picture to dispatch. Can you describe what she was wearing?"

"Yes ... Ginny has on her Dora the Explorer light-up sneakers on the wrong feet. Jeans. A pink T-shirt and her hoodie. Was that today? Yes, I think that's right. I could check the pictures on my phone if I could hang it up. The guy must be suspicious by now. I've been sitting here a really long time." Patty panted in quick, shallow breaths. The paramedic reached forward with an oxygen mask, but Patty twisted her head away. "He said I should play it cool. *Play it cool!* I don't know what to do! What should I do? I can't breathe! You have to help me!"

"Ma'am, you're not giving us a lot to go on here." Davis's words squeezed through gritted teeth.

"Then why don't you do your damned job and start investigating? You can start with Henricus. You can start with the weird message at the letterbox. There's a 7-Eleven right by Henricus. He probably got his coffee there. He was at McDonald's. Surely someone—"

"Wait. Back up. What weird message at the letterbox?" Cooper asked.

Patty briefly let go of Cooper's sleeve to push an auburn curl back behind her ear. "Do you know what letterboxing is?"

"You follow clues like a treasure hunt, find a box, take a prize and leave a prize."

"Right. And in the letterbox with the golden locket was a note from Barney that said something like 'I did what you said. This better be the end of it. I owe you nothing more.'"

Davis removed his hat and rubbed a hand over his close-cropped hair, blowing out an exasperated breath and shaking his head. Cooper cut him a glance that told him with no uncertainty that he needed to stop.

"Go on, Mrs. Clark," said Cooper. "Where can we find the box?"

"The instructions are in my purse."

Cooper looked over at Davis. "Get the purse and the GPS."

Davis took off at a jog and was quickly back with two purses. "Which one, ma'am?"

"Mine's brown. I found the red one in the shed." Patty reached for her purse, took out the folded paper and handed it to Davis.

Davis turned to the Chesterfield officer who trotted over with a hand on his gun. "Sergeant, we're investigating a homicide and possible kidnapping. We need this letterbox retrieved immediately." He held out the dirt-smudged paper. The officer took the cryptic directions, nodded and left.

"You thought to bring the dead woman's purse, ma'am?" Cooper asked.

"I thought it might help me find Ginny."

"And you hadn't thought to call the police?" he asked.

"He *told* me not to call the police. He didn't tell me not to take the purse." Cooper had to lean in to hear Patty's whispered answer. The road noise already made hearing difficult. Davis pulled up the last address on Patty's handheld GPS. He typed a message to dispatch, asking an officer to go by the residence to check the backyard for a minivan seat and to tape off the shed as a crime scene. Cooper pulled a wallet out of the red purse and flipped it open to the photos.

"Does this woman look like the deceased?" Cooper pointed at a brown-haired woman with her copious bosom spilling out of a frilly wedding dress.

"I don't know. The body had no face," Patty said.

Cooper turned over the plastic sleeve. On the back was another photo of the woman. In this one, she was sitting on the lap of a ponytailed man.

"That's him! That's the man from Henricus!"

Cooper pulled out the driver's license and typed the address to dispatch. He leaned over and said something quietly to Davis. Davis took off for the van again. When he returned, he held

Patty's phone in his hand.

"Mrs. Clark, we need to get this man's phone number *now* to help us trace him to your daughter. How do you hang it up?" Cooper asked. A massive dump truck rattled past, spewing debris from under its protective cover. Davis handed the phone to Patty.

Patty reached out her hands and put the phone to her ear in a habitual gesture.

"Hello? Are you still there?" she whispered with a cracking voice. " ... He's back at his patrol car, writing me a ticket ... No. Just a ticket for my tags. Ginny—is she okay? Can I talk to her?"

Officer Cooper narrowed his eyes, watching Patty intently. Suddenly, with a surprised gasp, Patty pressed the end button.

"She's at my house!"

"Your daughter? How do you know?"

"I heard Ginny say 'Cocoa.' Cocoa is my dog's name."

"How did your daughter get to your house if she's been kidnapped?" Cooper asked.

— 🐞 —

Cooper's lights flashed as he rocketed his car down the highway toward the Clark home on what he guessed would be the biggest goose chase of his career. He had left Davis in charge of the scene. Patty was strapped to the gurney with an oxygen mask on her face, a sedative going into her vein, ready for her ride to Chippenham Hospital. Patty had completely lost control after she said she'd heard her daughter's voice on the phone. *Chippenham's probably best. They have the mental health ward there,* Cooper thought as he checked his rearview mirror. Chesterfield had sent backup. Leading the three-car convoy, Cooper barreled off the exit ramp.

He swung into the Clark's subdivision, turning off his lights as he eased onto Patty's street. From the top of the hill, Cooper could see a green paneled van in a driveway up ahead. That surprised him. He stopped his car two doors down, hidden by a clump of evergreens. Cooper sprinted across the manicured lawn, past the red bicycle lying on its side, and charged up the three stairs. He banged on the door so hard that the pastel Easter wreath jumped and danced. The other officers stood at the corners of the two-story brick colonial watching for movement. No one came to the door. A dog barked ferociously from inside.

Cooper gestured at one of the Chesterfield policemen. This one—potbellied and wheezing from the short jog, red faced from the adrenaline rush—could guard the front door. Cooper and Officer Timmons made their way around to the rear. The back door hung slightly ajar on a badly splintered frame. With gun in hand, Cooper kicked the door fully open. He and Timmons raced in, quickly searching room to room.

Kitchen—empty.

Dining room—empty.

Den—Ponytail sat on a hassock with a slender, golden-haired child on his lap. Her eyes were as wide and white as Patty Clark's had been when Cooper first saw her.

The man's hands encircled the child's throat. "I wouldn't come any closer. She'll snap quick." Ponytail's voice slurred over the word "snap," drawing it out, giving it emphasis. He pressed his thumbs to the back of Ginny's slender neck.

Cooper took in the lay of the room with his peripheral vision. He didn't see anything that Ponytail could use as a weapon. He did see empty beer cans strewn on the brown carpet.

Cooper crept forward. Timmons moved slowly to the right.

"Put your hands in the air." Cooper's voice was commanding and strong. Ponytail must have had a lifetime of disregarding orders, or he would have heeded Cooper's authority.

"Nah. I got my ticket to ride right here. Although it didn't work out how I planned it."

"You planned to kidnap this child?" Cooper held the man's

attention while Timmons slid closer.

"Nope, lucky day for me. Kid got the locket. Mom got the key. I just sit around and eat some grub, have me a beer, wait for Mama to take care of things, and come on home."

"What did you think would happen when she came home?"

"Only three people knowed something about me and my problem with my wife. There's Barney, but he's up to his armpits in all this. Then there's little darlin' here and her mama. They were a simple fix. It's in the news all the time how a mom goes nuts and drowns her kid and then commits suicide. Women hormones." Ponytail stopped to belch loudly. Cooper was close enough now to smell the alcohol on his breath.

"But I see her mama cain't be trusted to follow instructions."

Timmons's massive fist cracked across Ponytail's jaw as Cooper grabbed Ginny. The child flailed her arms and legs with a high-pitched shriek as Cooper gathered her into his arms. Ponytail's head snapped to the side, his body slid to the floor, where he lay, unconscious.

Ginny turned her body into Cooper's and buried her face deep in the hollow of his shoulder. Her arms tightened noose-like around his neck; her legs vise-gripped his waist. Ginny's body shook as hard as her mom's had when Cooper pulled the minivan over. Cooper rubbed the child's back, calming her with the same soothing voice he had used with Patty.

Cooper looked over at the prostrate man with the dirty, white T-shirt and work boots Timmons was busy handcuffing. *I'll be damned. The woman was telling the truth,* he thought. A cold sweat glazed Cooper's skin as he realized how close this story had come to a horrific ending. "Thank God today wasn't shot to hell," Cooper murmured as he hugged Ginny tightly and stroked his fingers through her honey-blond curls.

THE CHRYSLER CASE

BY YVONNE SAXON

THURSDAY 6:45 P.M.

Beethoven's portrait scowled down the length of the darkened gallery, past the few remaining nineteenth century paintings, and over the vacant cases to Napoleon III's grand piano. Strains of jazz floated up from the event in the courtyard downstairs. A solitary figure stood in the shadows, listening, hands resting on the piano's parquet-inlaid casing.

But not for long. A moment later he pulled supports from behind a screened doorway, placing them under a masterpiece then deftly detached the artwork from the wall, maneuvering it into a padded crate below. Turning back, he attached a small sign in the now empty space. The music stopped. The figure froze. From downstairs he heard a muffled voice, laughter, then the music began again. Grabbing the supports, he deposited them on the wheeled cart that held the crate then hastily removed the screen blocking the entry to the gallery. Within seconds, he pushed the cart holding the masterpiece into the darkness, and disappeared.

Thursday 6:55 p.m.

The Chrysler Museum's Artsy Jazzy Norfolk Christmas Gala was in full swing. I was staring up at the full moon through the vaulted glass and timber ceiling of Huber Court or I might have seen who bumped me. I almost landed on the table, on top of my friend Katie, one of the art librarians at the museum.

"Are you okay? Who was that?" Katie asked.

"I didn't see," I told her, looking around.

With the lights down, the only illumination came from the candles and the softly glowing hand-blown glass ornaments in the garlands draped on every archway. The holiday lighting made the fifteenth century Florentine designed courtyard visually stunning, I thought, but you couldn't see anyone more than three feet away.

"Merry Artsy Jazzy Christmas, ladies!" Sam Moore greeted us, raising his punch glass.

"Merry Artsy Jazzy Christmas to you, Sam," I replied.

"Mind if I join you?"

"Not at all," Katie said. "We'd be honored to have the director of guest services at our table." She bowed in mock formality.

Sam seated himself on the opposite side of the table, looking around at the decorated courtyard. "A beautiful end to a year that started in an ugly way," he said.

"Oh," Katie said, "I'd almost forgotten about that."

"Me too," I added. "I guess the really horrible things you try to put out of your mind."

"Remember when they first put up that orange mesh construction fence? How we all complained that it detracted from the beauty of the grounds and architecture?" Sam said.

"Yes!" I said. "And then when that front loader knocked a tree over into the Hague and left a huge hole? We were all livid!"

"But that didn't seem to matter when they pulled the tree out of the water and a dead body came with it, did it?" Katie said softly.

"I haven't complained about the construction since then," I said. "Oh, that's right, you missed the excitement that day, didn't you Sam? Where were you again?" I said, teasing him.

"Yes, do tell," Katie said, laughing.

"You had to bring that up, didn't you?"

"Hmm, let's see—you went to pick up the visiting conservator from the airport and couldn't find him?" I prodded.

"Okay, so there was some confusion, and I missed his flight.

It happens," Sam replied grumpily.

"Don't pick on him," Katie told me. "He only missed him by an entire day!" Katie and I howled in laughter. Even Sam grinned at the memory.

"I still haven't figured out how that happened," Sam said, shaking his head. "Let me change the subject to something less embarrassing: I'm surprised your bosses aren't here enjoying the music and the company," Sam said to me.

I shrugged. "Zach's hiding in the studio, working on something, again."

Katie looked puzzled. "Zach was here about thirty minutes ago," she said. "He said he'd be back."

"Peter said that he'd make an appearance before the evening was over, but—"

"But?" Sam gave me a sharp look.

"I don't know, Sam. Peter seems preoccupied most of the time, and Zach's in the studio painting night and day. I didn't think we had that many canvases left to work on."

Zach Tunstall was the head art conservator at the Chrysler. Peter Marson, the visiting conservator, had been working with him for months on many of the masterpieces in our collection that needed to be cleaned and restored (or "conserved" as I had learned) before they were sent "on the road" to other galleries or stored during the upcoming renovation. As their assistant, I ensured they had what they needed when they needed it so they could continue working. Since Peter was "on loan" to us, I'd been working mostly with him.

Just then the trumpet player took off with the fastest swing rendition of "Sleigh Ride" I'd ever heard, with the sax player in hot pursuit.

"I hope they get here soon," Katie said when the applause died down.

"So do I," Sam agreed. "We've all been working nonstop to keep this art gallery open to the public while we've been closing it down behind the scenes. We deserve a little celebrating before we go back to the inventory and the packing."

"You've got that right!" I told him. "Speaking of packing, Katie, aren't you about done?"

She narrowed her eyes and gave me a mean look. "No. Do you know how much stuff is back there in the library stacks? And besides that, I hear these noises, so I keep looking over my shoulder to see if the ghost of Jean Chrysler is sneaking up on me."

Sam laughed at her. "Well, since she and her husband were responsible for the majority of the collection, and her name is on the art library, she probably wants to make sure you're doing things right! Seriously, you do know those are just legends?"

"Well, if they're not, and she appears, put her to work packing!" I said. "We've only got until Sunday before we start moving the first crates out."

"What happens Sunday?" Peter said innocently as he and Zach pulled up chairs on either side of Sam and sat down.

We all groaned.

Friday 10:30 a.m.

I stood in front of "The Finding of Moses" amazed at the skill of the conservators. The jewel-toned robes of Pharaoh's daughter and her attendants were as vibrant today as they were four centuries ago when they were first painted. I felt privileged that I got to watch as Peter and Zach worked their magic on the fading or flaked masterpieces. In addition to the many projects in the studio downstairs, every other Friday they demonstrated art conservation to the public by working on this painting in the gallery. But Zach hadn't come up yet today.

"Welcome to the Chrysler Museum of Art," I said to an older couple entering the gallery,

"Is this your first visit?"

They nodded at me then smiled and strolled around the

room.

The husband turned around and asked, "What happened to all the paintings?"

Two of the four dark-green walls were bare; the paintings had been removed. Patches of white dotted the walls where the accompanying signs had been pulled away, taking some paint with them. In place of the artwork, a small card was posted indicating the name of the piece taken and whether it was in a traveling exhibit or had gone to storage. I explained to the couple that the Chrysler was being renovated, and due to the imminent construction, pieces were gradually being moved off site to avoid putting any artwork in jeopardy.

"Oh, so that's why some galleries have screens across their entrances," the wife said.

Peter motioned to me, "I need more acetone. Can you get me more of this and another one of these?"

Excusing myself, I went to get the supplies he needed.

Halfway downstairs I realized I'd forgotten the keys to get into the studio. "Great." Wait: I could borrow Katie's key. I stuck my head in the door of the art library and saw no one at the desk.

"Hello. Anybody home?" I called out, walking to the doorway of the restricted back area. No answer. I was hesitant to go back there without another staff member (I'd heard the ghost stories), but I was in a hurry. "This place is huge!" I passed shelf after shelf in the stacks. So where was that connector door to the back—

"Aaeeehhh!" shrieked a voice.

"OOOhhhh!" I yelped, jumping away from the figure that appeared beside me.

"You scared me to death!" we said in unison and then started laughing in relief as Katie and I recognized each other.

"Oh, I'm really in a hurry. I forgot Peter's keys and thought there was a shortcut through the back here to the studio," I told her.

"I thought Jean Chrysler's ghost had me for sure! I've been

hearing noises all morning," she told me, grabbing her chest as if she were having a heart attack. "Between you and Sam—"

"Sam was back here?"

"Yesterday. He was just here from out of nowhere! I never heard him come in either. He was looking for something."

"That's strange."

"I thought so too," Katie said. "Anyway, the hallway to the back is through that door over there. Here's my key."

"Thank you so much."

Katie shook her head. "Just don't sneak up on me in here ever again!"

I was making my way through the hallway Katie had pointed out. It was more like a maze filled with crates of all sizes: some packed with art treasures, some empty—all signifying the coming change caused by construction—when I saw what I thought was the door to the back of the studio. The key worked, but, wait a minute, this wasn't the studio. It was more storage for frames?

We didn't store frames. The room contained several frames in various dimensions: gilded, carved, ornate. I recognized all of them. And then I saw the paintings that belonged to them: They were supposed to be going in storage! I had watched as Zach and Peter inspected and cleaned them. Why were they out of their frames? And why were they hidden down here in a locked room? Could I be wrong? What was this? I got closer and noticed something else—the end of a painting was sticking out behind this one.

Trembling, I pulled the other painting forward to reveal the one behind. I had seen this Renoir when it came back from Italy at the end of September before we had crated it for storage. It had been gone for months. Hadn't it? I looked around the little room. In the corner sat a crate on a rolling cart. I tried to open it, but it was sealed.

Was someone planning to steal all this art, pretending to crate it up and put it in storage until the Chrysler reopened after construction? It would be almost sixteen months before the theft would be discovered.

But then I stopped breathing, because behind the Renoir was another unframed canvas, one I knew was still hanging in the gallery upstairs at this very moment. That glare, the unruly hair, the monochromatic color scheme—I knew Beethoven's portrait anywhere! This wasn't art theft, it was forgery! No. It was both. I looked around at all the artwork. Which were real and which were fake? Were they all forged? I didn't know what to do. Should I call the museum curator? Security? The FBI? Taking a deep breath calmed me a little. *I'm just an assistant, using my education to run errands and get coffee*, I thought to myself. Zach and Peter! The conservators took turns checking every work of art before it went out and when it came back to see if any damage had occurred. My mind was racing. *Could it be one of them?* No, it couldn't be, I argued with myself. Besides, they weren't the only accomplished artists in the building ... just the best. Sam? He'd been acting strangely too. I grabbed the smallest canvas, the Beethoven, and fled for the door.

I stopped. Quiet footsteps were heading my way. *What if the forger saw me?* I hit the lights, backing into the corner between the crate and the wall, hoping the darkness would hide me. My ankle pressed into something hard but smooth. The doorknob rattled. *Please Lord*, I prayed, *don't let him find me!* I was afraid, really afraid, and wasn't even sure of what. Or whom.

More footsteps, louder this time, and a shadow passed in front of the door and joined them, the sound growing fainter. I didn't dare move.

When I was sure they were gone, I reached down and grabbed what felt like a box. In the light it turned out to be a small but rather expensive attaché case. It contained one-way tickets from Norfolk International Airport to Paris via Atlanta. Departure time: Sunday morning. The only other item was a French passport in the name of Andres LeBlanc. I stared at the photo of a dark-haired man with a slight mustache and goatee. There was something about it. *Who is he? The forger?* Whoever he was, he was leaving early Sunday, right when we were transporting crates to other destinations. I guessed some of those crates were going with him.

The acetone! I had forgotten all about it! *What if Peter comes looking for it? Or me? How could I explain?* Hurriedly, I closed the case, wedged it back into the corner, put the Beethoven back where I'd found it, and ran for the door.

Friday 3:00 p.m.

Somehow, I made it through the afternoon: paying extra attention to gallery guests, volunteering to pick up staff members' lunches, doing anything to avoid talking to Zach and Peter. I had this fear that they could see on my face what I had discovered downstairs. I suspected them; I suspected everyone. I scanned all faces for any resemblance to the passport photo. By the end of the afternoon I was so "jumpy" that I asked to leave early, saying I didn't feel well.

I left the museum as fast as I could, not stopping to talk to anyone, moving through the museum with a fake smile on my face and my phone at my ear, pretending to talk. I walked outside, around the orange construction fence, around the front of the building, and on past the heroic sculpture, "Passing the Torch." I didn't notice the winter sun dancing on the water of the Hague as I walked by. I just kept walking, my arms wrapped around me less for warmth than to keep me from falling apart. After an hour or more of wandering, I knew I had to go back and tell someone. I was afraid, more afraid than I'd ever been in my life. Whoever was doing this wouldn't think twice about getting me out of the way. You didn't have to be in the art world long to know that famous artwork brought in *serious* money from private collectors who hid their *purchases* away for their own enjoyment. But I was more afraid that the forger was going to get away with stealing art treasures that belonged here, in Virginia, for everyone to appreciate. Forgeries just devalued the whole collection, and when discovered, would be destroyed, leaving the Chrysler with nothing, and, I thought, this fallen world with one less thing of beauty to uplift it.

I found myself on Boush Street in front of the WTKR-TV station, a block over from the museum. I could tell the newspeople. "Tell them what? That I found some extra paintings and frames in an art gallery?" I said out loud to myself. Scared as I was, I couldn't let this happen, but I needed help. *Whom could I trust?* In less than two days the artwork would be gone, and I needed a plan. *Had someone really seen me in the little room?* I doubted it now. *Security was always making rounds, trying doors to see if they were locked, weren't they?* For the first time in hours, I relaxed. *I'll tell the curator. First thing in the morning. But I'll figure this out tonight. It's not as if the paintings are going anywhere yet.* I walked the block over to the Chrysler parking lot, found my car and went home.

Saturday 9:30 a.m.

Peter and Zach were in the gallery preparing for the final "Conversation with the Conservators" event. They were going to finish "The Finding of Moses" today while the public watched and asked questions. After making sure they had everything they needed, I slipped away.

On my way to the curator's office, I ran into Sam. Friendly, always smiling Sam. In an instant, I decided to take him into my confidence.

"Sam, I need your help. Please. I don't know exactly what to do. Can I trust you?"

Sam's face grew serious. "You know you can. What's going on?"

He listened to my story on the way to the locked room. Once in, he said, "So what did you bring me down here to see?"

Again I was in the little storage area; again I was unable to breathe or speak. The Renoir and the Beethoven were gone. The works supposed to be on the road were gone, and there were no extra frames. Even the attaché case was missing. There were no tickets, no passport, no proof of anything out of the ordinary.

"I know what I saw. I know what I saw," I repeated, blinking to hold back tears.

Sam cleared his throat, then said kindly, "I know you've been working with the conservators around the clock to help them get the paintings ready to move. I know you're tired, and I think that you saw frames and paintings, but you can relax. I'm sure Zach has a completely logical explanation. Every item will be accounted for before it leaves the premises. Just keep assisting your conservators and don't worry them with these ideas." He opened the door and held it for me. Like a child, I'd been dismissed.

Sam left me standing in the hallway. Stunned, my mind whirled. *What just happened? Where did everything go?* Then a horrible thought came: *Was it Sam? Had the one person I trusted been the wrong one?*

I don't know how long I stood there after Sam walked away. At some point I realized that being back here by myself wasn't a good idea. The forger had seen me yesterday, obviously. All the evidence was gone, along with my credibility. I couldn't stop this now; I had nothing. "Nothing but a name on a passport and a Beethoven on the wall upstairs ... probably fake," I said softly, starting to cry. Then I stopped. That was it! If I found the other Beethoven, the curator would have to start an investigation. I checked the time on my phone: less than twenty-four hours before the trucks would come ... and an airplane would take off from Norfolk.

Saturday 11:30 a.m.

"You made me go back there by myself. That's going to cost

you extra!" Katie said. "You're lucky the vertical file materials haven't been packed yet."

"Thanks for looking up all this for me, Katie. I'll explain all this soon."

"I hope so. Look how long his hair was then!" Katie exclaimed, pointing at a newspaper clipping from the file. "He looks so much different now."

I laughed then studied the photo. "Too different," I said under my breath. "Next question, how would I know if the Beethoven portrait was authentic?"

"I'm not supposed to help you find that information."

"I know, but it's more important than you can imagine," I pleaded with her.

Katie stared at me for a full minute, turned abruptly and disappeared into the restricted area. Returning, she handed me a folio-sized book. "You know you can't leave with that; you're not really authorized to see it," she warned me.

I balanced the book on the bronze head of a Moreau statue. It took a little while, but I found what I was looking for.

Ten minutes later I was upstairs in one of the last open galleries, face-to-face with the grimacing visage of the composer himself. I examined the Beethoven and again, found what I was looking for.

Katie breathed a big sigh of relief when I returned the folio to her. "Thanks," she said. "I was envisioning a career flipping burgers!"

I hugged her. "Did you find anything out about that name I gave you?"

"Yes. I searched the local news websites first, and found him," she said, handing me two printouts. "How did you remember his name?"

"What do you mean?" I asked her, puzzled.

"Andres LeBlanc was the dead man the construction crew pulled out of the Hague at the beginning of the year."

"No. He's not ... I mean ...," I stammered in shock.

"Look." She pointed at the two pages. "According to the Norfolk police, the body was identified as thirty-eight-year-old Andres LeBlanc from Quebec, a university art professor who had just been fired and arrived in Norfolk two days before."

I looked at the photo. "It's not the same person. He's got similar features but ... without the mustache ... no, it can't be," I gasped.

"What are you talking about? You've gone pale," Katie said, pulling out a chair for me to sit in.

"I have to find the original. I'll be back," I said and ran.

An hour later, I reentered the art library, got the keys from Katie and went to the back hallway where everything was being stored. Thanking whoever it was that liked me in the acquisitions department, I pulled out the barcode scanner and tablet they'd lent me and ran the laser over each label on the crates. All the information for every piece in the crate was recorded on the label, including who had packed it and when, and who had signed and sealed the crate, signifying its authenticity. After two hours, I had scanned and eliminated all but three crates. I broke the seals on all three. If I was wrong, I was going to lose my job. If I was right ... Inside these three, I found more than I was looking for. Now I needed to find Peter. And Zach. And Sam.

Saturday 4:00 p.m.

Late in the day I found Zach in the studio, examining Mary Cassatt's "The Family." There was an easel with an almost exact copy right beside it. But the faces of the mother and baby were different. He seemed to be comparing the two.

"Where have you been all day?" he asked without looking up.

"You know, running around, looking for forgeries."

That shocked him enough to turn and look at me. "Sam told me what happened this morning, so if you need some time off, we can arrange it."

Just then, Peter came in pushing his wheeled cabinet of solvents, pigments, brushes and the other tools of a conservator's trade. He sensed the tension in the room. "Am I interrupting something?"

"No," Zach said.

"Yes," I told Peter.

Then Sam came in. I had intended to confront Zach alone, give him a chance to explain, but now that was impossible.

"Zach's the forger!" I burst out. "His signature is on the crate with the Beethoven and the Renoir and—"

"How did you get that portrait?" Peter yelled.

Sam and Zach looked startled.

Zach motioned for me to sit down. "Do you know how serious an accusation this is? This is my life, and my entire career could go up in smoke."

"I know that you won prizes for your imitations of the Impressionists when you were in college—works so good that you played an April Fool's prank and switched your Degas with the real one at an exhibit, and were placed on disciplinary probation for it," I said.

Zach smiled. "That was a long time ago."

I continued. "Your signature is on the packing slip on unlisted crates in storage. They contain the Renoir that was already sent to storage, a Monet and this Beethoven that has a twin still on the wall upstairs. The Monet wasn't even scheduled to be taken down until today. When I was looking at Beethoven's portrait, the staff that came in to get it was really surprised that it had been removed early. You must have taken it Thursday night while we were waiting for you at the gala because the label says it was sealed Thursday night at seven-ten. Only staff would have been allowed anywhere besides Huber Court."

Zach looked at me, then looked in turn at Sam then Peter. "I didn't."

"I went looking for you, Zach" Peter said. "I saw you in a

service elevator upstairs."

"I did leave and go upstairs to look at a painting, but not the Monet. I was taking this down so I could work on it in here," Zach said, pointing at the Cassatt. "Here's the paperwork." He delicately brushed a speck of pink on the baby's rosy cheek.

"I've been working on it in the gallery after hours. If you must know, my wife loves the paintings of Mary Cassatt. So for Christmas, I'm giving her a painting in the same style but with my wife's and my children's faces. I haven't had time to do anything else."

"How are we supposed to believe that?" Peter shouted. "If you can copy the Cassatt, you can copy the Renoir. You've got three crates of evidence against you."

Zach got up and faced him. "You know as well as I do that I didn't do this. I'm an artist, not a thief."

Sam pulled out his phone. "I think it's time we called the authorities."

"Wait a minute, Sam." I looked at Peter. "How did you know there were three crates?" Peter turned a little too quickly and knocked over the supply chest. Two drawers rolled open spilling jars, brushes and a barcode scanner/tablet combo. Zach grabbed it.

"This is mine!" he accused Peter.

"So that's how you did it," I said to Peter. "All these months you've been copying masterpieces, putting your forgeries in the original frames and locking up the originals in that storage room. While Zach was working on his Christmas present Friday night, you were sealing the crates with his digital signature."

Peter reached inside the overturned cabinet and pulled out a gun. Backing toward the door, he motioned us to the opposite corner of the studio. "It all would have been over tomorrow. You had to stick your nose in where it didn't belong, didn't you?"

"Put the gun down, Peter," Sam said. "No artwork has left the building yet. You can work a deal with the prosecutor."

Peter sneered, and the resemblance between his face and the passport photo became clearer to me even without the mustache and goatee.

"There's no deal for murder, Sam," I told him. "This isn't Peter. This is Andres LeBlanc."

Peter pointed the gun straight at me. "You're too smart for your own good."

"What happened to Peter?" Zach asked.

"This." I reached down and carefully picked up a bottle of solvent that had rolled away from the chest. I started to hand it to Zach, but with a quick flick of my wrist, uncapped it and threw the contents toward Andres's face.

Startled, he jerked back so far that he lost his balance and fell sideways. Sam and Zach were on him in a heartbeat, rendering him unconscious.

Sunday 11:30 a.m.

"I can't believe how close he came to getting out of here with those paintings. Those crates were being shipped to a phony museum in Europe, with his name as curator!" I told Zach, Katie and Sam. We were sitting around a cafe table in Huber Court, enjoying the winter sun streaming through the glass ceiling as we ate lunch and celebrated being alive.

Katie turned to Sam. "So you didn't miss Peter at the airport."

"No," Sam said. "It turns out that Andres e-mailed us the wrong information. He picked up Peter from the airport late the night before and killed him in the car, then dumped him in the Hague. The construction accident actually helped solve a murder."

"With a little help from the intern," Zach said. "By the way, what were you doing in my personnel file?"

"Trying to frame you for something you didn't do. I was almost sure it was Peter, I mean Andres, but the crates had been sealed by you. So I brought the Beethoven to the studio to see what reaction I got. You're really good. If it weren't for the faces, we'd have another Cassatt in the room." I stopped. "Will you forgive me?" I asked him.

Sam also looked embarrassed. "I'm sorry I didn't believe you. It just seemed so far-fetched! Forgive me?"

"Of course!" I said, smiling at him.

Zach reached under the table and pulled out a large portfolio that he had brought with him. He pulled out three smaller unframed canvases that had been in the crates I had found. The paintings had red bows attached.

Zach said, "Last night, I made a few modifications to these excellent imitations. They will never be confused for the real thing now, and since Andres will be away from us for a very long time ..."

We laughed at that.

Zach continued, "... a very long time, I thought he would want you all to have something to remember him by."

He handed me Beethoven; it was his portrait that had helped me figure it all out.

"Zach?" I asked.

"Yes," he replied.

"I didn't know Beethoven had a mustache!"

DEATH IN THE HOUSE

By Rosemary Shomaker

"MR. SPEAKER, DOES THE delegate from Fredericksburg yield for a question?" asked Phillip Exeter.

"The gentleman from Amherst asks if the delegate from Fredericksburg will yield for a question. Do you so yield?" iterated Steven Harrison, Speaker of the Virginia House of Delegates.

"I do, Mr. Speaker," Carolyn Flournoy responded, lifting her snack-bar drinking cup in Exeter's direction as if to toast him.

"Delegate Flournoy, a resolution directing staff to assemble data from other states is pointless. What happens elsewhere is immaterial. Virginia prides itself on its independence."

This will go on forever, and it won't be pretty, thought Hampton Delegate Pamela Taylor. She knew Flournoy's "Pro-Gay" resolution was on the House of Delegates calendar of daily business, and she had received her Republican marching orders to vote *nay*. Resolution language likened the state's disallowance of civil unions to historical miscegenation laws. As if that wasn't enough to rile conservatives, other language equated the pursuit for gay rights with the Civil Rights struggle. Still, the resolution merely directed committee staff to report on the legal status of civil unions and domestic partnerships in other states.

Pamela sent a message to her legislative aide Paul Bailey and asked him to send her some files; she might as well get some work done. Well-muscled college-boy Paul, however, was probably on his lunch break working out with his buddies in the basement gym of the General Assembly Building. He wouldn't check his messages until later.

Well, she could do some Internet shopping on the sly. Tapping away on her laptop, Pamela found the perfect silk Nanette Lepore dress. Her friends decried this designer's items as too youthful for Pamela, but she liked the look. As she shopped, she looked up occasionally at Flournoy and Exeter. She found herself looking past her colleagues and admiring the dark rose, ivory and tan hues of the Chamber's restoration and how the faux gold leaf on the wall and ceiling moldings shone in the brightness from the newly uncovered skylight. This majestic and classical Thomas Jefferson-designed building, with its breathtaking interior, truly inspired and distracted Pamela. She included exterior Capitol Building photos and a panoramic of the House of Delegates Chamber on her legislative webpage and print newsletters. Her real estate business cards also featured the shots.

Pamela considered the annual General Assembly, the "Session," a lively break in her routine. She looked forward to her two months in Richmond's parklike Capitol Square. The iron spear-and-fasces fenced area housed the Capitol and the Italianate Executive Mansion, built in 1788 and 1813, respectively, plus other legislative and state agency office buildings. Her service in Virginia's part-time "citizen legislature," a winter practice harkening back to when plantation- and farm-owning gentry could afford to be absent from their dormant lands, allowed Pamela to serve her constituency, rub shoulders with influential Virginians and grow her real estate business all at once.

Delegate Exeter paused for a long drink from his snack bar cup then continued his stentorian oration. "Furthermore, Delegate Flournoy, this body has traditionally defeated legislation that includes 'sexual orientation' as a protected class."

Pamela found it amusing that some of the legislators opposing gay rights on the basis of indecency or immorality were the ones with extramarital and lascivious sexual appetites of their own. She'd accept a committed gay partnership with monogamous private sexual practices over the unusual habits of some legislators. Even those activities, however, were private as long as no one's rights were infringed, and that was the point exactly.

The actionable language in the resolution read:

Be it RESOLVED by the House of Delegates, the Senate concurring, that the House Health, Welfare, and Institutions Committee staff be directed to compile a catalog, of no more than one hundred and thirty pages, of the current legal status of civil unions and domestic partnerships in each state. The catalog shall, in addition, list legislative actions in the past three years in each state that specifically include or exclude "civil unions" and/or "domestic partnerships" in state statutes governing social service benefits, adoption and custody, and those governing insurance and education.

Flournoy's masterful final sentence justified the new Speaker of the House, a Democrat, assigning the resolution to the House Health, Welfare, and Institutions Committee. In a ten to nine vote, the resolution was reported from committee to the House for further action. In past sessions these types of resolutions faced certain tabling in the Rules or Courts of Justice committees.

The Republicans had enlisted Democrat Phillip Exeter as a partner in the their efforts to challenge Flournoy on the floor. Exeter was old-school Virginia aristocracy, a throwback to 1960s segregation. He worked to defray any widening of freedoms and rights that detracted from traditional white-male-landed privilege. Yet Pamela couldn't help admiring his courtly manners, his Brooks Brothers suits, his deep voice and his air of breeding.

Pamela had tuned out the debate once again and was twirling her long, well-coiffed blond hair and admiring her flawless red nails. A few ladylike coughs caught her attention, and she realized Exeter had finished talking.

After a few more coughs, Carolyn Flournoy said, "Mr. Speaker?"

"The Chair recognizes the gentlewoman from Fredericksburg."

"I respect my colleague's position, but insist that—" With a strangling gasp, Delegate Flournoy collapsed to the floor.

Now Pamela was fully attentive—here was something dramatic. Was it a tactic? Pamela did not think so. Carolyn Flournoy was the most direct and unadorned woman she knew. Ann Taylor-attired and Princeton-trained, Carolyn was a Democratic Party leader known for her forthrightness and even dealing. Carolyn's seatmate, tall, gaunt Lillian Nelson, clothed as usual in black, gray and navy hues, knelt down and checked Carolyn's breathing. The Charlottesville Democrat's elongated face and impossibly long arms and legs, coupled with her penchant for turtleneck sweaters, long skirts and boots, projected an aura of gloom. There was something ghoulish about Lillian's presence next to an unconscious Carolyn, but no one else seemed to notice as delegates crowded around Carolyn's desk.

"Sergeant at Arms, *Code Alpha*," the Speaker said, and within twenty seconds a stretcher bearing a pair of white-coated emergency medical technicians arrived at Carolyn's desk. Medical assessment and stabilization began.

Thumps from the Speaker's gavel pierced the din of the Chamber as Carolyn was spirited out the glass-paneled double doors. Maryanne, Carolyn's legislative aide, grabbed Carolyn's laptop and purse and attached herself to the departing train of the Sergeant at Arms, the medical personnel, an insensate Carolyn and two Capitol Policemen. Pamela saw them crowd the elevator.

Pamela begrudged Carolyn her quick-thinking—although plain—assistant. Maryanne had acted immediately, and her presence alongside Carolyn was accepted; aides were tantamount to delegates' proxies or shadows. Young Paul Bailey, although attractive and well mannered, was, to Pamela's disappointment, less than brilliant. His patron, the president of a prominent conservative college, dubbed him "a promising student leader," and she'd been maneuvered into hiring him as a contingency to closing a deal on an exclusive residential property. Well, as a real estate agent, she'd made worse deals, and her seller's commission put bread on the table and her in Gucci.

Pamela darted through the Chamber's ladies lounge into the limestone and marble checkerboard-floored hall and down the brass-railed stairs in time to see the EMTs retracting the gurney's legs and passing through a nondescript doorway. A serious Capitol Police officer stood at the door.

"May I follow my dear friend in her time of need?" Pamela asked, almost ashamed as she uttered this patronizing falsehood. She and Carolyn tolerated one another, but were not friendly.

"No, ma'am. Speaker's orders: No one enters," he replied, staring forward and not looking at her. *He doesn't know who I am. He must be new.* Well, that was that, she thought, for now.

She returned to her desk in time for the Speaker's pronouncement of a House adjournment until six, "in light of the disruption." She packed up her belongings and turned to see Paul near the wall, whispering with Lillian's young aide, Robert, his arm over Robert's shoulder in a companionable way. Robert was tall, thin and a Democrat. His glasses, tweed blazer and sweater vests gave him a geeky but intellectual air, and Pamela was pleased to see Paul with someone different from his usual fraternity boy group.

Solicitous and apologetic, Paul came to her side. "I'm sorry, Delegate Taylor. I didn't get your message until after my workout. I e-mailed you those files."

"Thank you, Paul. Please take my briefcase back to the office. I'll be back shortly." She would take another crack at finding

Carolyn.

"How horrible that Delegate Flournoy fainted," Paul said, and they both looked toward Flournoy's desk where a young female worker from the snack bar was mopping up Flournoy's spilled fountain drink.

Paul, ever gallant, went to help her. The girl—Pamela read "Tina" on her nametag—backed away as Paul approached, her eyes downcast, almost deferential. They were both soon shooed away by a Capitol Police officer, and they left the Chamber with wads of wet trash. Pamela caught Tina's dreamy look at Paul's leading form. Pamela left also and again slipped through the lounge, down the stairs and to the mystery door, which was guarded by the same officer. Just then her most besotted admirer, Capitol Police Officer Grady, emerged from the door.

"Well, hello, Delegate Taylor," he said with a huge smile.

"Officer Grady, please escort me to Delegate Flournoy's location. Delegate Deason wants to know what's going on," Pamela demanded. Nothing in this statement was a lie. She never said that Republican Minority Leader Deason actually sent her.

"I'll bring her down and tell her the nonconfidential information while I check with the Governor's Office," Officer Grady said to the stoic young officer as he took Pamela's hand and pulled her through the door. They were instantly in steam tunnels that mazed below Capitol Square. Pamela had forgotten these tunnels. She'd dashed through them once before to avoid bad weather and the press as she responded to a hastily called Nominations and Confirmations Committee meeting in an obscure Washington Building conference room to defeat some proposed judgeships.

Today, Grady guided her north toward Virginia Commonwealth University's Medical Center. Pamela kept a brisk pace and kept Grady talking. He never made the call to the Governor's Office. In his version of events, two nurses and a movie-star handsome doctor had met Delegate Flournoy's retinue in the tunnels.

"He's the doctor assigned to handle General Assembly problems," Grady said, "but usually the only business he'd get is teenage pages with the flu or an occasional senator with bad heartburn. Today is different."

"Then Code Alpha worked as planned?" Pamela inquired, supposing this was a reasonable question the Minority Leader might ask, as well as giving Grady an opening to divulge more. Grady explained the existence of confidential VIP quarters and a priority team of doctors in the hospital that handled exceptional cases at the Governor's, *or the President's*, discretion, and that Code Alpha was the order to activate the team and covertly transport the patient.

After many turns through echoing subterranean cement hallways and an elevator ride to the seventeenth floor, she and Grady exited into a blue-carpeted corridor leading to an open door. The Governor's press secretary stood at the door, and as she approached, he reached for his phone and partially blocked the door. Pamela strode confidently past him and into the room.

"Why all the long faces? You look all right, Carolyn. What do the doctors say?" Pamela asked, noting Carolyn's pallor, intravenous line, oxygen mask, her husband, David, at her bedside and a furious looking Maryanne Compton striding from the window.

"Not YOU! You insincere phony! Did you come to see the train wreck? You are not welcome here!" shrieked Maryanne.

Pamela stopped in her tracks at this vehemence. Carolyn took off her mask and spoke to David, who intercepted Maryanne.

Leading Maryanne out of the room, David said, "Carolyn *wants* to talk to Pamela."

— 🐾 —

Pamela stood by the suite's windows, crying softly. From the view, she knew they were in the University's 1940s art deco West Hospital. Minutes earlier, Carolyn had lain back to rest and had fallen asleep, but first she had dropped a bombshell that made Pamela sink into the bedside chair.

"I am sick because I have been, according to the doctors, poisoned," Carolyn began. "The doctors are isolating the substance, but already my liver and heart have been damaged. The police are investigating, looking at links to terrorism, David's business and my politics. I do not know what to think.

"The one thing I do know," she continued, with a laugh, "is that you *are not* involved. No way you would allow drama like this to center on anyone but you, let alone me."

She went on, "I remember something about poisoning being a personal act. When I passed out, I had a vision of people close to me handing me my usual drinks.

"I saw three arms extended. One wore a classically tailored dark suit jacket. The white shirtsleeve cuff with gold cuff links enclosed a rough, age spotted but immaculately manicured hand holding an iced tea. Phillip Exeter. He and I share a passion for sweet tea. He sends me one whenever he orders one from the snack bar.

"The next arm, in a beige blouse with a functional Timex watch at its wrist, proffered coffee. Maryanne. The last arm, clothed in a burgundy robe edged in lace at the wrist, ended in slender, long fingers and delivered a cup of herbal tea. Lillian Nelson, my suitemate at the Commonwealth Park Hotel."

"Carolyn, do you really believe anyone would do this?"

"Well, someone has. Pamela, you are expert at getting people to talk more than they should. See what you can uncover, please, and then tell me ... or tell the police."

— ※ —

Looking now at the sleeping Carolyn, Pamela wondered

if the collapse had addled Carolyn's brain. David returned and corroborated the poisoning premise and Carolyn's failing medical condition. Pamela divulged nothing of her conversation with Carolyn, and David did not ask. She left the room feeling sick and uneasy.

The press secretary accosted her in the hall, demanding she sign a non-disclosure form protecting the Code Alpha details and sealing her lips on Carolyn's condition, including the suspected use of poison. She signed.

Officer Grady walked her to the elevator.

"I am posted here until ten o'clock p.m., so I can't walk you back. You can't leave the way we came," he said with a wink. "Do you know where you are?"

Pamela, glad to ditch her escort, assured Grady that she would be fine walking back to Capitol Square.

By dinnertime, Delegate Carolyn Flournoy was dead. The Speaker of the House announced it to the reassembled House. The Lieutenant Governor notified the State Senate at about the same time, and both chambers adjourned for the evening. No one mentioned foul play or poison.

Pamela noted that Delegate Lillian Nelson was not in attendance, so she rushed to Carolyn's Commonwealth Park Hotel suite. A shaking Lillian opened the suite's door with panic in her eyes. Pamela talked her way in by admiring the suite's homeyness. The flowering plants and designer pillows gave the suite warmth and appeal. Lillian was jittery, seemingly taking the news hard, but as she and Pamela had a cup of tea, Lillian relaxed into her usual morose manner.

They both cried, and together they tidied up and gathered Carolyn's belongings. The tea calmed Lillian, and Pamela left assured that Lillian would rest. She concluded that Lillian's grim persona was nothing macabre but was a true aspect of sadness and despair. Lillian's origins and upbringing must have been unhappy, even desperate, to weave into such a personality.

———— ⚉ ————

The next morning in her office, Pamela wondered, *With the state police and the Capitol police on the case, what can I do? And why had Carolyn wanted me to do something?* She'd found an envelope on her desk this morning. The note inside, eerily signed by Carolyn said, "The poison was oleander."

Pamela's mind ranged to her dear Grandmamma's tales of how Southern belles flirted with Union officers and soldiers, offered them tea and then continued their coquetry while the gentlemen sipped the tea—oleander tea.

Grandmamma would say, "This was how good women defended their people in the War of Northern Aggression," never deigning to call the conflict the Civil War. Reputedly, two of Pamela's great-great-great-aunts in Savannah employed this technique successfully four or five times. The Union men would ignore or disavow their symptoms in the gentle company of the ladies until they collapsed and became pale and cold. If heart failure did not kill them, the concomitant vomiting and diarrhea finished them off, and loyal household staff disposed of their bodies.

Pamela broke out in a sweat remembering Carolyn's vision of the three extended arms and her own evening tea with Lillian. To clear her mind from this paranoia, she walked outside. Her nose tingled with each inhalation of chilly air. Her foggy exhalations evaporated her fear but not her suspicion. As her mind whirled, her feet took her to the observation deck atop City Hall. At nine-thirty, not many employees came to the observation deck, especially on a cold February morning. That suited Pamela fine. She wanted to be alone, and she had discovered that a mere block off of Capitol Square she had all the anonymity she wanted. Around the always busy City Hall, city employees recognized their own, and a state delegate could walk, eat and even sit alone undisturbed.

The shock that held her now high above Richmond was the news of Delegate Flournoy's death and her proprietary knowledge of the poison. What she viewed off the Observation Deck oddly paralleled the actors in Carolyn's vision: Maryanne, Phillip and Lillian. City Hall, built in 1971, was a colorless, rectangular skyscraper, efficient and functional but with few obvious charms. It reminded her of Maryanne.

Beyond the plexiglass, as she faced south, stood the 1880s-era Old City Hall, gothic-spired, crenellated and made of gray-blue granite. The towers and spires called to mind Lillian's tall form and angular face, framed by her trademark longish, blue-sheened black and gray hair, cut in an asymmetrical bob. Old City Hall was complex, dark and irregular. That's how she'd characterize Lillian.

Beyond Old City Hall stood the clean, white, restored Capitol. Regular, classic, balanced and stately. That's how she'd describe Phillip Exeter.

"I can't report to you now, Carolyn," Pamela said aloud, "but I'll see what I can find out." With determination, she marched to the elevator, left the building and returned to Capitol Square.

In the House Chamber at noon, the Morning Hour, typically reserved for recognizing persons visiting the Chamber, truly became a *mourning* hour as delegates memorialized Carolyn's extensive work for Virginia's citizens. Pamela sat on the fringes of the Republican's power seats to the left of the center aisle. A single pink rose lay on Carolyn's desk, a row back and across the aisle, firmly in the midst of the Democratic leadership's desks.

Delegates Nelson and Exeter were present and subdued, Nelson mostly in tears. Exeter remained stoic and grim. He would jerk his head away each time his eyes absently or purposefully fell on the empty desk's rose.

Maryanne entered ten minutes into the Morning Hour and sat in a staff chair near the door. For the next thirty minutes, members and staff quietly approached her and shared words of comfort. Pamela too went to Maryanne. As she expected, Maryanne glared at her.

"What do you have to say, Pamela? Aren't you Republicans pleased with yourselves? This means certain defeat for Carolyn's resolution and for many of the appropriations amendments she championed."

"No, Maryanne. How can you say that? Please accept my condolences. We have all suffered a loss."

"Your party's attack on Carolyn wore her down to where she was sicker than anyone knew! Your aide is learning party tactics, too. He's overzealous, causing trouble among the aides, interns, and even the pages. He bullies Lillian's aide Robert. You better rein him in, Pamela."

"Paul?" a confused Pamela asked. Had not she seen Paul and Robert acting friendly yesterday? "Yes, of course I will speak to him," she said, and then, hoping to deescalate the conversation, continued. "Maryanne, do you have suggestions on what flowers to send to Carolyn's church in her honor? What did she like?"

This disarmed Maryanne, and she became quieter, even melancholy.

"Roses. She loved roses. The rose on her desk today was a perfect gesture, whoever placed it there."

"Do you like flowers and plants, too, the way Carolyn did?"

"Yes. I studied biology in college. Botany was my specialty." Maryanne looked at Pamela, seemingly in wonder at the kindness of her words.

The Speaker called a short recess signaling an end to the oratories for Carolyn. Pamela stepped outside into the dim sunlight of a Richmond winter. She saw Paul and his friends on the brick path leading toward Richmond's Main Street business district, probably on their way to lunch. Robert was returning from that direction, walking alone toward the group. They began yelling insults at Robert, Paul leading the harangue, calling him a weakling, shouting gay taunts. Robert moved to the sidewalk on the other side of Capitol Square's iconic green fence and went on his way, maturely ignoring the group.

With the problem of Paul on her mind, she headed back into the Capitol, destined for the snack bar before the recess ended. Phillip Exeter was there, as was Tina, the timid employee with eyes for Paul. She was stocking the drink cooler. Phillip was paying for iced tea.

"Hello, Phillip." Pamela finished filling her plate at the salad bar and asked if he'd join her at a table. As she paid the cashier, she considered thin and mousy Tina at work and guessed she was seventeen years old.

At their table, Phillip said, "Pamela, this is a sorrowful day for the House of Delegates. How are you holding up?"

"I'm quite shaken by Carolyn's death."

"Yes. She had all the markings of success. Perhaps her constitution was not hearty enough for the rigors of leadership."

"Phillip, I think she was plenty hearty. Have you heard the details of her passing? Had she some underlying health issue?" Pamela angled for information.

"I don't know. It's such a shame. She had a good chance of getting that resolution passed. She was the future of the Democrats. She could have been Governor one day."

"I'm surprised you say that, given the way you excoriated her resolution on the floor."

"It's not Virginia's time yet. Her resolution sought to open a door that is not ready to be opened. It is just not Virginia's time," Exeter answered cryptically.

"Do you do much gardening?" Pamela offered, diverting the conversation.

"Why, yes. Especially since my wife died three years ago. You can see my home on Amherst's Garden Week tour in April." Phillip beamed. Then, as a second thought, he added, "Or before that, if you'd like to visit."

The House of Delegates adjourned at seven. These February days marked the middle of the Session, and the House and Senate worked late to finish action on their business in readiness for "crossover," when one chamber's approved legislation moved to the second chamber for review. A tired and troubled Pamela headed for her office, completely dissatisfied with her lame questioning of Phillip and Maryanne. She was letting Carolyn down. Perhaps she'd call David Flournoy and also talk to the police investigators. Purposeful now, and with a plan, she decided to tackle another problem.

As she climbed the General Assembly Building steps, she called Paul. She was concerned about Paul's behavior, and she owed it to his parents, and to his college president, to check on him. The young people working at the General Assembly contributed a contagious freshness and energy that the legislators appreciated. The compressed work of the two-month legislature was stressful, and, as the young people bonded, the intensity often manifested as sexual energy. Pamela considered that Paul's troubles could be romantic.

A phone sounded as someone exited the General Assembly Building, and that person answered the phone the same time Pamela's call connected to Paul. Oddly, Pamela found herself face-to-face and on the phone with Tina.

They both stared. Tina closed the phone.

"Tina? Is that Paul's phone?"

"Yes, ma'am. I'm sorry, ma'am," she said.

"Does he know you have it?"

"Yes, ma'am."

"Tina, you've got to offer me more than that. I'm trying to locate Paul, that's why I called his number. Have you seen him?"

"He let me borrow his phone. He's down in the gym now. He's got plans after that, but he said he'd call me later."

"But you have his phone, Tina."

"What?" Tina asked.

The conflict was lost on her, Pamela realized, so she thanked Tina for telling her where to find Paul and said good night.

Once inside the General Assembly Building, Pamela headed for the basement. From the stairs she could see Paul at a weight bench.

"Hello, Paul? It's me, Delegate Taylor. I'd like to talk with you." Her words echoed off the concrete walls.

Paul stood as Pamela crossed the floor. No one else was around.

"Paul, would you like to get some dinner with me? We haven't had a chance to debrief on our legislation's progress in the House. We should talk about Delegate Flournoy's passing also."

Before she took another step, he rocketed toward her. His clenched jaw, raging eyes and sheer bulk alarmed Pamela, and she mentally pictured Paul as a poster boy for the dangers of steroid use.

"What about Flournoy's death?" Paul asked, spitting his words.

"I know it's a pressure cooker here. Adding in a death makes work even harder," Pamela began. "You seem anxious, Paul, and I'd like to help."

"Help? You can stop those pantywaist Democrats from allowing sexual deviants near my little brother! You can help Virginia renounce homosexuality! That's if you would actually do your job and not socialize. You're a typical woman. You are not fit to be a delegate!"

Now she understood Carolyn's comment that she had a way of getting people to say more than they should. She awed, flattered or *irritated* people. She could feel Paul's tension. He was irritated, defiant, angry, misogynistic and self-righteous.

"Flournoy was a dangerous woman, a gay-loving liberal."

Oh, Paul! Methinks thou doth protest too much, Pamela thought, paraphrasing Shakespeare. He was impressionable, and his conservative upbringing and college environment had strangled him. His developing sexuality didn't have a chance.

Pamela extended her arms. "Paul, let's go upstairs and talk about this. We'll ask to meet with the Minority Leader. He'll want to hear your ideas," Pamela offered, wanting only to get to the building's Capitol Police check-in desk for help.

"I don't need you or the Minority Leader's help. You and the other Republicans said the resolution had to be defeated, that it was not Virginia's time, but you didn't *do* anything about her. Well, *I did.*

"You can make a strong tea with oleander leaves and twigs. All parts are poisonous. You can boil it down with sugar into clear syrup. Ingenious, right? You can find oleander hedges everywhere. Even in Capitol Square!"

*I certainly stumbled into thi*s, Pamela thought. Carolyn had thought the poisoning was personal; no, it was just *convenient.* She withdrew her arms and moved toward an equipment counter. The jump rope, stretch bands and hand weights might be her only defense.

"Paul, Delegate Flournoy's resolution didn't permit civil unions. It was just about information."

"Yeah, information on how to make Virginia a haven for sodomites!" Paul seethed. "I can bench-press two hundred pounds," he said quietly. "I can easily break your neck."

"Don't do this, Paul. It will link you to Delegate Flournoy's death too."

"No. If anything, that ditzy chick Tina will get the blame. I can get girls to do anything. They are useful tools. She's a pest, though. I lent her my phone just to get her to stop calling me.

"I had her sneak oleander into the coffee Flournoy's aide picked up in the morning and into the iced tea that Exeter sent to her in session. It worked! She died within hours."

"You can still get help, Paul. I know you really didn't want any of this to happen."

"No! You won't be able to tell anyone, you fake, frothy-haired bitch!" Paul screamed.

Her eyes were glued to Paul, but she heard a thundering from near the locker room.

"That fake, frothy-haired bitch, as you *mistakenly* call her, figured you out, you moron," said a broad-shouldered man in spandex as he landed a right hook into Paul's face and a left jab into his unprotected stomach.

"Pamela, are you all right?" asked Phillip Exeter, standing over a downed and moaning Paul.

"Phillip? You look ... so ... so .... fit!"

"I was in the locker room changing into my workout gear when you arrived. I heard it all," said Phillip, moving to embrace her. "I alerted the Capitol Police on my cell, and when Paul insulted you I lost my head and punched him. I saw you put your hand on the equipment table. What were you going to do? Thrash him with the jump rope?"

Shaking in his arms, Pamela replied, "Just looking for any kind of weapon, Phillip. I didn't expect that a tall, distinguished knight would save me!"

WASHED UP

BY HEATHER BAKER WEIDNER

DOGS BARKED AND CHASED their jogger down the sand on Chic's Beach, while the gulls squeaked and darted in and out of the surf. Ten-year-old Tom ignored the serene morning on the Virginia Beach side of the Chesapeake Bay as he concentrated on the beeps and blips of his metal detector. The red and green lights danced across the tiny screen. He waved to his younger brother, Tim, who joined him at the water's edge in the shadow of the Chesapeake Bay Bridge-Tunnel.

The beeping crescendoed as they found a small ring of keys near the rocks. Tim tossed them into his backpack with the loose coins and a bent iPod Nano and said, "Dern. I thought we had something with all those flashing lights."

Tom climbed onto the rocks and replied, "Hey, come here. Look at this."

The boys unwedged a red box. Tom grasped the plastic handle and pulled it out into the sunlight. "I think it's a suitcase."

"You sure?" asked eight-year-old Tim. "It doesn't look like one. There aren't any wheels."

"Nana had one like this. It's a hard case. See, the lock under the handle."

The boys leaned on the dented leatherette case and pulled on the faded red handle. They took turns gouging the lock until Tom grabbed the key ring in the backpack and tried each one until he found a flat one to pry open the box. The lock clicked and the gold-colored latch snapped. The boys squealed and a crab walked away when they got a glimpse inside. Their shrieks drew a couple of onlookers from the early morning beach inhabitants, including Lucy, who was dumping trash in the cans under the deck of the Land Shark, a local eatery and fixture on Ocean View Avenue for close to thirty years.

—— 🐾 ——

Lucy looked over one of the boy's shoulders as a male jogger poked a brown, hairy hand with a stick. The curled fingers were frozen in a crooklike pose. Nobody was curious enough to touch a mummified hand. Lucy wasn't sure if it was from a human. The brown, clawlike hand, some bits of burned paper and an old rusty gun bounced around in the salty water in the satin-lined case. Lucy snapped a couple of photos with her phone then called the police.

The boys and Lucy sat in the sand to await the authorities. Lucy forgot all about prepping the pub for the lunch crowd. She figured that Uncle Leo could handle any breakfast orders. This was probably the most interesting thing that had happened in this quiet community in a long time.

Lucy spent more of her twenty-five summers than she could remember helping Uncle Leo at his beach restaurant and bar, several miles away from the flashy tourist areas of Virginia Beach. For the last couple of summers, she supplemented her second-grade teacher's salary by waitressing and bartending at the Land Shark. Unlike some of the other smaller places, Uncle Leo kept his place open year-round, even though it had been a struggle some months.

The morning sun felt good on Lucy's face. Pushing her blond hair behind her ears, she watched a few moms and dads dragging small kids and beach gear over the dunes. The umbrellas and colorful towels dotted the beach in both directions. After what felt like hours, she saw two Virginia Beach police officers climbing the dunes in their dark uniforms and black leather shoes. Lucy didn't recognize them. The two who stopped in frequently for sandwiches, wore shorts and rode bikes. She stood and waved, and they headed toward the group surrounding the red case.

After taking pictures and everyone's contact information, the policemen carried the suitcase back over the dunes, and Lucy wandered back to the darkness of the Land Shark. When her eyes finally focused, she found Uncle Leo prepping for lunch. "Hey, Uncle Leo, where's Rex? I thought he'd be here by now."

"He called and told me that he was quitting last night. He got a job at the new steakhouse on the boulevard. He said he needed more money."

"I'm sorry. He'd been here for a while," said Lucy as she was interrupted by someone at the walk-up window, facing the patio. After she handled his breakfast order, she returned to help Uncle Leo, who had moved on to prepping the bar in the restaurant area that faced thirty small wooden tables with beat-up captain's chairs. The dark paneled walls were decorated with years of memorabilia from Uncle Leo and Aunt Lila's travels and life at the beach.

"Where've ya been?" he asked as he wiped his hands on his already dirty apron.

"Out by the dunes. A kid started screaming when I was at the trashcan. He found a suitcase with some freaky shriveled up hand."

"Interesting," said Uncle Leo as he walked through the swinging doors to the kitchen. "Roy was in here last night, and he was talking about something weird on the bridge."

"Roy's always in here," said Lucy, referring to Roy Brown, Uncle Leo's childhood friend. They had joined the Navy together after graduating from Princess Anne High School. Roy did a short stint in the service and returned to Virginia Beach to live with his mother and look for the latest get-rich-quick scheme. Uncle Leo married Aunt Lila, and after twenty years of being stationed around the world, they returned to open the Land Shark near the neighborhood where Leo and Roy grew up.

Later that evening, after a disappointing lunch crowd, Lucy flipped on the TV to the local news and caught the story about the unusual find at Chic's Beach earlier that morning. Roy wandered in during the segment and found his usual stool at the end of the bar.

"Hey, they oughta interview me," said Roy as he pointed at the TV. "My story is better. Hey, it may even be related."

"What?" asked Lucy as she wiped down the tables that probably no one would use tonight.

"Last Sunday night, I was coming back across the bridge from my secret fishing spot. As I came out of the second tunnel, I saw something up ahead on the bridge. It was a person who threw something off the bridge. When I got closer, I could tell it was a woman in old clothes. By the time I got up near the spot, she was gone."

"Did you tell anybody?" she asked.

"Just the guys in here," he said.

"What did she look like?"

"Old. Well, okay, she looked young, twenties or thirties, but her clothes looked nineteen-fifties or sixties."

"What did she throw over the side?"

"Dunno. It was small enough for her to heave it over her head," he said as he nursed his bottled drink.

"You should report it. People aren't supposed to be standing on that bridge. They could get killed. Come to think of it, it's illegal to throw anything off the side," Lucy said as she headed back to the kitchen.

When she returned, Roy hadn't moved. He was peeling the label off the bottle. "I have an idea. Let's send a message to that reporter. I bet she'll contact you. Here, we can tweet her," Lucy said as she grabbed her phone.

Roy scowled for a minute then nodded. Lucy wasn't sure if he fully agreed or understood.

Later that evening, Lucy's phone beeped. "Roy, hey Roy.

Look, Angelina Torres from WAVY 10 wants to talk to you. I got a message."

"Really. When?" Roy replied with that confused look again.

"You tell me," Lucy replied.

"How about tomorrow? Tell her to meet me here on the deck," said Roy as he wiped the sweat on his round forehead.

"Okay," said Lucy. "She confirmed. She'll be here at ten o'clock tomorrow morning. Will you be up by then?"

"Yep," he said as he went back to his beer.

As promised by the petite reporter in the low-cut suit, Roy, in his best jeans and a pressed shirt, was on TV for about four minutes the following evening. It replayed again on the six and ten o'clock newscasts. Roy recounted his story and his time with the lovely Angelina to anyone in the bar who would listen. His role had taken on epic proportions.

Angelina was on the news the next three nights in search of the mystery bridge woman. By the end of the week, Roy miraculously had been able to remember more of his encounter, and he recounted some of the missing pieces with the drama and flourish of his own one-act play. Roy, now the hero of the Land Shark, held court on his favorite barstool, and his following was growing each day. Stunned by the social media chatter about the mystery bridge woman, Lucy was amazed that it was standing room only at the bar.

On Sunday morning, Lucy found Uncle Leo whistling as he set up the bar. He was dancing around listening to old Jimmy Buffett songs.

"What has gotten into you?" Lucy asked as she walked in with a tray of clean glasses.

"I like it when we're busy. We've done better this week than we did the first part of the summer. Did you see how many people were out on the beach this morning with metal detectors?"

Lucy laughed, and it was nice to see the Land Shark full again throughout the day. Before she could reply, Roy burst through the back door in a navy blazer and khakis. Lucy almost didn't recognize him.

"Hey," he said. "Angelina's coming right before lunch. She wants to interview me. I've been talking to folks at the historical society. I think I know more about this woman."

"The historical society?" said Lucy.

"Isn't this getting out of hand?" asked Uncle Leo as he walked into the kitchen.

"No, this is great," Roy said. "I love this Twitterface thing. Did you see how many people were on the beach this weekend? It's hard to tell that we're in the middle of a recession. Anyway, I have to get ready. Angelina and Doug will be here soon."

"Doug?" Lucy asked.

"Her cameraman," Roy replied as he slicked back his thinning hair and rubbed his cheeks.

Lucy busied herself until the WAVY 10 crew arrived and set up camp on the patio. Angelina interviewed Roy again with the bridge tunnel as the backdrop. Lucy froze in her tracks when she heard Roy say, "Well, Angelina, I had this feeling that there was more to that night on the bridge that I couldn't recall, so I went to a hypnotist, and she helped me bring up some of the things I had repressed."

Lucy rolled her eyes, but she stayed to listen to the rest of what Roy was dishing. "Angelina," he said as he leaned in toward the young reporter, "it was dark that night and very odd. The woman looked like she was dressed in clothes from the fifties or sixties. Everything was white or gray except the red suitcase. I saw her raise it above her head and toss it into the bay. Before I could get to her, she disappeared. I didn't see any other cars, and it wasn't near the pull-off ... but now that I think of it, her outfit was kind of provocative and out of place for the middle of the night on the bridge. I think she was an apparition. That explains how she disappeared so quickly without a trace."

"A what?" asked Angelina as Doug made a face off-camera.

"An apparition," Roy replied. "I've been talking to the historical society and doing some Internet research. The spirit world is very active in this area. There were a lot of shipwrecks and bad stuff around here through the years."

Angelina didn't reply, so Roy continued with, "Don't you know the local history? That lake back there behind the dunes is Lake Pleasure House, and the main road that way is Pleasure House Road. You don't know about that?"

"What does that have to do with your story?" she asked as she looked off-camera and frowned slightly.

Roy straightened up and replied, "There was an old farmhouse there that they tore down in the seventies. It sits on the site that's been a tavern or roadhouse since the 1700s. It was a brothel at one time. What if the mystery woman had something to do with that? A lot of freaky stuff went on there over the years. What if she was destroying evidence from something that wasn't on the up-and-up? There was burned money and a dismembered hand in that suitcase, and an old gun. Somebody told me that the tavern that was there burned down."

Angelina asked a few tamer questions then they wrapped up and quickly left. Roy puffed up like a peacock and returned to his favorite spot in the pub to recant his latest additions to his story. After the fourth rendition, Lucy went outside to sit on the patio. The beach had always been her peaceful place, the perfect escape. But today it was packed with thousands of beachgoers as far as the eye could see, and it was anything but quiet.

Uncle Leo interrupted her thoughts when he called her inside to see Roy's latest appearance on the news. Tonight, Roy's interview was much shorter, and it seemed to highlight the more farfetched parts of the conversation. After Roy, Angelia interviewed Dr. John Harlow, president of the historical society.

Angelina asked him about the brothel, and he talked for a few minutes about the myth. The historian stated emphatically, "Pleasure House Road was named for a pre-Revolutionary tavern that was run by the descendants of Adam Thoroughgood, one of the earliest settlers in the new land of Virginia. It doesn't have the same connotation it does today." When his story went on with dates and facts of Virginia Beach's early history, Uncle Leo turned off the TV, and the crowd cheered for Roy, even though his story had taken on a life of its own.

By the following Wednesday, the media attention moved on to other things, but the crowds at Chic's Beach were at record levels. The police directed traffic throughout the day as people came to see where the boys had found the suitcase. And Roy talked about his experience with the mysterious woman to anyone who would listen. There was even a new craze prompted by the social media buzz. Hundreds of people shelled out the seventeen dollars to drive over and back across the bridge at night in hopes of getting a glimpse of the ghostly suitcase woman.

Growing weary of the story, Lucy worried about Uncle Leo as she cleaned the restaurant's dining room. Uncle Leo didn't have much to say lately about Roy or the good fortune that the suitcase woman had brought to the pub.

After stirring up enough dust, she sat down at one of the back tables to refill the salt and pepper shakers. She daydreamed about all the places Uncle Leo and Aunt Lila had visited. There were hundreds of their souvenirs on the Land Shark's walls. In the Okinawa section near the restroom, Lucy saw something that she hadn't noticed before. It was a picture of Uncle Leo and Aunt Lila outside at the airport. On the shelf next to the photo in the gilded frame was a small makeup case that looked exactly like the one in the picture and some Japanese dolls.

Lucy bided her time until Roy showed up. Growing weary of retelling his story to the tourists on the deck, Roy wandered in for a beer. Lucy set the opened bottle in front of him. "So Roy, how are you?"

He nodded and took a long pull on the beer. "Guess what?" he said. Before she could continue, he replied, "The ghost hunters may do a story on our bridge lady. I contacted them through their website. They may send a crew out here to film a reenactment."

Lucy nodded and said, "Really? This story has snowballed. It's made you somewhat of a legend around here. You sure of what you saw that night?"

"Yep, of course. I saw a woman on the bridge. And the suitcase washed up. It's proof. Plus I remembered even more from the hypnosis. This is incredible. I can't believe how many people have come by to see where it all happened."

"And you. They've come by to meet you. I'm surprised you're not signing autographs."

"No, no autographs," he said. "But some folks have asked me to be in their pictures."

"It has been interesting. And the tips are great here at the Land Shark," she said as she smiled. Roy smiled back, and she leaned in toward him. "Where'd you get the shriveled-up hand?"

"What? What are you talking about?" he sputtered.

"You know what I'm talking about. Do I have to walk you over there to the back wall and show you part of the red luggage set that Aunt Lila used to have? It's hanging next to a photo of them in Okinawa, right back there by the restrooms," she said as she pointed.

Roy stammered, but no complete words came out. Lucy glared at him. "What were you thinking? Somebody is going to figure it out sooner or later."

"I just wanted to help," he said in almost a whisper. "I was cleaning out the attic the other day with Leo. He's thinking about selling this place. This is the worst summer that he's ever seen. He wanted me to take a bunch of stuff to the Goodwill in my truck. There was a box from overseas. I don't even know if he knew what was in it. I took some of the stuff to the donation center, but I kept the monkey's paw and the suitcase. This place has been my home for years. I didn't want him to sell it. Where would we go?" Roy sniffed.

Lucy patted him on the back even though she really wanted to smack him in the head. "I would recommend that you stay off the TV and let this thing die down. Hopefully, it'll become some urban legend after the summer season. You better hope that no one digs any deeper into your cockamamie story."

Roy nodded and wiped his eyes and nose with the back of his hand as Uncle Leo came in with a tray of clean dishes. "What's going on in here," he asked as he pushed the rack under the bar.

"Not much," said Lucy. "Roy and I were just talking about his mystery woman. And if I were you, I'd do a little redecorating back there with your Okinawa souvenirs. I'd pull a few of them down before anyone else notices," she said as she grabbed a beer and headed out on the deck to watch the pelicans.

Virginia is for Mysteries Authors

Meredith Cole

Meredith Cole started her career as a screenwriter and filmmaker. She was the winner of the St. Martin's Press/Malice Domestic competition. Her first book, POSED FOR MURDER, was nominated for an Agatha Award for Best First Mystery Novel. Her second book, DEAD IN THE  WATER, continued the adventures of photographer Lydia McKenzie in Brooklyn. Her short stories have appeared in anthologies and Ellery Queen Mystery Magazine. She also contributed to the recent book MAKING STORY: TWENTY-ONE WRITERS AND HOW THEY PLOT. She teaches writing at the University of Virginia and WriterHouse, and lives in Charlottesville. Her website is www.culturecurrent.com/cole

Maria Hudgins

Maria Hudgins is a full-time mystery writer and a former high school teacher of oceanography, earth science and biology. She has served on mystery writers' panels at Malice Domestic, Left Coast Crime, Bouchercon and Thrillerfest. She is active in local writers groups, a member of Mystery  Writers of America, International Thriller Writers, International Association of Crime Writers, and Sisters in Crime. Her Dotsy Lamb Travel Mystery novels, all published by Five Star / Cengage Learning and by Worldwide Mysteries (Harlequin) including Death of an Obnoxious Tourist, Death of a Lovable Geek, Death on the Aegean Queen and Death of a Second Wife. Maria lives in Hampton with her two Bichons, Holly and Hamilton. Contact Maria at www.mariahudgins.com

Teresa Inge

Teresa Inge grew up in North Carolina reading Nancy Drew mysteries. Today she doesn't carry a rod, like her idol, but she hotrods. She juggles assisting two busy executives and is president of Sisters in Crime, Virginia Beach Chapter. Love of reading mysteries and writing professional  articles led to writing short fiction and a novel. Look for her short story "Fishing for Murder" in Fish Nets: The Guppy Anthology (Wildside Press, 2013) along with "Guide to Murder," and "Shopping for Murder," in Virginia is for Mysteries anthology (Koehler Books 2013). Visit Teresa at www.teresainge.com

Smita Harish Jain

Smita Harish Jain has published three short stories – "Cosmic Justice," Chesapeake Crimes 4; "The Body in the Gali," Mumbai Noir; and "An Education in Murder," Chesapeake Crimes 5 – and is currently working on her first novel, a mystery set in Mumbai, India. When she isn't writing or  working as a college professor, she is cheering her husband on at triathlons. One day, she expects, her worlds will collide, and she will write a mystery set at a triathlon in Mumbai.

Maggie King

Maggie's first book, Murder at the Book Group, comes out in 2014 from Simon and Schuster. Maggie is a member of Sisters in Crime and the American Association of University Women. She has worked as a software developer, retail sales manager, and customer service supervisor. She did a stint as an administrator at the Kent-  Valentine House, the setting for "A Not So Genteel Murder." She lives in Richmond, Virginia with her husband, Glen, and cats, Morris and Olive. Visit Maggie at www.maggieking.com

Vivian Lawry

Vivian Lawry is Appalachian by birth, a social psychologist by training. Her short story "Good Works" won the Sandra Brown Short Fiction Award for 2004. She is co-author of two Chesapeake Bay Mysteries, Dark Harbor and Tiger Heart. She lives and writes near Richmond, Virginia, where she  is a charter member of James River Writers and the Central Virginia Chapter of Sisters in Crime. She has served as president of the chapter, Tell Tale Heart, in 2011 and 2012.

Vivian has combined her twin loves of teaching and writing by conducting writing workshops for academics, elementary school children, and adults. Her short work has appeared or is forthcoming in more than thirty literary magazines and anthologies from Aljembic to Xavier Review. To learn more about Vivian, visit her at www.vivianlawry.com

May Layne

May Layne lives and works near the Great Dismal Swamp in Virginia. She writes mystery, history, and a little bit of poetry.

Michael McGowan

Michael McGowan is a teacher and an author of two novels and assorted short stories. He lives in Virginia Beach.

Jayne Ormerod

Jayne Ormerod is the author of the cozy mystery, The Blond Leading the Blond, first published by Avalon Books and now available through the Thomas & Mercer imprint. Her indie-published novella, "Behind the Blue Door: 230 Periwinkle Place" is available

on a Kindle-platform near you. Her humorous short mystery, "When We Were Middle Aged and Foolish" is included in the WG2E All for Indies Anthology, Spring Hop Edition. Her first big publishing break came with a short mystery, "The Tide Also Rises" in the Chesapeake Crimes 3 anthology. When not writing, Jayne is a real estate agent, which gives her plenty of fodder for her Misadventures in Moving blog, where she shares the hilarities and horrors of her many military moves. Jayne served 30 years as the wife of an active-duty U.S. Naval officer. Her husband is now retired and, after living in 19 different homes, they have settled down to spend their reclining years in a cottage by the Chesapeake Bay. Learn more about Jayne at www.jayneormerod.com

Fiona Quinn

Canadian born Fiona Quinn has rooted herself in the Old Dominion. She spends her days un-schooling her children, devouring books, popping chocolates, and typing into her laptop. She is currently working on the Lexi Sobado Series about an unschooled heroine and her out of the box

thinking. Visit Fiona at www.thrillwriting.blogspot.com, www.FionaQuinnBooks.com

Yvonne Saxon

Yvonne Saxon, a former high school English/history teacher and librarian, lives in Chesapeake, VA, with her family and the cat. When not homeschooling her son, she's writing mysteries at her local coffee shop, or traversing downtown Norfolk in search of its secrets. Her love of art, music, books

and puzzles influenced her choice of the Chrysler Museum in Norfolk as the setting for the short story The Chrysler Case.

Rosemary Shomaker

Ms. Shomaker, born in New England and raised in the mid-Atlantic states, calls Virginia home. Two of her short stories appear in the Mozark Press Shaker of Margaritas series and one in the Columbia Chapter of the Missouri Writers' Guild's 2013 Well Versed anthology. She is pleased  to have her first mystery included in Virginia is for Mysteries, a joint project of Sisters in Crime's Chesapeake and Central Virginia chapters. Ms. Shomaker is a government data and policy analyst by trade, an urban planner by education, and a fiction writer by choice. She lives with her exceptional husband and fine children in Richmond, Virginia.

Linda Thornburg

Linda Thornburg is one of two authors of the Cool Careers for Girls series, fourteen books written to inspire career exploration in teen and pre-teen girls that are used in schools throughout the United States. She runs the website Memoriesintostory.com, which offers advice and vignettes from the memoir genre.

Linda has been a writer and editor for thirty years and is currently at work on a full-length mystery featuring Ham Cohen.

Heather Baker Weidner

Heather Baker Weidner, currently the Program Chair and chapter vice president, has been a member of Sisters in Crime – Central Virginia since its foundation in 2010. She enjoys reading, writing, and traveling, and she has been a mystery fan since Scooby Doo and Nancy Drew.  In addition to mysteries, she also writes the blog, Crazy for Words. Heather lives in Chesterfield County, Virginia with her husband and a pair of Jack Russell puppies. Contact Heather at Heatherweidner.com

CPSIA information can be obtained at www.ICGtesting.com
Printed in the USA
LVOW12s1750060314

376328LV00005B/372/P